First American edition published in 2012 by Gecko Press USA,
an imprint of Gecko Press Ltd.

A catalog record for this book is available from the
US Library of Congress.

Distributed in the United States and Canada by
Lerner Publishing Group, Inc.
241 First Avenue North
Minneapolis, MN 55401 USA
www.lernerbooks.com

This edition first published in 2012 by Gecko Press
PO Box 9335, Marion Square, Wellington 6141, New Zealand
info@geckopress.com

Design by Luke Kelly, Wellington, New Zealand
Printed by Everbest, China

ISBN hardback: 978-1-877579-03-5

For more curiously good books, visit www.geckopress.com

THE TRAVELING RESTAURANT

JASPER'S VOYAGE IN THREE PARTS

~ A NOVEL FOR CHILDREN ~
BY BARBARA ELSE

GECKO PRESS

Dedication

from A to Z—
Abraham, Olive, Rosa, and Zachariah

CONTENTS

FIRST PART
BREAKFAST ON THE
TRAVELING RESTAURANT

SECOND PART
LUNCH WITH THE SECRET PRINCE

THIRD PART
BARBECUE WITH THE TRUE CROWN

MAPS OF FONTANIA

See inside front and back covers

FIRST PART

Breakfast on the Traveling Restaurant

A BIRTHDAY AND THEREAFTER
IN THE CITY OF SPIRES

Jasper wanted something good to happen on his birthday, but he didn't hold out much hope. His parents were too busy to buy presents. There wouldn't be a party in the little palace because he had no friends (you couldn't count the chickens and the horses). Besides, they had to go to afternoon tea at the Grand Palace. It would be torture, but he'd be in big trouble if he complained.

The door bell clanged, then he heard the housekeeper's voice float up from the lobby. "You can't see him! Please go away!"

Even though the little palace was near the middle of the city, they hardly ever had visitors. So Jasper took three leaps down the curving staircase. "My father's at the Workroom of Knowledge till Lady Gall's afternoon tea," he called. "Can I help?"

Emily, the housekeeper, was trying to close the door. She flapped her apron in Jasper's face, so all he saw was a man's black shoe and the hem of a black cape.

"Jasper Ludlow?" The man tried to dodge under Emily's

arm, but she shoved him back. Jasper still couldn't see him properly. "I'm a journalist. I believe it's your twelfth birthday."

Jasper's face flamed with surprise. "Why do you want to talk to me?"

"Aren't you twelve today?" the man asked.

His mother's voice rang behind Jasper, quick and sharp. "Twelve? No! My son is ten!"

"Lady Helen …" began the man.

"Good day!" cried Jasper's mother. She was carrying Jasper's little sister, Sibilla. "Emily, shut the door!" Emily did. "Jasper, hurry and find your velvet jacket. We mustn't be late for the Grand Palace." She beckoned Emily, and her satin skirt swished as she ran upstairs.

Jasper followed to her dressing room.

"It's two years since I was ten!" he said. "Add ten and two. It's always twelve!"

"Jasper—please." Lady Helen used silver clips to fasten her red curls.

The housekeeper dampened a comb to flatten Jasper's mousy hair. There was no point in trying to make Sibilla's hair stay down. It always stuck straight up as if she'd had a huge surprise. His mother stuffed Sibilla's blue rag monkey behind a pillow so she would forget she had to lug it everywhere. Then they had to dash down to the carriage and set off for the Grand Palace. The torture began. This was not the way a birthday ought to be.

~

The reception room glittered with seven chandeliers,

two hundred and nine mirrors, and gold curtains on the floor-to-ceiling windows. There were other children, but Jasper didn't know how to talk to them. They didn't seem keen to talk to him either. Perhaps they just thought he looked skinny, plain, and dull. Or maybe everyone was shy because his father was head of the Workroom of Knowledge. His father, Dr. Hannibal Ludlow, arrived in a rush at the last minute.

Jasper expected the cakes to be as dry and sour as last time, and the orange juice to be full of pips. He was right. He also expected he would be the only one who couldn't stand Lady Gall. Again, he was right.

She appeared in a slender pink dress, and glided to a pink and gold platform. There was a murmur of *Oo, beautiful, more beautiful than ever.* To Jasper, she was so skinny and her golden hair so puffed she looked like a walking mushroom. She made his skin creep. You couldn't ever tell what she was thinking.

"Welcome!" Her voice was sweet as syrup, as sticky as glue. "This is the seventh year since the Great Accident, when our little world was changed forever. Though it was very terrible, we have managed amazingly well!"

There was rustling in the crowd, some nudging, then a few cries of *Oo, haven't we! Oo, yes!*

"I am humble and proud to be the Provisional Monarch of Fontania," she continued.

"Provisional means temporary!" called a little boy with a lace collar. "She's just the temporary Queen!"

In a terrified stillness, Lady Gall raised her skinny hand

(with at least six glittering rings) and pointed a sharp fingernail. Four guards in mustard-colored jackets hauled the boy and his parents away. There was no more murmuring. Mothers and fathers kept hands tight on their children's shoulders. The speech went on and on. Boring. Torture.

At last it was over and Lady Gall, Provisional Monarch, moved around to greet her guests. She swept up to Lady Helen and Dr. Hannibal.

"Jasper. Plain boy, hard to remember. But clean," she said in her syrupy voice, hardly giving him a glance. "He must be twelve?"

Jasper opened his mouth to say yes, but Lady Helen said, "Ten!"

Dr. Hannibal said, "Eleven! Oh—nearly eleven!"

The Provisional Monarch might have frowned if her forehead had let her. "Is he tall for his age?"

"No," said Lady Helen.

"Yes," said Dr. Hannibal at the same time. "That is, yes and no."

"And not at school? No sign of any talent?" asked Lady Gall.

His parents shook their heads and smiled politely.

"How sad." But Lady Gall seemed pleased. "There is always military college. I would have been splendid at military college, but even I cannot do everything. Besides, I've become Commander-in-Chief of the Army and Navy anyway." She glided off to shake hands with other guests. People looked wary of her nails, gleaming pink and sharp as knives.

"She's *Provisional* Commander," Jasper muttered. His father jabbed him with an elbow.

Other children drank the orange juice and picked their teeth till their parents made them stop it. Jasper longed to be invisible, though that was just an expression, because really wishing for anything like that was against the law. (Even saying the word with five letters that began with "m," had a "g" in the middle and ended with "c" was completely and thoroughly forbidden.)

He saw Lady Gall move to the corner where toddlers were playing with pots and wooden spoons from the palace kitchen. (Lady Gall didn't spend a single dollero on toys for guests. Any spare money went to the Workroom of Knowledge, so it was said.) The Provisional Monarch picked Sibilla up and twirled to a window where a gold curtain almost hid them. She pressed her fingers to the toddler's lips. Sibilla reared back in Lady Gall's arms and looked as if she was trying to spit out something nasty. Lady Gall's sharp nails held his sister's mouth shut tight. It gave Jasper a horrible feeling.

Sibilla threw up her orange juice soon after, and the Ludlow family had an excuse to hurry home.

~

Sibilla had a fever for several days and couldn't eat. She lay in her cot, tiny fingers quiet around her grubby monkey toy. Her hair was dark with sweat, her blue eyes closed. Not even Jasper's father knew what was wrong. Jasper nearly said what he'd seen, but he was sure his parents wouldn't believe him and he'd be in trouble. The longer he left it, the harder it was to say anything and the worse he felt.

Then, after a week, Sibilla sat up. Her hair was a white-blonde tuft again. She dressed herself in Jasper's old leggings, which made her look like a pair of walking concertinas. Emily bustled her into the high chair in the kitchen, and tied her bib on.

"Thank goodness!" cried Lady Helen. "I've been neglecting my desk terribly!" She dashed upstairs to the library. That's where she wrote letters about orphans, and about money and food for people who had no money, food, or family.

Dr. Ludlow took a sip of coffee, buttoned his jacket quickly and jammed his hat on (slightly crooked). He strode out into the City of Spires. Neither of them waited to see Sibilla eat. Jasper didn't understand them. They didn't understand him either, but he supposed that was usual with parents and boys, especially boys who weren't allowed to have twelfth birthdays.

Sibilla didn't want her breakfast. Jasper sat with his own plate and watched Emily coax and plead. "The child will starve!" Emily threw down the spoon. "Does she think I'm trying to ram poison down her throat?"

Sibilla rubbed porridge-covered fists into her tuft of hair and in her ears.

Jasper squirmed with guilt. He got up, took her plate away and wiped the tray of the high chair. From the cupboard he chose a yellow plate shaped like a duck. On it he dolloped a small amount of porridge. Around that he arranged seven raspberries and three strawberries. On top of the dollop he dabbed a curl of honey, then he set the plate in front of her. Sibilla stared at it. He handed her a new spoon for messing about with, and sat next to her with a spoon for actual feeding.

"It's good," he whispered. "It's not like at Lady Gall's. Look—mmm!"

In less than five minutes, all that was left was one squashed raspberry.

"Wonderful!" Emily cried. "Just like magic!" Then her face turned the color of dishwater. She had used the forbidden word.

~

Nobody but Jasper and Sibilla had heard what Emily said, and with a child of two it didn't matter. But Jasper figured he'd better leave the kitchen while Emily calmed down after her mistake.

He was near the chicken coop, fixing a back wheel on his cart, when he heard a wordless whisper. On the kitchen step, Sibilla held an arm out to him. The stuffed monkey was underneath her other arm.

Jasper heaved her into the cart, along with the monkey. She chuckled and gripped the steering bar. He hauled the cart up to the top of the garden, squeezed in behind her and put his hands beside her little ones. She let out her wordless squeal.

"Ready—steady—go!" he yelled.

They whizzed down the path, around the elm tree, past the herb garden, through the chickens, under the rose arch and straight at the ramp into the pond. As they hit water,

Jasper hauled the steering bar to the left. A satisfying wave swished over the path. The cart turned full circle. Before they could sink, Jasper paddled for the ramp. Up they trundled and got stuck halfway. The chickens were in riot. Sibilla laughed and waved for more.

Emily rushed from the back door and whisked Sibilla up. "You boy!" she said. "You dreadful boy!" She kicked a gasping goldfish back into the pond, and stalked inside.

At the library window was his mother, hair wild with fright. He trailed up to his room to read a geography book. His heart ached for a geographical adventure with some friends. But he hadn't had a friend for years and years.

~

Toward the end of the afternoon he had to practice his trumpet. It was small and could almost hide in a large man's hand (if a large man should want to do that). Jasper tried it in the stables first because the horses were old and deaf. After ten minutes their ears twitched so much it was kinder to move on. The palace balcony would do.

A seagull perched on the curly iron railing. As soon as Jasper started playing, it screeched and flew off. But the racket in the street drowned Jasper's worst mistakes. Sailors shouted for the quickest way back to harbor. Coachmen pleaded with bad-tempered horses. People talked loudly about the Provisional Monarch, especially in front of any soldiers: *Oo, how beautiful she is, our Lady Gall. How lucky we are to have her for our monarch.*

His mother came into the room behind him. She was carrying her green sewing box and a shirt that needed a button. Sibilla followed, holding the blue monkey and a picture book, trying to walk on tiptoe. Jasper puffed his cheeks to make the monkey-bum face. You never knew if Sibilla would laugh at it or scream. Today she tried to make the face herself. His mother frowned.

He'd better apologize for the pond incident. He bowed. "I am sorry that I upset you and Emily, Mother. I would never hurt my sister."

"The thing is, Jasper, we must be careful." Some of Lady Helen's hair escaped its clips. Jasper pressed his teeth together. It did not do to laugh at his mother's hair when she was upset.

"I wouldn't be a nuisance if I were at school. Like, military college," Jasper said. "I am old enough, at twelve." (He said "twelve" loudly.)

His mother looked worried, and put the sewing box on the fat blue sofa.

Jasper kept trying. "I don't understand. Am I so stupid that I'll never be allowed to say I'm twelve? Is it one of Lady Gall's rules, like the one that Father can't work for anyone but her?"

Lady Helen tugged his collar straight. "Oh, darling," she said, as mothers do. It's never much of a reply.

"I'm sorry," said Jasper. "If I say what I want to say, I know I'll be punished."

"My dear ..." Lady Helen's eyes were even more worried. "I really think it's time you understood a few things. But please, wait till your father's home." She sat down beside the sewing box.

It was so hard to stay quiet. Through the balcony doors late sun gleamed off the city spires. In the distance, banners from ships entering port fluttered like birds circling before night. Real birds circled for the night as well, a thousand gulls and sparrows chattering their million secrets in the evening gossip. And suddenly it all exploded out of Jasper. "It's a waste of Father's cleverness to treat nobody but Lady Gall! She's …"

"Jasper, your father tries to find time for his own research but …"

"Her face is scary as a billiard ball! She's cruel! Why does everyone believe she's wonderful?"

Her mother put a hand up over his mouth. "Your father will be home any minute, and we'll explain." She opened the box and rattled through: cotton reels, scissors, broken clasps, the puzzle of wire circles and red beads that Jasper had never managed to take apart. His mother said it didn't come to bits, but he was sure you only had to figure out the knack. She pulled a piece of paper from the bottom of the box. "In the meantime, look at this. I wrote it when I was seventeen."

He unfolded it and read:

LADY HELEN, COUNTESS OF THE NORTHERN HILLS.
REASONS WHY I SHALL MARRY HANNIBAL LUDLOW:
1: He likes everything to be fair and he doesn't like cheats.
2: He has many excellent ideas for helping people to have a better life.
3: He is not rich, but I am. If I marry him, I shall help other people too by using my wealth and position.

"What use is being rich, when we're bossed around by Lady Gall?" Jasper burst out. He expected his mother to be angry, but she only pointed to the next item.

4: *(This is a selfish reason, and I am ashamed.) Hannibal is not handsome, so the ghastly Gall will never try to weasel him away from whoever marries him.*

The word "ghastly" was a shock, and so was "weasel."

"You actually wrote that about Lady Gall?"

Lady Helen's lips tightened. "It was years ago. We were at school together."

How horrible that must have been. "What was she like?"

His mother gave a glance at the balcony as if someone might be listening, and whispered, "In my last year at school, young Lady Gall said we should have a beauty contest. A dreadful idea! But she went on and on about it. In those days she had a snaggle tooth, her eyes were too close together for comfort—such things don't matter in themselves. The problem was, whatever anyone else tried to talk about, she only talked about herself."

"She still does," Jasper said.

"She did it so often we used to run to the bathroom and make faces. Even so, we tried to be pleasant to her." His mother's hair had become a big red tangle. "I refused to enter the contest. So did my friends. On the day, a strange thing happened. It wasn't just the girls who voted. Even the poorest person in the city cast a vote in the form of one penny." Her hands flew up. "One penny is a lot of money if you are poor and want to feed your children! One penny can buy enough oatmeal for a week of breakfasts!"

"She won, when she shouldn't have," said Jasper.

Lady Helen leaned close. "She'd been around the whole town asking even the poor people to vote for her."

Jasper frowned. "Why didn't they refuse? Or why didn't they say yes and just not do it?"

His mother screwed up her lovely nose. "She said she ought to win because everyone thought so. If you say something often enough and loudly enough, people start to think it's true."

"They fell for obvious weasling." Jasper shuddered.

"When she was given first prize at school assembly, she said she felt astonishingly humble. There was a terrible crush in the bathroom—we all dashed in and pulled faces." Lady Helen's hair stood straight up with curly ends. "So you see, you're not alone in your opinion. But we have to be careful."

Sibilla put her book down, looked at Jasper and gave a fake cough. *Ach-ach!*

"Jasper?" asked his mother. "Are you all right?"

He certainly was. The minute Dr. Ludlow came home, Jasper could tell his parents that Lady Gall had poisoned his little sister.

UNCLE TRUMP IS UNEXPECTED

Now, below, the front door opened. Dr. Ludlow trudged upstairs. He kissed Lady Helen and Sibilla, and gave Jasper's shoulder a friendly thump.

"Mother and Father," Jasper said. "You have to listen …"

Lady Helen patted her husband's cheek. "Hannibal, enjoy the sunset on the balcony. It will be a long evening." She smiled at Jasper with a finger to her lips, then went to talk to Emily about dinner. On the floor, Sibilla was going through the picture book, upside down.

Jasper followed his father outside. "I—um—wish you didn't work for Lady Gall."

He knew why his father did, though—two reasons. First, Dr. Ludlow had invented the special fluid called beauteen to inject into wrinkles and smooth them away. Lady Gall demanded injections of beauteen most days. It was expensive to make and took ages. It had to be done in the Workroom of Knowledge because Lady Gall wouldn't let anyone else use it.

Second, if you said "no" to Lady Gall, you vanished. A few months back, a mad beggar had roamed the streets crying out that Lady Gall would be defeated at the return of (that thing you couldn't mention). A squad of soldiers whisked the man away. *Defeated?* said the people. *Lady Gall? Who could say such treason? We have science now. We don't need nonsense. Oo, yes, we have our wonderful Lady Gall.* If you didn't vanish, you ended up with jobs like cleaning public toilets or hosing down the elephant house. Lady Gall had the only elephant in the city. She kept it because of an old saying about the greatest monarch having affinity with the greatest creature. But affinity means fellow-feeling, and Jasper had no idea why it ended up with Lady Gall keeping an unhappy elephant.

Jasper's father lay back in a balcony chair. He sighed, and said simply, "We don't have a real King or Queen, so Lady Gall must be obeyed." His voice was weary.

So what had happened to the real King or Queen? Jasper might have a chance to ask tonight, because his mother had promised they would talk. Mind you, his parents often forgot promises—this was probably true with most parents and most boys. But, for once, Jasper had a bit of hope.

If he was lucky, they might tell him something about the Great Accident as well. He didn't know much, except it had caused the death of (that "m" thing). Since he didn't play with other children, he'd never been able to ask them. His tutors stuck strictly to their subjects. His parents had never listened to his questions about it. He had asked Emily, but all she did was grumble under her breath and make a bitter soup for lunch. It was incredibly difficult to ask questions when you were not allowed to say a certain word out loud.

A bright boy might have managed. Jasper couldn't.

Now and then he'd wondered if his father's own research was to try and bring (that thing) back. But Dr. Ludlow wouldn't have time, quite apart from the fact that (that thing) was illegal.

Boots clanged on the cobblestones below. Jasper looked over the railing. Six guards in their ugly jackets marched along with swords and rifles.

"They always look as if they want to fart," Jasper muttered.

Dr. Ludlow stretched out an arm and yanked him back. "So would you, if you were fed on beans and cabbage." His face was strained as if he was trying not to laugh, though he also looked fearful.

Lady Helen returned to the balcony room and clapped her hands. "Dinner time, Sibilla."

Sibilla shook her head and turned the pages, backward, with her pixie fingers.

There was a cry of seagulls, then a soft knock at the street door. Another visitor? Jasper's father left his chair and looked over the railing. His nose went pale.

A man's low cry came up. "Have you time to chat with a long-lost layabout?"

Dr. Ludlow held out a warning hand to whoever was below, and scrambled inside. Jasper saw his father put his hands on Lady Helen's shoulders, murmur something and rush downstairs. Jasper stretched over the railing. He glimpsed the top of a hat with a long feather.

"Who is it?" Jasper asked his mother. "What's the matter?"

"It's your uncle," she answered. She had turned extremely pale too.

~

Jasper had met Uncle Trump once or twice when he was younger. He thought Trump traveled about making sketches that he usually couldn't sell.

As soon as he entered the balcony room with Jasper's father, Trump set his artist's satchel down against the wall. He flicked the tails of his coat straight, clicked his shabby heels, and bowed to Sibilla, who was still sitting on the floor.

"Dear young lady," he said. "Your wicked lazy uncle is honored to meet you." Sibilla held out her wiggling fingers, and Trump bent down to take her hand as if she were a grand princess.

"Emily can feed her and put her to bed. I'll be back as soon as possible." Lady Helen went to whisk Sibilla up, but Sibilla screamed and wouldn't leave without her monkey. Jasper managed to find it, hidden among blue cushions on the sofa.

Then he set himself down quietly and waited for his mother to come back. He still hoped there might be a family talk, though Uncle Trump's arrival had unsettled things.

The men sat down too, but they scowled as if they'd love to punch each other on the nose.

Jasper observed his uncle closely. A marvelous little leather scabbard hung at Trump's waist. It was decorated to look like the scales of a fish or lizard.

At last Lady Helen returned. Her nod at Jasper said he must be quiet. He would obey. Family talk or not, he might learn something.

He certainly did.

"Lady Gall is going on a voyage on the flagship," said Uncle Trump. "The *Excellent Hound.*"

"She does it all the time," said Dr. Ludlow. "She's the Navy's Provisional Commander, after all."

"But this time she's going to the Eastern Isle, where—" Trump glanced at the balcony.

Dr. Ludlow got up and chased a seagull off the railing. "That's better," he said.

"She's having a particular object made there." Trump kept his voice low. "When it's finished, she'll change the law. She will become the actual monarch."

Lady Helen went so white that Jasper thought she'd faint. "But she doesn't have the true crown," she said.

"The object she's having made is another crown," Trump whispered. "If she says it's as good as the true one and sets up a coronation, who will stop her?"

Dr. Ludlow put a hand over his eyes. "That will be the end of any hope for the return of ..." Nobody said the word, though Jasper knew what it must be.

"Well, where is the true crown?" Jasper asked quietly. "Who's got it? And who is the real monarch? Where is he? Or she?"

There was a heavy silence.

"You don't send the boy to school, sister?" Trump observed. "Quite right, of course."

So his uncle thought Jasper was dim-witted too. "I have tutors in arithmetic, geography and trumpet," he said. "And nobody is answering my question."

His parents looked at each other with hopeless angry faces. "Actually, Jasper, the answer about the real monarch is not yet clear," his mother said.

Disgust clogged Jasper's throat. "But Lady Gall's a cheat. She gets rid of people. Someone should have stopped her long ago."

"That's why I've come," said Uncle Trump. "Better late than never, as they say."

There was the tramp of boots on cobblestones again. Soldiers, a lot of them. They milled about, then passed by. Trump let out a long breath. Lady Helen put both arms over her head as if her hair might fly off at any moment. A flock of seagulls whirled past the balcony, screaming.

Trump unhooked the scabbard from his belt and slipped out a dagger. What a princely hilt it had. Jasper was spellbound by the glint on that sharp blade.

His uncle turned the dagger in his hand and eyed Jasper. "I believe you've had a birthday?" he asked.

His mother and father opened their mouths, but Jasper spoke first.

"I was twelve last week," he said.

"I thought I'd counted right," said Uncle Trump. He slid the dagger back into the scabbard and grinned again with one side of his mouth. Then he stood up, bowed to Jasper, and presented the dagger and scabbard on outstretched hands. "I was given this at your age. Use it wisely."

Lady Helen flung out her hand to protest. Dr. Ludlow stood up so fast he nearly fell over.

But in the same moment Jasper took hold of the gift and politely said, "Thank you."

Then he said in a clear strong voice, "Listen. There is something you have to know. I saw the Provisional Monarch putting something in Sibilla's mouth. That's why she was sick."

THIS IS WHEN JASPER REALIZES SOMETHING DANGEROUS HAS STARTED

Lady Helen turned so pale Jasper thought she'd melt like mist. Dr. Ludlow and Trump gripped arms, as if they held each other steady in a rocking boat.

"Leave the city at once!" said Uncle Trump.

Jasper's mother ran out, calling for Emily. The men talked like two heads on one person.

"Must get away at once. Have to keep the children safe."

"By horse—too slow." (That was Trump.)

"Carriage—dear heaven, far too slow!" (Dr. Ludlow.)

"By sea!"

"But Lady Gall will be at sea on the *Excellent Hound*!"

"Decide while you're packing?" Jasper suggested.

"Decide while we're packing!" said Dr. Ludlow as if he'd thought of it himself.

There was hardly any sleep that night. Jasper had no chance to ask exactly why they had to run. They were too busy. Anyway, it was to do with Lady Gall. That was enough.

Lady Helen rushed up and down stairs, fussing. "Warm coats for the children! Woollen socks!"

"Only one bag each, my dear. We must be calm!" cried Dr. Ludlow.

Uncle Trump chewed his fingernails, held his satchel and got in everybody's way. Sibilla began to cough again—a real cough—and clung to the stuffed monkey as if it meant life and death.

"Disguise the children!" said Dr. Ludlow.

"Old borrowed clothes for everyone," Trump insisted, "so the hounds of Lady Gall can't sniff our tracks."

"I don't want to stay behind and care for the wretched chickens!" grumbled Emily.

"Someone has to look after the little palace! That includes the chickens and horses!" Dr. Ludlow's nose was red with worry.

"But I will not be responsible for the valuables!" The housekeeper tipped the rubies and pearls from Lady Helen's jewelry box into a cloth bag, tipped in everything from the sewing box as well, including the puzzle and all the odd buttons, and thrust the bag at Lady Helen.

Then Emily scolded Jasper for getting underfoot, told him to pack for himself and find room for his trumpet. She also made him roll up an old wool jacket and strap it to his backpack. He longed to examine the dagger, but knew he'd better wait.

Eventually, with only a bite of toast for an early breakfast (Jasper shoved a second slice into his pocket), Emily hustled them out of the palace by a side door.

He still had no idea where they were going, but he hoped at least Sibilla would be safe from Lady Gall.

Lady Helen grabbed Jasper's arm. "What's that on your belt!"

It was the dagger, of course. That's what you did, buckled a scabbard on your belt.

There were several cross but hushed words. His mother made him take it off and stow it in his backpack. But at last Emily shooed them down the step and closed the door quietly. Jasper knew she'd rather have slammed it.

Wearing old clothes and carrying their own bags (Sibilla with her monkey), they edged through the streets, dodging soldiers in mustard jackets and naval officers in dark green. Dr. Ludlow kept a grubby gray scarf over his big nose so he wouldn't be recognized. Lady Helen had a scarf over her hair. They headed for the wharves. But when they reached the red iron gates, there was already a squash at the ticket office.

Trump pulled his hat with its feather over his forehead. "We mustn't be seen together," he muttered.

"It's a bit late for that," Jasper said.

"For goodness sake, Jasper!" Dr. Ludlow tugged his scarf off his nose and glared.

"I'm afraid I have no money," Trump said.

"For goodness sake!" muttered Jasper's father again. He shoved some coins and notes at Trump.

Dr. Ludlow bought tickets for himself, Lady Helen, and Sibilla. Trump bought tickets for himself and Jasper, and handed Jasper's to him. They struggled through an even thicker crowd and found Wharf Three and a five-masted sailing ship, the *Blue Swan*.

"Why can't we go by steamship?" Jasper asked. "If we have to go quickly, it's much faster."

"Keep your voice down," said his father.

"If you're not traveling with me, you shouldn't talk to me." Jasper meant it as a joke, but his father growled (probably curses) into his scarf.

Trump bent down to Jasper's ear. "We're heading to Battle Island for a start," he whispered. "We'll tell you more when we've set sail."

"But you've got time to tell me now," Jasper complained.

Sibilla had another fit of coughing.

"I forgot her medicine!" cried Lady Helen.

"Wait here," said Uncle Trump. "I'll dash to the nearest drugstore ..."

Dr. Ludlow gripped his sleeve. "Not you! Remember, we're not supposed to know you."

"This is ridiculous!" Jasper crossed his arms.

His mother shook him. "Will you behave!"

"You're not supposed to know this boy!" Trump said.

Dr. Ludlow's face was grim as thunder. "Trump and Jasper, wait here. Jasper—do not budge. Do not board the *Blue Swan* before we're back, and speak to nobody." He took Lady Helen by the hand, scooped Sibilla up in his arms, and rushed off.

"I'm not as stupid as everyone thinks," Jasper mumbled. He pushed out of the crowd, found an upturned barrel and hoisted himself onto it. Trump flicked back the long tails of his coat, sat on another barrel and looked about him.

A tall thin man in a thin black cloak strolled past, scribbling in a notebook. Trump went very still, then turned to Jasper.

"Move slowly and sit over there," he murmured. "Wait out of sight."

Jasper slid off the barrel and sat on a small crate hidden between two bigger ones. He had to take off his backpack to squeeze into the gap. Who was his uncle frightened of? There was something familiar about that cloak. It couldn't be that journalist who'd come to the door to talk to Jasper on his birthday, could it?

He took the chance to examine the little scabbard. The scale pattern was actually more like feathers. He slid the dagger out. Its handle was curved for grip, but plain. The steel blade had a wicked point. There were creatures, part-dragon and part-bird, etched round the top of the blade. He didn't dare practice a stab or two in case someone noticed. But he carved a slice off the side of the crate, then used the point to clean his nails. It drew a drop of blood. Jasper stowed the dagger and scabbard away again and sucked his finger.

Up and down the wharves, carts and carriages made a hollow rolling clatter. Horses champed at their bits and snorted. Passengers jostled to board a hundred ships as well as the *Blue Swan*: sailing vessels, steamships, a paddle steamer. People shouted a thousand questions, to which there were five thousand answers. Officers shouted and gave a hundred orders, at which hundreds of sailors cried, "Aye aye!"

By now, it had to be mid-morning. The sun was hot. Little waves sparkled silver and gold. Seagulls called, rigging clanked in the breeze. The voices of the passengers and sailors grew fainter. The sensible part of Jasper's mind said, *You'd better not fall asleep. They'll go without you.* The frustrated part said, *It would serve them blasting well right.*

~

Something jabbed Jasper's leg. He glanced down. A big seagull hopped away. Jasper realized the day was colder now. The sky was half covered in cloud, the horizon dark with rain. The waves sparkled now in shades of gray. Only three carriages were passing. Just a handful of people wandered about. The barrel his uncle had been sitting on was gone. Uncle Trump was gone as well.

Jasper was suddenly on his feet, upright with shock. The tall masts of the *Blue Swan* were so far out beyond the harbor mouth that they looked the size of toothpicks. Most of the other ships had disappeared too. There was only a frigate from Lady Gall's Navy, a steamship, and a rusty fishing boat. And, at the end of Wharf Three, where the jetty looked as if it had been chopped off with a giant cake knife, a boat that looked more like a circus tent than something seaworthy.

Heart pounding, Jasper glanced around for anyone who might help. Someone in a black cloak was down at the red gates. Was it the man Trump had warned him to hide from? Could it really be that journalist from his birthday?

He started to shiver, untied the jacket and slipped it on. The first lights of evening twinkled behind him in the City of Spires.

The seagull sat watching. Its yellow eye was mean, but it

might be hungry. Jasper felt in his pocket and hauled out the slice of toast. It was squashed, and fluffy with lint. He broke a piece off and held it out. The gull hopped nearer, stabbed Jasper's hand so he dropped the toast, and flapped away with it. Jasper nibbled his half to make it last.

If he were sensible, he'd do what Dr. Ludlow had made him promise, stay exactly where he was. But the rest of his family must all be on the *Blue Swan*. They couldn't come back. They might not even have realized that Jasper wasn't on board too. They probably thought he'd gone on with his own ticket and was hoping to make friends with the cabin boys. How stupid he had been, to get in a temper. Why hadn't Trump woken him? Why had his parents trusted a useless artist uncle to look after him!

In the circumstances was what his parents had said a lot last night. *In the circumstances*, they had to travel without drawing attention to themselves. *In the circumstances*, they hadn't dared tell Jasper yet what it was all about.

In the circumstances, he did not want to be found by Lady Gall's guards. He had better not go home. He had better not go into the city.

The only other direction was up the jetty.

~

The solitary boat at the end of the wharf was the most unusual vessel Jasper had ever seen. She seemed almost circular. Instead of being painted in sensible colors with a smart stripe, she had segments of orange, yellow, red, and purple like a set of paints, so tempting he wanted to dab his finger out and have a lick. Orange dinghies hung on orange davits on either side. The sails were furled but seemed to be bright green. There was also a smokestack. The portholes were edged with crimped metal, as if they'd once been pie plates. On the bow and round the funnel there were painted shapes of flying birds.

From inside the ship came a light voice singing, a nice voice—perhaps. The ship's appearance might be misleading. What came to Jasper's mind was the story about the lollipop house and the witch who fattened wandering children and ate them for lunch. You were forbidden to tell fairy tales, of course, but it is hard to keep a scary story down, and Jasper had discovered a box of old books under a blanket in the attic.

A white gull screamed. Another gull squawked in the growing dark over the harbor. Jasper leaned against a bollard, trying not to feel hungry.

The cabin door opened. A woman came out, wiping her hands on a white apron. In the light from the cabin, Jasper saw she wore a blue headband. She was slender and graceful, younger than his mother and as tall as his father.

She cupped a hand above her eyes. "Who's there?"

What should he say, *in the circumstances*? "Jasper."

She pointed up to the side of the cabin where a wooden sign was folded in half so you couldn't read it. "Well, Jasper, we're not opening tonight."

"Actually, I'm in a bit of trouble," Jasper said.

She didn't say anything, but tipped her head for him to continue. He explained a little—only that his parents had left him behind by accident. Could he sleep in a corner of the deck, just for tonight?

When the woman answered at last, she was not helpful. "I'm sorry. I don't know enough about boys. You'd better find a policeman." She went inside and shut the door.

Jasper said several bad words. He settled his backpack to make a sort of nest for some shelter from the wind. It grew darker, as night does.

The cabin door opened again, and Jasper saw a man walking toward the stern. The light from the cabin made him a cut-out shape with a bald head and stiff beard. A seagull screeched.

"Who's there?" the man asked.

Jasper thought he'd better stand up while he spoke to such an old man. Being polite might help. He explained again that his parents had sailed without him. The man listened, one hand behind an ear. When Jasper had finished, there was a moment's silence.

The old man turned back to the cabin. "Sorry, I don't know enough about boys."

"Sir, you were once a boy yourself." That might not have been polite.

"It's a very long time since then."

Jasper heard the door shut with a firm click.

He tucked back into his awkward nest. He was afraid a night watchman would find him and drag him off to Lady Gall. How cold it was, and growing colder. He gritted his teeth. A seabird called.

There was another click, then a clanking, scraping sound. The old man had come on deck again and was putting out the gangplank.

"Come aboard," he said. "I remember enough about boys for just one night."

—

THE NEXT DAY GOES LIKE THIS

Jasper found a corner on the deck, but it was as hard as the wharf had been. The wind grew chillier. It started to rain. Finally he knocked on the cabin door. The old man opened it. He didn't say anything, just let Jasper carry in his backpack.

The man went back to a table where he sat with rolls of maps, a pencil in one hand, the other rubbing his bald head. The woman had been reading. She snapped the book shut and rose to her feet. She didn't smile. Neither the man nor the woman seemed to smile at all. They seemed as wary of Jasper as he was of them.

Through folding glass doors Jasper saw a larger area with several tables. This smaller space must be the main living area. It had three brass poles from floor to ceiling. A counter divided off a surprisingly large galley—he had better not be a landlubber and call it a kitchen. There was a set of steps up to the wheelhouse. Did this odd-shaped ship actually sail? He supposed she must. Otherwise, how would she be tied up at a wharf?

The young woman pointed at a bench under the portholes. It had a thick cushion. Jasper took a step toward it.

A boy could sit there eating gingerbread while he daydreamed. There was an old wooden booth where a boy could sit and eat pies while he teased his little sister. There was a swaying lantern hanging from the ceiling, with patterns of birds that would make Sibilla smile …

His throat hurt with missing his parents and Sibilla. Even though she could be a pest, she loved him. They made each other laugh. He hoped her cough was all right—that if his parents had forgotten him, at least they'd found medicine for her. They and Trump had better be taking more care of her than they had done of him!

The woman pulled a quilt out of a box built into the walls, and handed it to Jasper. It was soft, warm. She led him two more steps toward the bench, and showed him how to lift a little metal barrier and lock it into place so he wouldn't tip out of the narrow bed if the boat pitched. Jasper suspected she thought he was nearly in tears. A ten-year-old might have been. He certainly wasn't.

Soon the old man tidied his papers away, said good night, and slid open a door that had been hidden in the wall. It led to some stairs—a companionway. The man disappeared down it. The young woman dimmed the lantern, gave Jasper a nod, opened a second door and disappeared too.

He lay in the gentle rocking of the strange ship, with the swaying of bird shadows from the faint glow of the lantern. The birds sometimes took on the shape of dragons. Moonlight glinted through the porthole onto the brass poles. He smelled spices and other scents that reminded him of the big kitchen at home, with Emily and Lady Helen laughing and gossiping together. His feet were cold. He hadn't asked for anything to eat.

~

The next thing he heard was a door sliding open. He blinked. The woman came in, her yellow hair not yet tied back. For a moment she seemed like the rising sun.

"So," said the woman, "your name …"

"Just Jasper," he said.

"Jasper. I didn't give you my name last night. That was appalling manners. We're not used to visitors, you see. Customers, yes, but not visitors. I'm … Polly."

Jasper had a feeling she wasn't too sure she should have told him. He glanced at the door that led to the companionway.

"And he," said Polly, following his gaze, "is the captain."

Beneath the cabin floor was grunting and huffing, some banging, and a roar that sounded as if a fire had taken grip. The door opened and in came the captain. His beard was gray, like a worn-out hearth brush. He stopped and stared at Jasper.

"I thought I might have dreamed you." He came over to the bench. For a second Jasper thought the captain was going to prod him, to make sure he was real.

Jasper scrambled up and tried to straighten his shirt and trousers. "I'd better go."

"The boy hasn't had a chance to say much." Polly looked at the captain with a rather sharp eye. "I've told him that I'm Polly and you're the captain."

The captain's eyes crinkled. Just a little. He rasped a

hand into his stiff gray beard. "Well, Polly," he said, "I've recalled enough about boys to believe they usually like breakfast."

~

Most grown-ups who have to give breakfast to a boy without much notice might put cereal on the table with a rapidly sliced banana and a glass of milk. That's all Jasper expected. He wished they'd hurry. He needed to get off the ship and try to find his family. The trouble was, if he went to the city or port officials, they'd ask awkward questions and Jasper had no answers. All he knew was that his parents wanted to protect him and Sibilla from Lady Gall. Would she poison his whole family, one by one? Surely she wouldn't poison his father? He was the only person who could make beauteen.

The captain pushed back the folding doors between the small cabin and the bigger space with all the dining booths. Polly began to clatter in the galley. There was a long wide bench where knives and cooking spoons were lined up. There was the roaring of fire from the very large oven.

"Oh," said Polly. "Through there. Obey the notice." She pushed Jasper toward a door with a picture of a short fat man.

It turned out to be a bathroom. Jasper was glad. A notice told him how to flush, and how to use the taps to wash his hands. He had not been on a boat before, and wanted to try it all out, but it would be embarrassing if he wrecked the plumbing.

When he came out again, Polly had tied her hair in the blue headband. The galley was full of rattling and clinks, the sound of batter being beaten with whisks. Sizzling scents rose up. Jasper clenched his hands into fists to stop himself begging to be fed.

The captain rummaged about, brought out a scrap of pie, sniffed it and tossed it into a bin. At last he waved toward the dining room. "Sit!"

Jasper slid into a booth. Polly placed a tray in front of him. There was orange juice with no pips. Two eggs, sunny side up. Three huge rashers of crisp bacon. Four pancakes. Toast with curls of yellow butter, dabs of golden jelly and pieces of cut-up apricot.

He was so hungry, it was hard to eat politely, though he could slow down after a while. Jasper hoped it was good manners to leave plates absolutely empty. And it must have been all right because the captain didn't look surprised or cross when he whisked the tray away at last.

Jasper thanked Polly and the captain with a bow, hand over his heart, then heaved up his backpack. They gave him their half-smiles. He went out into the rays of morning sun. Polly turned the crank that let down the gangplank, and Jasper stepped onto the wharf.

At the sound of metal scraping, he looked back at the ship. Polly was climbing an iron ladder—she had bright green high-heeled boots on, with striped stockings—to undo the wooden sign. It fell open with a musical *clash!*

THE TRAVELING RESTAURANT
ALL-DAY BREAKFAST
RECOMMENDED ALL OVER OLD OCEAN
BY WELL-FED FOLK

Before Jasper had finished thinking, *But how will anybody know the restaurant is here?* a scattering of people came through the far-off gates of the wharf. Hurrying and chattering, they came nearer. This was good—if the wharf was busy, he would have a better chance of avoiding Lady Gall's guards.

The crowd came right up to the ship. Some went aboard. Many simply stood on the jetty, admiring the colorful paintwork and pleasing bird shapes. They talked about wonderful meals they'd had there, or amazing meals they'd heard other people had eaten there. After his own breakfast, Jasper believed them.

A baby sitting like a parcel in its father's arms gave Jasper a round-eyed stare. Jasper made the monkey-bum face. The baby blinked.

A mother pointed to one of the bird shapes high on the funnel. "See its feathers?" she asked her child. "The tuft on its head just like a crown? It holds happiness or sadness, so it does." She ruffled her baby's hair.

Several people turned and hushed the woman as if she'd said something wrong.

From the dining cabin of the *Traveling Restaurant* came cries of happy breakfasting. Curly bacon-scented clouds rose from the funnel (or was it a chimney?). People threw back their heads and sniffed deeply. Some had tears in their eyes and said things like *Remember when we could afford bacon?* Jasper even heard someone murmur *Remember what it was like before the Great Accident?* And someone started to weep but quickly stopped.

Then, way down through the red iron gates, marched a platoon of soldiers. The crowd hushed.

The soldiers in their ugly jackets stood at attention for a moment, then the officer pointed to Wharf Three. The crowd seemed to be expecting the soldiers to visit the fishing boats or the frigate, but they marched straight past them. Everyone tensed. The soldiers reached the crowd, and the officer called, "Halt!" Rifles on their backs, swords at their sides, the soldiers stared straight ahead. Morning sun struck reflections off the ripples of the harbor, and must have shone right in their eyes. Jasper hid behind a well-built family.

"We're looking for two gypsies traveling together," the officer shouted. "An old man, name of Dr. Rocket, and a young woman with a lot of yellow hair."

The crowd shuffled. The baby in its father's arms blew a bubble and gave a squeal.

The officer glared, and shouted again. "We are also looking for a boy on his own. Name of Jasper Ludlow. Ten years old. Hard to notice. Skinny and plain. Apparently not very bright."

Boys could easily be overlooked, especially plain ones. Even his parents had overlooked him yesterday. Fed up, Jasper swung the backpack onto his shoulder.

"Excuse me!" he said.

The well-built family moved to let him through.

"Hello!" he said to the officer. "My name's just Jasper. Same as the chap you're looking for, but I'm twelve. Good luck with finding him!"

The officer reached to grab his collar, but Jasper sprang aside.

"Late for work, sir!" He leaped onto the gangplank of the *Restaurant*. He gave a salute, a little smile, and marched into the cabin. Behind him, he heard a thread of laughter in the crowd. Very cheekily, he had marched just like the soldiers.

In front of him were tables crammed with people. Polly—if that was her real name—had a chef's hat covering her yellow hair and headband. The captain was in an apron, waiting on tables. Perhaps his name was Dr. Rocket, because there was no reason why a doctor could not also be the captain of his own ship. They didn't smile when they saw Jasper.

"What's the job this morning, Captain?" he cried. "Sorry I'm late!"

The customers stopped eating and glanced up. They didn't smile either. A couple of small boys were sitting on the bench where he'd slept the night. Right in front of Jasper, a toddler flung some pancake to the floor.

"Cranky babies, is it?" Jasper said. "Toddlers who refuse to eat what's good for them?"

Before Polly could order him to leave, a woman with a scrawny baby on her lap called out. "My baby won't!"

The father of the pancake toddler beckoned. "Mine's just made this 'orrible mess."

"Just a jiffy, madam and sir!"

Jasper swung himself around a brass pole and into the galley. He saw a quarter of a smile on Polly's face. He stuffed his jacket and backpack behind a sack of onions.

"Little plates?" he whispered as he tied on an apron.

Polly pointed to a latched cupboard.

"Jam?" he muttered. "And berries?"

Polly nodded toward another cupboard.

He found a plate shaped like a leaf, and arranged the breakfast dollops that always pleased Sibilla. He set it before the scrawny baby.

The officer and three soldiers entered the cabin. Jasper's heart thundered. But in front of the messy baby he set a round plate with three slices of banana to make eyes and a nose, a segment of orange for a smile, and little squares of brown toast for hair. By now, the scrawny baby had gobbled half of its dollop. Other parents had begun to call for Jasper.

The officer and soldiers tried to ask Polly and the captain if they were gypsies. They had no chance against the uproar of parents who wanted their babies to eat breakfast, not just smear it and drop it. The parents, as parents do when their children are concerned, were even bold enough to shout (carefully) at the officer to go away. "Gypsies don't run restaurants!" one man yelled, then ducked so he wouldn't be spotted.

The officer glanced around, and stooped to Jasper. "My little boy stuffs baked beans behind his ears instead of eating. Any tips?"

Hands shaky, Jasper held up a rectangular plate with a row of tiny blobs of porridge and a row of berries. Along the rim was a strip of bacon cut into bits. "Look and learn, sir."

One of the soldiers gave a cough. The officer stood up and scowled. "All right, boy. On you go."

Away the soldiers went about the business of Lady Gall, Provisional Monarch of Fontania.

~

When the customers had gone, Jasper's eyes had spots of dizziness from relief. Polly climbed the ladder and bolted the sign shut. The captain made a pot of tea and offered a mug to Jasper. They sat in deckchairs, listening to ripples slap the hull. Further down the wharf, all the ordinary business of making ships seaworthy was going on. Up here, where the jetty still looked to Jasper as if it had been sliced off with a cake knife, it was peaceful, though his heart jolted now and then.

The captain held his mug in both hands as if he were a giant sea-going squirrel. "Boy?" he asked. "What next for you?"

Jasper's eyes smarted and he stared at the horizon. "I have to find my parents and little sister."

"You didn't mention a sister last night," said Polly. "What's her name?"

Should he risk telling her? Heaps of boys were called Jasper, but not many would have a sister called Sibilla. If Dr. Rocket and Polly knew exactly who he was, they might give him up to Lady Gall. If they didn't give him up, having him on board might make it dangerous for them. But then again, it might be worse later if he lied.

"Sibilla," he mumbled.

Dr. Rocket went still as a rock. Polly took off her

headband and twisted it in her hands. After a while, she spoke in a low voice. "We can't take every stray that comes our way."

"I'll fetch my stuff." Jasper's voice cracked a little, which was embarrassing.

Inside the cabin he took a steadying breath, then he went back on deck, backpack over his shoulder.

Polly and Dr. Rocket were standing side by side, blocking the gangplank.

Dr. Rocket held up a hand. "We must always be loyal citizens of Lady Gall," he said.

"As everybody is," Polly added.

The captain's beard twitched. "We heard the officer say he wanted a ten-year-old boy called Jasper Ludlow." Jasper stared at the deck. "Ludlow is a name we used to know. However, your name is just Jasper and it is clear that you are twelve."

"So!" Polly slipped her headband back on. "We have a third crew member, Dr. Rocket. Temporarily. We'll see how it goes."

She still wasn't smiling. But Jasper's heart lifted. They all sat back in the deckchairs and clutched their mugs of tea.

"I'm deciding," said the captain, "to follow the *Blue Swan*."

"She's heading to Battle Island," Jasper said.

Polly glanced at Dr. Rocket. "That's the quickest route to the Eastern Isle."

"I don't know where my parents were going after Battle Island," Jasper explained.

"An interesting destination all the same," said Polly.

"The Eastern Isle being the place of the Great Accident." Dr. Rocket gazed into his mug.

"When that thing that can't be mentioned came to an end." Polly frowned.

Dr. Rocket cleared his throat. "There are possibly signs that the worst of the Great Accident is mending. That might be right, it might be wrong. Old Ocean is as full of rumor as it is of fish."

"All the isles on Old Ocean belong to Lady Gall," said Polly. "Provisionally."

"Just as all the people on every coast and all the isles are her loyal subjects," said the captain. "Provisionally."

"Provisionally, which means in the short term," Polly added.

Jasper didn't dare look at them but his heart lifted further.

Polly swirled her mug of tea. "Battle Island is several days away. I suppose we're seaworthy for that distance?"

Dr. Rocket shrugged. "If I'm as truthful as I can be, we'll have to find out."

THIS IS WHEN IT BECOMES VERY DANGEROUS

It was one thing to run a floating restaurant with the ship moored by iron hawsers to a city dock. It was another to set out across Old Ocean. Jasper was not sure that Dr. Rocket was a good sea captain. But it was not his place to say anything. His mother had often annoyed him by being firm about politeness. She said that apart from anything else, being polite didn't hurt and it could pay off. People remembered politeness more kindly than they remembered rudeness. (That made sense.) Even if it didn't pay off, that was no reason for bad manners.

Anyway, if Jasper was going to stay on board, he had to have faith in Dr. Rocket. It was only till they caught up with the *Swan* at Battle Island. How embarrassed and ashamed his parents and Trump would be for leaving him behind!

Dr. Rocket clambered up the outside ladder to the wheelhouse. Jasper—being polite—offered to help tidy the galley. Polly, still not smiling, thanked him. The kitchen was soon remarkably clean after serving fifty breakfasts. So was the dining-room floor.

"What shall I do now?" Jasper asked.

"Look and learn," said Polly. "Don't do anything on the ship till we've shown you how. Not a thing. I mean it. Not one." She disappeared up the inside companionway to the wheelhouse.

Jasper felt snubbed, and punched the counter. It hurt, and didn't make him feel better. He went on deck. Another seagull was on the bollard where Jasper had sat the previous day. It watched him with a sly yellow eye.

Wharf workers had loosened the hawsers that tied the vessel to the dock. Jasper looked at the rope that hauled the gangplank. It was a simple mechanism. Surely it wouldn't hurt to lend a hand. He took the rope and pulled hard.

There was a grinding sound, a bang, and a splash as the gangplank hit water.

Jasper teetered. Before he knew it, he was over the side too, sinking between the vessel and the wharf.

He struggled for the surface, caught a breath and heard the harsh laughter of gulls. Then he was under water again, between the ship and the piles of the wharf. For a dreadful moment he thought the *Restaurant* would crush him. He was forced to sink down, down, so that the hull of the ship was far above.

So this is what it's like to die, he thought. *I won't have a chance to get the better of Lady Gall. I won't be alive for the return of magic.*

His lungs hurt. Then it was as if a huge silver wing opened out above his head. His eyes blurred in a cloud of bubbles. He felt himself scooped up.

Next he was gasping and dripping, flat on the deck beside the railing of the stern. The *Traveling Restaurant* must have floated away from the jetty a little, and Dr. Rocket and Polly must have heaved him out. Now they were both at the gangplank, heaving that too and lashing it firm where it belonged. They were each saying many bad words.

Further down the wharf were shouts and the tramp of marching. The captain's feet thundered up to the wheelhouse. Polly rushed over, grabbed Jasper, and bundled him back into the cabin and onto the bench where he had slept.

"Stay low, you stupid boy," she whispered fiercely, and dashed out.

Jasper raised his head and through the porthole saw the wharf already at a distance.

Standing on it was the officer who had talked to Jasper. "Ahoy!" he shouted, waving a pistol.

Jasper ducked down.

"Is that skinny boy on board? I want to talk to him again."

"Do you see him?" Polly called. "I don't!"

"I saw that splash!" the officer shouted.

"I was butter-fingered," Polly growled. "I dropped the gangplank."

"Trust a woman, eh?" Dr. Rocket yelled from the wheelhouse.

Jasper snuck another look. The officer lowered his pistol, grinning. The laughing of the officer, soldiers, and wharf workers mingled with the slapping of waves and creaking of ropes. Jasper was wringing wet and scared, but mostly he was angry: with his parents for leaving him with Trump; with Trump for leaving him behind; and with himself.

~

Soon the wharf was far enough away for it to be safe to sit up properly. Jasper wrestled into dry clothes from his backpack and stumbled on deck. Spangles of light danced on the waves of Old Ocean. He stood near the stern, where the arms of the wake stretched back to say farewell to the arms of the harbor far behind. His throat hurt again. Missing his parents and being angry was a strangling, painful thing.

Dr. Rocket set course and came down from the wheelhouse. Polly went to take his place. The bright green sails billowed in a brisk wind, though Jasper hadn't seen who had unfurled them.

"A bit seasick?" Dr. Rocket stood beside him.

Jasper shook his head. The captain continued to stand near him, being quiet.

"It is really partly my fault that I'm here." Jasper hadn't known he was going to say that, but it was true.

"It is usually the case."

"I was in a bad mood. I'll have to tell my parents I'm sorry."

"There is one rule on this ship," said Dr. Rocket. "No sentiment. No soppy stuff."

"But it wasn't all my fault," said Jasper.

"Each of us has our own burden," said Dr. Rocket.

Polly climbed down the outside ladder to the deck, gave

Jasper a grim look, and used the hem of her skirt to polish her green boots. "I suppose we should have lunch," she said.

The sky over the horizon had turned jet black. Jasper wondered if he'd better mention it. Sailors could be offended if you pointed out something they should have seen themselves.

The *Traveling Restaurant* rocked more and more. The wind was stronger.

"All large vessels should heave to," remarked the captain.

"Like the *Blue Swan*?" Jasper asked.

"Indeed." Dr. Rocket rubbed his brush-like beard.

"What about small ones like the *Restaurant*?" Jasper asked.

"Small vessels," Polly answered, "better keep their fingers crossed."

~

Jasper would have needed many pages to describe how terrible the storm was, far more terrible than Dr. Rocket had thought it would be. Large and small vessels should have run before it in hopes of escape. It would take a very large page indeed to draw how high the waves became. It would need pots of blackest paint to show how dark those waves were, how dark the clouds.

There was no lunch. Nor dinner. Nor breakfast. Nor any lunch again.

Jasper needed only three words to describe himself during the storm: scared and sick.

There are three words to describe where the *Traveling Restaurant* ended up: far off course.

~

At last, Old Ocean calmed again. Jasper lurched about at first when he tried to walk, but soon felt better. The horizon was level and blue. Gradually it seemed to have a bump in it. Dr. Rocket steered toward it.

"Is it Battle Island?" Jasper asked.

Dr. Rocket shook his head. "It's Little Skirmish."

Eventually, a small harbor reached out its arms to welcome them.

Eventually, Polly threw out a rope. Wharf workers caught it and eased the vessel in. When they were close enough, Polly jumped out and helped the men loop an iron hawser around a bollard. At last the strange ship was tied up in this small harbor at this small wharf on this island far away from Jasper's home.

—

THIS IS WHEN IT BECOMES
VERY DISTRESSING

The *Traveling Restaurant* was not the first to come in once the storm had past. The wharf at Little Skirmish groaned as fishing boats and traders of all sorts pressed against it.

"What news?" cried Dr. Rocket from the wheelhouse to the gathered townsfolk.

There was plenty offered up in shouts and gestures. In parts of the island, huge orchards had blown down. The school had lost its roof. Several factories had lost chimneys. The streets were littered with broken branches, drifts of paper, and items that had been torn from washing lines. Apparently there was an enormous collection of odd socks and underpants.

Jasper dared to speak to Polly. "I hope there'll be news of the *Blue Swan.*"

She had her eyes on a vessel at the town end of the wharves. A sloop-of-war, with masts and funnels. "That's Her Provisional Majesty's ship the *Lively Beagle,*" she murmured.

Jasper felt stupid and scared. He had thought that once

they left the City of Spires he would be safe from Lady Gall. But the Provisional Monarch ruled over all of Old Ocean, every island in it, and as much of the coast as anyone wanted. Polly and the captain obviously thought Lady Gall would hunt everywhere for him. He realized that his parents had always lived in great fear of Lady Gall and kept it from him. Perhaps he shouldn't blame them for any part of what had gone wrong, though he'd still blame Trump, who had left him behind.

"We won't ask about the *Swan* outright," said Polly. "We'll wait, and keep our ears open."

"The thing to do," said Dr. Rocket, "is offer breakfast."

Polly squinted at the sun, nearly overhead. "Let's make it early lunch."

At once, Polly and the captain set about opening the *Traveling Restaurant.*

Polly asked Jasper to wash down the decks. It was useful to do something active when he was worried. The *Restaurant*'s paint was still bright, or even brighter as if the storm had rinsed it clean. Other ships seemed very shabby. Jasper swished buckets of sea water over the davits where the orange dinghies hung, then oiled the moving parts. He splashed water over the portholes (Dr. Rocket advised him to check first that they were shut). He noticed properly, for the first time, that there were two anchor-wells toward the bow: one large, one small, with the anchors hanging out. Toward the stern, on the side of the ship that didn't face the wharf, was a third very large anchor-well. That was odd, wasn't it? Most ships only had one or two, up at the bow.

But this was an unusual ship. After being so stupid with the gangplank, Jasper didn't fancy another dunking, but leaned over as far as he dared. This third anchor-well was a brass cavern. Deep inside was a hint of carved metal, almost like a bird with its head beneath a wing.

It was not as windy on the afterdeck near the stern. Jasper sat there and sorted out his backpack. Perhaps it would be all right to buckle on the dagger. He had just done so when Polly came out of the cabin. It was time to let the sign down. Polly raised her eyebrow. It was a half-smile. Jasper realized she was saying he could do it.

He leaped to the bolts. The noticeboard fell open with a musical clash.

THE TRAVELING RESTAURANT
VERY LONG LUNCHTIME
AUTHENTIC ROYAL
RECOMMENDATIONS
(OTHER FOLK SAY IT'S EXCELLENT AS WELL)

Jasper read the sign again. In the City of Spires, hadn't it said *all-day breakfast*? The words were painted. How had they been altered? Had the captain done it while Jasper was asleep or being seasick? Because it couldn't be (magic). His heart twisted with the sorrow of it—not even a fragment had remained after the Great Accident, no matter what Dr. Rocket said about rumors. Not even Lady Gall used (magic) to make herself beautiful. She relied on Dr. Ludlow's beauteen injections, twice a day if there was a party.

Polly hadn't even glanced at the sign. She was staring at the scabbard on Jasper's belt.

"Oh—my uncle gave it to me," Jasper said.

"You didn't mention an uncle. Did you mention an uncle to Dr. Rocket? How long ago did your ..." She pressed her lips tight as if some people chose their uncles very unwisely. "Put that dagger in the back of a kitchen drawer," she continued. "In case it scares someone."

Well ... lots of men wore daggers. It was simply something that people did. But Jasper stuffed the dagger in its scabbard into a drawer as she said, because someone might try to steal it. Like a feather, the thought brushed through his mind that definitely none of Lady Gall's troops should ever see it.

~

Now that the sign was down, the townsfolk of Little Skirmish crowded around. Once again, a lot of people simply admired the vivid paintwork and the images of flying birds on the funnel and the bow. They eyed the sign and nudged each other, but didn't say anything aloud.

The people who wanted to eat in the restaurant made an orderly, though noisy line. The captain, a grin behind his bristly beard, asked Jasper to let down the gangplank. This time, he did it carefully. Up people filed, and the captain and Jasper handed out menus.

"Don't forget the special plates for babies!" called a woman with twin boys.

"Plates for babies!" roared other parents and several children.

Jasper blinked. How did the people here, such a distance and a wild storm away from the City of Spires, know about the special plates already? Still, it all went as before. Jasper made sure that small children were given food arranged like faces or funny creatures. Instead of whining, grizzles, and vegetables on the floor, there was pleased munching and gurgles of delight, plates cleared and fingers licked clean.

Jasper's hardest job was to keep smiling. All around were happy families. Where were his own parents? How was Sibilla's cough?

"Oi!" a father shouted. "Don't use your fingers! Use your spoon!"

Jasper pushed down self-pity. "Sir, your little girl is using her spoon."

She was less than two years old. Jasper had made her lunch look like a fish: curves of tomato for fins, rims of green pepper for its tail, a green olive for its eye. And yes, she was using her spoon, for banging the table. However, with her other hand she stuffed lunch into her mouth sliver by sliver.

"You're right, boy," the father said. "Well done! She's eaten it up like mag … I mean … as if it was a m-muffin … oh blazes, look at the time! I've got an appointment, to get my second Lady Gall tattoo!" The man gathered up his daughter, paid Polly, and left in a rush.

There was a throbbing moment while everyone obviously thought that if he was getting a Lady Gall tattoo, then they were all a crowd of monkeys. Then they began chattering more loudly and ordering pudding. It's best not to write the puddings down. They were far too delicious.

Toward the end of lunchtime, the captain's beard was

like a very old brush with lopsided bristles. Polly's apron was smeared from cooking and from cleaning up as she went along. Jasper had done some cleaning too, whirring the eggbeater in the dishwater, and pushing the colander down so bubbles spurted through the holes.

During the long lunchtime many ships had left port. Others had entered. Many customers had come and gone. But Jasper heard nothing about the *Blue Swan*, nor about Lady Gall's *Excellent Hound*. He hoped his parents were safe. He hoped the *Excellent Hound* was far away.

~

A soft breeze ruffled the harbor. As the last customer strolled down the gangplank, Jasper asked if he should close the sign. Polly came out to check that he did it properly, and her hand flew to her mouth. Staring at the sign, she walked backward till she bumped into the captain. He stared at it too.

"Who changed it?" asked Jasper. "When? Isn't it spelled right?"

"Er … yes … I'm just never sure how many *m*s there should be in recommendation," said the captain. But he wriggled his eyebrows at Polly as if something really was a bit odd.

"Oh," she said. "Spelling. Yes, that's all right. Just bolt the sign up, Jasper."

A blue and white duck landed on the deck near her and piped sadly. One wing drooped as if it had been hurt. Polly glanced at the bird, then looked toward the harbor mouth. The bird fluttered off.

The horizon held a sketch of cloud. And there, in the east, was a ship. For a moment Jasper hoped it was the *Blue Swan,* but the shape was wrong. This was a battered three-master. At least, there was one mast and two broken stumps. The mast still standing had a tattered sail. It came into harbor slowly, making careful use of the light breeze.

"A credit to the seamanship of the crew," Dr. Rocket muttered.

They shaded their eyes to watch the scruffy newcomer approach. The usual shouts and cries of sailors berthing a ship, the ringing of bells, the flinging and looping of ropes and hawsers ... the name of the ship must have been smashed away by waves in the storm. All Jasper could make out was a small y, a capital P and a small d.

Her gangplank clattered to the wharf. The first sailors stumbled to the dock.

Dr. Rocket put a hand on Jasper's shoulder and glanced over at Polly. The three of them strolled down their own gangplank and along the wharf until they reached the sailors, who were now talking to some townsfolk.

"Ahoy," said Dr. Rocket. "The *Ruby Partridge,* is she? Had a hard time of it, maties?"

"Hard enough," said a small fat sailor with a fresh red scar on his brow. "But not as hard as some."

The captain's hand tightened on Jasper's shoulder. He made a gruff noise that meant, "Tell on."

The sailor rubbed a hand across his forehead. "We was heading to the City of Spires when the storm struck. All we could do was run ahead of it. That took us close to the

Isle of Storms. No chance of shelter there, with all them reefs. We made it past with the results you see." He pointed to the broken masts. "And on we came to lick our wounds in Little Skirmish."

"Any news of other ships of your line?" asked Dr. Rocket.

"Not good news," said the sailor. "Not if you mean the *Blue Swan*."

Jasper could hardly breathe.

"We saw her, in a flash of lightning. She was ahead of us, then we lost her. A ship that size—we hoped. We prayed. But she ran onto the reefs."

Jasper felt Polly's hand rest on his other shoulder, light and warm.

The sailor glanced at Jasper, then back at the captain and Polly. "Didn't see her go down," he said. "But once the storm was past, we did see wreckage. That color o' blue paint you can't mistake, even when the waves have scoured it." He gave a little shrug. It meant he was sorry.

Polly and the captain kept their hands firm on Jasper's shoulders as the whole world seemed to move beneath him. His clever father, beautiful mother, his little sister …

Through a dreadful buzzing of grief in his ears came the sound of marching feet. He seemed to be lifted up and hurried along the wharf. Then he was back on the *Traveling Restaurant*, being carried through the dining cabin and the hidden door, down a companionway and tucked into a bunk in a small dark cabin.

His body shook as if he wept, but this was too big for tears. He felt someone stroking his forehead, like his mother used to do when he had a fever.

"Was your uncle on the *Blue Swan* too?" whispered Polly.

He managed to nod.

"Don't give up hope," he heard her say. "Don't ever give up."

—

THIS IS WHEN JASPER
HAS TO COPE

He didn't know how much time passed. He had no strength to move. Finally he rubbed a hand over his dry eyes and thought, *I must do something.*

Just then he heard the boots of many soldiers on the deck overhead. He sat up.

Above, there was a groan or two. Soldiers who had eaten too much cabbage must be bending to hunt under the dining tables. It would be a disaster if they found his backpack.

He heard gruff talk along these lines:

"How are we expected to find a boy when we don't know what he looks like?"

"All boys look the same."

"Right. Find any boy, he'll do."

"No, thick-ears, we have to find a particular boy."

"A boy who isn't handsome, that's what I heard."

A great shout: "No boys are handsome!"

"I was."

"You're not now, thick-ears. Have you looked in that cupboard?"

There was a crash as plates spilled out.

"Now you've done it, ugly-mug."

Jasper hoped they wouldn't see his dagger in the galley drawer. He hoped they wouldn't come down to the cabins.

"All right, there's no boy here. Move out, men! Back to the *Lively Beagle*! On the double!"

After more pounding on the deck from many boots, everything was quiet except for waves smacking the hull.

Soon the door to the tiny cabin opened. Polly's shape was outlined in dim light. "Jasper?" she said softly. She came over and sat down. "Jasper, our plan was to follow the *Blue Swan*. That's still what we must do. We'll put our worries and sadness aside and set to work."

His throat choked up. Even in the shadows, he saw her bite down on a sob as well. She gave a smile. It wasn't a wide smile and it was full of pain, but it was also full of kindness.

"I've come to say I know you're an unusual boy," she said.

"I'm ordinary," he said.

"No boy is ordinary." She put her hand over his. "We'll find out where Lady Helen is, and Hannibal Ludlow. Most important, we must find your little sister."

"What about Uncle Trump?" Jasper said.

Polly drew her hand back. "Your wicked lazy uncle has much to answer for."

Not for the first time, Jasper thought she might know Trump. But the look on Polly's face stopped him from asking.

~

"Have a wash and clean your teeth." Polly got to her feet. "It makes you feel better. Come on. Up with you."

"No toothbrush," Jasper said.

"In your backpack, I shouldn't wonder," Polly answered.

Actually, dirty teeth could wait. His toothbrush was one thing Emily hadn't remembered in the mad business of leaving the city. But he rinsed his mouth and splashed water on his face in the ship's bathroom. In the galley he opened the drawer where he'd hidden his dagger—yes, right at the back. He buckled the scabbard back on. It hung comfortably against his hip. He tugged his shirt to cover it.

After a deep breath he went on deck. It was late afternoon, the sun buttery. A wharf worker was there to help cast off. Dr. Rocket had already drawn up the gangplank and Polly was about to climb the rigging. They both looked anxious.

"Go back inside. Be quiet," called the captain gruffly.

But a white chicken staggered past along the dock. It had a tuft of feathers like Sibilla's hair. Three squawking seagulls chased it. It looked almost as if they were herding the chicken toward the *Lively Beagle*. Somewhere past the *Beagle*, Jasper heard the barking of great dogs. The chicken struggled on. The gulls began stabbing it with their beaks and drawing blood.

Jasper sprang over the rail and knocked into the wharf worker. Behind him, Polly cried out. The captain shouted.

Jasper said sorry to the worker and stumbled to his feet. The seagulls had picked up pace, stabbing, jabbing, herding. Jasper darted round a horse and cart but couldn't catch up. He dodged another horse and passed the *Lively Beagle*.

Finally he thrust his hands into the crowd of birds and gripped the trembling chicken. The gulls flew off, screaming with laughter as if they'd got exactly what they wanted.

Gasping, he sank onto a decorated platform and set the chicken down. It flurried away—to safety, he hoped. His hands were streaked with red.

Something pushed him. "Get off there, boy!" It was a soldier.

He scrambled up and wiped his hands on his backside. The decorations on the platform were banners of the Provisional Monarchy—pink, with dark pink fringing. Directly opposite was the foot of the very grand gangplank of Lady Gall's flagship, HPMS *Excellent Hound*. She had five tall masts and three fat funnels.

Sailors were still working on her moorings, so she had only just arrived. That's why Dr. Rocket had told him to stay quiet and out of sight—Jasper felt far worse than merely stupid.

The baying of dogs grew louder. At the head of the gangplank Lady Gall appeared, three large black hounds on either side. Behind her, a guard carried a pink banner with the emblem her most loyal (or foolish) subjects got tattooed on their chests or arms or elsewhere: a crown, a bird with its wings up, and LADY GALL FOREVER BEAUTIFUL.

Jasper trembled with fright and rage. But he had to admit she seemed pretty from a distance. Her cloak was dark pink, her gown pale pink, and her face was smooth and pink to match. Her hat dangled with pearls, as if their job was to keep flies off. She swept down the gangplank, followed by the Admiral of the Fleet. He wore a dark green jacket with many gold buttons and a hat with twists of gold braid.

The soldiers and sailors stood to attention. The few townspeople nearby stood absolutely still. Jasper realized he shouldn't move either. There were murmurs of *Oo, beautiful. Oo, wise.* The dogs slavered, though they had stopped baying.

With her face so smooth (as well as pink) nobody could ever tell if Lady Gall was pleased, surprised, or angry. A face stiffened by beauteen made a person really very strange. It was amazing what Jasper's father could invent, especially by accident when he knocked over an experiment.

"Where is the crowd?" asked Lady Gall.

The soldiers led her to the platform, and drew their swords. People gathered in an instant. Wharf workers shoved and nudged, everyone trying to squeeze close to the platform to show how much they wanted a good view.

She is so beautiful, they said, *she is so talented. Oo, beautiful. Oo, wise.*

The Admiral raised his hands. The crowd fell silent. The Admiral bowed and Lady Gall stepped forward.

"I am so proud of you, my people," said Lady Gall. "We have made great strides. Fontania used to rely on …" she lowered her voice, "… the Great Nonsense." The crowd caught their breath at this mention of the thing that was forbidden. But of course she was Lady Gall, not an ordinary person, and she hadn't said (magic) directly. "But now we know the Great Nonsense was old-fashioned, as well as dangerous.

Now we have science, in which everyone can share. The Workroom of Knowledge is making great strides. You will see, my people, we will all continue to make great strides."

What she said was twaddle to Jasper. She certainly didn't share beauteen with anyone. But the crowd cheered. Pink flags were handed out by soldiers, and people waved them.

The Admiral bowed to Lady Gall again. "It is time the people of Old Ocean and all its lands and islands had an actual monarch!" he declared.

People glanced at each other as if to say: Fat chance of that.

Lady Gall held up a hand. "Searching for the actual monarch is honorable work. If we seek, we shall find!" Her fingernails glinted, purple this time but still sharp as knives. "We may find that the true crown is not a real object, but a state of mind! An honorable state of mind in an honorable monarch that can be symbolized by a wonderful new crown, created by the orphans of the Eastern Isle."

"I don't understand," said a boy near Jasper.

"Not a word of it," said a man near the boy. "What does symbolized mean?"

"Shut up," hissed his wife. "Smile and cheer."

"I bet it means she plans to cheat," the husband muttered. His wife jabbed him with her elbow.

"Lady Gall cheats?" asked the boy in a high shocked voice.

Lady Gall looked as angry as her face would let her. Two soldiers grabbed the boy. Four others grabbed the woman and the man. They were hauled off kicking, the soldiers' big hands clamped over their mouths.

The Admiral waved his hands in rapid circles, encouraging the crowd to cheer. Then he bowed to the Provisional Monarch.

"I must say this!" he cried. "We no longer rely on the nonsense of seven years ago. Therefore, we are free to choose a monarch for ourselves! To choose an honorable King—or Queen!" He bowed again to Lady Gall.

The crowd was suddenly as still as statues.

Lady Gall pointed very prettily at herself with her sharp nails. It looked to Jasper as if she'd practiced in front of a mirror. "Admiral, you can't mean me? Oh! If I were chosen as the actual Queen, I would be so humble!"

She spread both hands to show how humble, and smiled as widely as possible for a woman with a face that couldn't move. It wasn't wide at all. Small children trembled. Men and women quaked as well.

"But I am simply taking care of those poor orphans from the Eastern Isle. We must take great care of those whose homes were ruined in the shocking, shameful accident."

Oo, said the crowd. *Oo, generous. Oo, wise.*

Lady Gall waved toward the *Excellent Hound*. Between two guards at the railing stood a child about Jasper's age (twelve, not ten). Was it a boy or a girl? It wore a white tunic. Its hair was a mass of dark curls, its eyes were huge.

The Provisional Monarch flicked a hand, and the child bowed. It raised a flute to its mouth and began playing. Boy or girl, it was good at the flute.

Jasper nudged a woman next to him. "Who is that?"

"One of the orphans," she whispered.

"From the Eastern Isle?" he asked.

She frowned at him. "Be quiet."

He stared as the child's dark eyes scanned the crowd, glanced over him, then glanced back. The orphan probably thought Jasper was a happy ordinary boy. His throat cramped. The orphan couldn't know that Jasper, too, might be an orphan.

As the tune flowed on, the late sun grew more mellow. "Oh," the woman next to him breathed, "how beautiful it used to be …"

"At the Eastern Isle, before the accident?" Jasper whispered. "Or do you mean (that thing we shouldn't mention)?"

The woman's eyes were pools of tears. Her voice was so soft, he hardly caught it. "If only the Great Accident hadn't happened."

Lady Gall flicked her hand a second time and the music stopped. The child looked again at Jasper, who raised his hands as if he played his own small trumpet, and made a face to show that he was hopeless. The child blinked and pulled a face back, showing it wished it was no blazing good either.

A guard led the orphan away inside the *Hound*.

An officer walked past and the woman straightened herself quickly. "How kindly she cares for the orphans of the Accident," she said in a loud voice. "Oo, she should be Monarch. Oo, she cares for us all."

Jasper didn't have a clue what to say, so he just said, "Oo."

"Her ships have been rescuing folk who were wrecked in that great storm. Oo, fighting to rescue them."

Jasper widened his eyes so he'd look ten years old and innocent, to keep her talking. "Oo!" he said. "Oo! Fighting?"

"Fighting with pirates for the rich ones. Rich folk will give Lady Gall a reward for being rescued, and the pirates will charge them a ransom." The woman waved her pink flag. "Hooray," she shouted. "Hooray."

Had the Navy rescued Jasper's parents, or had pirates captured them? Which would be worse? Nobody would want the puzzle and the sewing things that Emily had stuffed into Lady Helen's bag, but his mother would be able to sell her pearls and rubies. And Dr. Ludlow still had plenty of money in his wallet after he'd given some to Trump.

"Did the *Excellent Hound* rescue anyone?" he asked.

"Stupid boy," the woman said. "Lady Gall's too important to stop and rescue …" She frowned, and stepped away as if Jasper suddenly had an illness she might catch.

Lady Gall glided down from the pink platform. She was so skinny you couldn't see her in the crowd except for the wide pink hat.

Jasper moved to pretend he was with some men in builders' aprons, but a large hand gripped his shoulder.

"A boy!" a soldier yelled. "We have a boy!" Soldiers dragged him to the foot of the gangplank and waited at attention. One had a rifle ready.

Jasper should not have worn his princely dagger. He dipped one shoulder to make sure it stayed hidden by his shirt.

There was a long line of people with requests or

messages for Lady Gall, but at last she swooped through the crowd, the Admiral striding behind her. The soldiers saluted.

"What boy is this?" asked Lady Gall. She kept her chin up, probably because looking down to boy-level would give her wrinkles.

His mind scooted with thought after thought. He had met Lady Gall many times, but he was too plain for her ever to have looked at him closely. And he'd always been well dressed, hair brushed, face clean. Now he was in old clothes and his hair was a bird's nest. He was streaked and blotched with wharf dirt and blood from the poor white chicken.

Jasper, shoulder still dipped to hide the scabbard, gazed at the pink ruffle around Lady Gall's neck and made himself go cross-eyed. Keeping his shoulder down, he stood on tiptoe like Sibilla. He put his head to one side like Sibilla. He wiggled his fingers (like Sibilla), and spoke with no sound, *Oo, 'ello, wha' a bootiful lady*. He smiled at Lady Gall's ruffle as if it was the best thing he'd ever seen—just as his sister did when he offered her cut-up banana on an interesting plate.

Lady Gall stepped back as if Jasper were a smell. She would have been frowning if the beauteen had let her.

"I grant you, this is a very ordinary boy. He is not handsome. But it should be obvious that I am looking for a clever boy. Dr. Ludlow pretends his son is not intelligent, but I know better. Does this child look clever to you?" she asked the Admiral.

The soldiers shoved Jasper away and he fell over. As he

looked up from where he lay, Lady Gall pointed a glittering purple fingernail under the soft bit of the Admiral's nose. No anger showed upon that terrifying face, but her voice was a hiss.

"If the family has all drowned, that's excellent. If they've been rescued, they must be brought to me as soon as possible! Is that so difficult?" She stabbed with her nail. A drop of blood trickled down to the Admiral's lip. The man didn't flinch, but his eyes went red and watered.

The son of Dr. Ludlow was intelligent enough to pick himself up very slowly and pretend he had hurt his knee. He kept his face down.

A man's voice called. "Lady Gall! Admiral! Permission to speak, Madam!"

Jasper thought he had been discovered. But it was a naval officer in a smart green coat, breathing hard as if he'd run a race. He saluted.

"News from the *Red Wolf*, Madam!"

Jasper listened as hard as he could, but the officer's voice dropped to a whisper. Lady Gall gave a yelp of glee. The officer said something more and she let out a little scream of rage. The pearls rattled and swung on her hat as she dashed up the gangplank with the Admiral.

The son of Dr. Ludlow was intelligent enough to limp away on tiptoe and keep wiggling his fingers. Why had Lady Gall rushed onto the *Hound*? Was it news of his parents? Good news or bad? Not knowing was a knife blade in Jasper's heart.

~

"Wretched boy!" scolded Polly as he came aboard. "We warned you to stay out of sight!"

"Sorry," said Jasper.

For the next hour, he sheltered behind an orange dinghy on the *Traveling Restaurant* and watched the *Excellent Hound* speed out of harbor. It headed north into the dusk. The *Lively Beagle* headed out faster because she was smaller and therefore speedier. Something was definitely up.

"Safe now," Dr. Rocket said at last. He and Polly untied the *Restaurant*. A group of townsfolk and their children waved sad goodbyes. They must have been hoping to have dinner.

Leaving harbor, they had to thread through the crowd of other ships. The *Restaurant* was so unusual that many sailors yelled and waved, with rude remarks as well as compliments.

"Goin' fishing in a puddin' plate? Ha ha!"

"I 'ad a pie from your galley once! I still taste it in my dreams!"

It was polite to wave back, though Jasper kept out of sight as much as possible. You never knew who was a spy. He was beginning to think that even birds could work for Lady Gall. It would be by clever training, of course. It couldn't be (m–g–c).

The captain called from the wheelhouse. "No time for cooking till we're at sea."

"Should I make sandwiches?" Jasper offered.

"Good idea. Hop to it!" said Dr. Rocket.

"Aye," said Jasper.

"Aye aye," the captain corrected him. "Aye on its own means yes. Aye aye means I hear you and I'll do it at once." He grinned, a frightening sight, big white teeth in that hearth-brush beard.

Jasper busied himself in the galley on his own. When he thought about his parents and Sibilla, he had that stab of awful pain. But he found fresh bread and cut it with the jagged-edged knife. He spread it with mayonnaise, and grated cheese. He washed lettuce from the chiller cupboard. A strong-smelling salami swung from a hook over the bench. He cut thick chunks and snuck a piece to taste. It was a farmyard of deliciousness in one mouthful.

When they were far out at sea, Jasper carried a tray of sandwiches to the wheelhouse. At last he was up here with the great spoked wheel, a cabinet of thin map drawers and the telescope on a brass swivel. Dr. Rocket sat on the steering stool, a hand on the wheel. With the other, he held Jasper's sandwiches and took great bites. Polly wrapped herself in a blanket and set a chair on the deck below. She sat with her boots on the railing, a sandwich in both hands, and nodded up at Jasper with her mouth full. With his own plate, Jasper sat in the outside doorway of the wheelhouse. The last rays of sun struck the tops of the waves. The sails flapped like strong green wings. For a while they chewed in silence.

Polly eyed Jasper. "You heard Lady Gall speaking to the crowd?"

What should he say? He still wasn't sure how much he should trust Polly and the captain. "She said some stuff about the true crown."

Polly examined the inside of her sandwich. "Oh?"

A small bird landed on the rail and blinked a ruby eye at Jasper.

"She said if the crown was never found, it wouldn't matter."

Dr. Rocket stopped mid-chew to stare at him too.

"She said we didn't need—she calls it The Great Nonsense."

"Nonsense, eh?" the captain rumbled.

"That a King or Queen with a new crown and an honorable mind would do the job," Jasper continued.

Dr. Rocket finished his mouthful. "Fair enough, in its way and as far as it goes. A new crown—easy to come by. The honorable mind—that's not so easy. An honorable mind—and Lady Gall?"

The bird made a strangled noise, like throwing up. It was just the right comment on Lady Gall, and Jasper was surprised into a laugh.

"The Great Nonsense," murmured Polly. "Really. Nonsense." She looked as if she was absolutely on Jasper's side.

"There's something I haven't told you," Jasper said.

"Only one thing?" The captain's old eyes held a faint twinkle.

Jasper took a breath and plunged on. "I saw Lady Gall putting something in my sister's mouth. It made her sick for a whole week. That's why we left home in such a hurry."

Dr. Rocket and Polly both lowered their sandwiches.

"She wants my family dead, or gathered alive," Jasper said.

"I don't know why."

Waves churned against the hull. Wind beat in the sails.

The captain cleared his throat, then cleared it again. "We're heading for the Isle of Storms as fast as possible. There will be news there of the *Blue Swan*." He turned to the wheel and clamped both hands on it, breathing hard.

"Thank you." Jasper's voice cracked.

Polly smoothed her apron, but Jasper saw her hands shake. "You don't have to thank us."

"By the way a second time," said Dr. Rocket gruffly, "I noticed a new toothbrush in the bathroom."

"You don't have to thank me for that either," said Polly. Then she jumped from her chair and hurried inside.

Dr. Rocket glanced at Jasper as if he knew enough about boys to be sure none would ever be grateful for a toothbrush. "I'm never going to ask if you've cleaned your teeth. I'm going to say, go clean 'em. And I'll expect to hear …"

"Aye aye," Jasper said. It didn't seem a burden in the circumstances. Besides, the son of Dr. Ludlow was intelligent enough to understand that neither of them wanted him to know how deeply they were upset.

~

Next morning, the horizon was a stretch of haze, the sky a delicate eggshell blue. After the usual fiery noises below, the captain came up to breakfast.

"Half a day to the Isle of Storms," he rumbled.

"If we manage to find the right map," Polly said.

The captain frowned. She gave a tiny fraction of a giggle.

Dr. Rocket stomped up the ladder to the wheelhouse,

then tossed a rolled-up map down the ladder. Polly spread it open in a dining booth and put jelly dishes on the corners. A map of Old Ocean. She showed Jasper where the *Traveling Restaurant* was, and in what direction they were sailing.

Jasper loved the maps in his geography book—the shapes of the land, the designs around the edges, the names of all the places. It was very different looking at a map when he was trying to see where a particular ship had been wrecked, a ship that had been carrying his family. He clenched his teeth and punched the table. Then he helped Polly tidy the galley and went on deck to do some odd jobs with the oil can. Small birds with cheerful eyes came, hoping for snacks.

For the first hour the sea was empty of other vessels, as if Old Ocean were still scrubbed clean after the great storm. Polly spent some time checking the rigging. With a worried chew on her lip, she set a pile of thick canvas and ropes in a corner of the deck. She threaded a huge needle with stout cotton. It looked as if she was sewing trousers for one-legged giants.

"What are you making?" Jasper asked.

"It's baggy-wrinkles."

"But what are they?" he said.

"Chafing gear, for winding round the iron hawsers."

"Why?" At once Jasper wished he hadn't asked. People would keep thinking he was dim.

"It's like canvas sausage skins. It stops the metal wearing out so fast. D'you think everything on this ship is done by..." She stopped, frowned, and stabbed the needle into the canvas.

He didn't dare ask if she'd meant (magic). It would be only an expression.

A sail appeared on the horizon, and a puff of black smoke from the funnel of another ship. Polly shaded her eyes for a moment, put the sewing aside and joined Dr. Rocket in the wheelhouse. They didn't invite Jasper to join them. As usual between Dr. Rocket and Polly, they weren't saying much but seemed to understand what the other one meant. Were they father and daughter? They were often annoyed with each other, though it never lasted long.

Dr. Rocket spent ages peering through the big brass telescope, then Polly used it. Her face became even more grim.

~

Jasper longed to use the telescope as well. He was pretty sure they wouldn't let him, for fear of what he might see. Not knowing about his parents felt awful, like someone using a kitchen grater on his heart.

Polly came down and worked faster on the baggy-wrinkle gear.

"Shall I fetch you and the captain more coffee? A piece of cake?" He didn't wait for an answer in case it was no. He climbed to the wheelhouse and passed a mug and plate to Dr. Rocket. Then he sidled to the telescope and put his eye to it.

He saw a blur of waves, and a close-up of Dr. Rocket's big earhole (shiny and clean). Then, in the middle of his vision was a five-master. It flew a pirate flag.

He swung the telescope to another vessel. It too flew a

pirate flag. So did a third—they were a flock of scavengers picking up wreckage. So much wreckage, even days after the storm.

"Dr. Rocket," he said, "it's possible that my parents might be aboard one of … that they've been captured …"

"Possible," said the captain. "Possibly not. Whichever it is, we mustn't let ourselves be captured."

But how could the *Traveling Restaurant* not be noticed? The storm hadn't eaten off her paint as it had on other ships, so her colored segments really stood out, and her shape was so unusual. And though she had an engine, it wasn't a strong one—a five-masted pirate ship would easily run her down.

The captain kept the wheel steady. On deck, Polly was wrapping a baggy-wrinkle round a hawser. Jasper went to help but she brushed him aside.

Stop! Jasper wanted to say. *We're mad to sail toward danger!* The only thing he could do was take some kitchen scraps aft to give to the little seabirds. "These might be your last," he told them. "But let's hope." Nobody but the birds would hear him here near the stern. He took in a breath and said, "If there were magic, I would trust in it completely."

A tendril of white floated past him like a moth's wing. He clambered back into the wheelhouse. Another tendril— mist—drifted up. Soon the *Traveling Restaurant* was in fog thick and syrupy enough to scoop up with a ladle. It even smelled a little sweet. Without speaking, Dr. Rocket steered on. Polly left the hawser half-wrapped and climbed the rigging to trim the sails (now and then there was a flash of those green heels). The fog looked thickest around the *Traveling Restaurant* but it was hard to be sure. What was certain was she sailed between the pirate ships, unchallenged. The captain seemed to hold his breath in disbelief.

Junk and rubbish floated past. A red armchair. Bottles—crates—barrels, and a tuba. As Jasper watched, a wave tipped into it and the big silver instrument sank down, down. A dinghy, full of pirates arguing as they gathered any useful-looking objects, scooted in and out of the thickest edges of the fog.

All at once the *Traveling Restaurant* was almost on top of a broken slab of wood. And sprawled on it was a man. He peered up at Jasper through a damp fringe, then collapsed. "Captain!" Jasper pointed.

A black ship, sails billowing, overtook them on the port side. How did it dare to go so swiftly in a fog? Jasper supposed pirates would dare anything. Then he thought—if the black ship's sails were bellied with wind, why didn't that same wind blow away the fog?

He still had sight of the makeshift raft. You couldn't tell if the man was a sailor or a passenger from some wrecked ship.

"Dr. Rocket!" Jasper tugged his sleeve. "We must do something!"

"Sorry, boy," the captain said. "We mustn't risk it."

The *Restaurant* was drifting further from the raft at every moment. What if Jasper's father, or Uncle Trump, were stranded in the middle of Old Ocean and a ship simply sailed by? He must do something!

Just below the wheelhouse, Jasper knew, was an orange dinghy on its orange davits. How difficult could it be to lower a dinghy? He'd tie a rope to the rail of the *Restaurant*, so if he lost one of the oars Polly and the captain could haul him back …

Jasper leaped out of the wheelhouse to the davit. The dinghy hit Old Ocean with a splash. There was a shout from Dr. Rocket. Jasper slung a rope ladder over the side of the *Restaurant* and scrambled down. He nearly toppled into the water, but wrestled into a seat and grabbed the oars from underneath it. Ignoring more shouts from the captain and screams from Polly, he set off toward the raft. What was the point of having an adventure if it was not at least a bit scary?

He knew how to row. You do it with your back to where you're going, and look over your shoulder. There, he saw, the fog was lifting. The man on the raft was up on one elbow.

Jasper glanced at the *Restaurant*. Drifts of smoky mist still swirled around the funnel. The captain, at the helm, was wrenching the wheel and shouting at Polly. Jasper had forgotten the important step of fixing a rope between the *Restaurant* and the dinghy.

He pulled harder on the oars.

The raft was awash. Jasper hadn't quite reached it when the man struggled to his knees and plunged off. With a splashing one-armed dog paddle, he soon had a grip on the dinghy's side. In the other arm he clutched a black bundle. He thrashed about—a rope from the raft was tangled around his wrist. His head went under. Jasper slid his dagger from its scabbard and sawed at the rope hard. At last, he cut it through. The raft disappeared below the waves and the man floated up, coughing and choking. Somehow, Jasper grappled him aboard. The man blinked through his fringe at the dagger, tried to say something but collapsed on the floor of the dinghy.

Jasper yanked on the oars. By the time he reached the *Traveling Restaurant*—rather, by the time the *Restaurant* reached him—he ached all over. The man was unconscious, face down. Even so, his arms were tight around the bundle. He'd lost one of his shoes.

With grumbling sounds like a volcano, the captain climbed down the rope ladder. He heaved the man over his shoulders, up onto the deck, and into the cabin.

They stowed the man and his bundle beneath a dining booth. Polly covered him with a rug, put a basin next to him in case he wanted to be sick, and vanished back into the rigging. Dr. Rocket hurried up into the wheelhouse. Neither of them had said a word to Jasper. He had put himself in danger, but he had saved somebody's life. It didn't seem fair to be in trouble because of that.

~

An hour passed. Polly stayed in the rigging and the man remained lifeless. Only threads of mist still hung in the air. A few ships were in the distance—a safe distance, Jasper hoped.

He sat in the cabin doorway and tipped out his backpack again. Emily would have told him to put on fresh underwear. He had not liked the way the man had stared at the dagger, so he stashed it at the bottom under his trumpet. Perhaps he ought to practice his trumpet, since it was there. He could play whatever tune or not-a-tune he liked—but it might keep the seabirds away.

Dr. Rocket stuck his head out the wheelhouse door. "Any sign of the Isle of Storms?" he shouted to Polly.

She called from the crow's-nest. "It's on the horizon. Fingers crossed."

Jasper shoved his backpack under the bench. On deck again, all he could see was the shimmer of waves under the mist. Then a movement caught his eye. A tiny green bird darted, so far from land that Jasper thought it must be lost. It dipped and swooped, small feet almost pattering over the surface of the water. When it reached the ship, it soared into the rigging close to Polly. Jasper began to climb up to see it better, but Dr. Rocket grabbed his collar. For an old man, the captain had moved very fast.

"Stay on deck, thank you," the captain said politely. "It will be no good finding your mother if we've lost you overboard. She's a most ferocious woman, is your mother."

Jasper stared. Above his hearth-brush beard, Dr. Rocket flushed as if he'd given away a secret. Did the captain know his mother? She could certainly lose her temper. Most mothers can. But more often she was gentle—sometimes scatty, but a lot of mothers are, aren't they?

The green bird, with a piping sound, pattered off again across the waves. The captain clambered back to tend the wheel.

The *Traveling Restaurant* moved faster. Jasper glanced

behind them. The mist was disappearing. Bearing down on the *Restaurant* were a pirate ship and a sloop-of-war close enough to see soldiers milling on deck. Had those ships been near them all along? Had the mist been conjured up to hide the *Restaurant*? The *Restaurant*'s sails spread like wings. She almost flew over the surface until the other ships were far behind.

Polly, looking as frail as sea foam, tumbled neatly back on deck. She climbed into the wheelhouse. Dr. Rocket put an arm around her shoulder, and they murmured. Again Jasper wondered if they were father and daughter. Dr. Rocket cleared his throat and spoke to Jasper.

"All passengers from the *Blue Swan* are safe on other vessels."

Relief made Jasper dizzy. His parents were safe! So was Sibilla! "Did the green bird tell you?"

Polly's shoulders went stiff. "There are such things as signal flags, you know."

"Yes, and you can train birds. I didn't mean—well, I did wonder if the mist might be …" His heart was huge with hope, but he couldn't say the forbidden word aloud again.

"The mist," said Polly, "is an unexplained but not uncommon natural event. The hull of the ship is cold, which could be part of the scientific explanation."

Dr. Rocket put a steadying hand on Jasper's shoulder. "The important thing is we're safe. At least, we're safe for now. You have been very lucky, boy. Let's hope that luck continues."

THIS IS WHEN IT
BECOMES FRAUGHT

The captain tucked a napkin under his beard. Sun bathed the dining table in yellow light, and the scent of mashed potato and lots of butter filled the galley. The rescued man (one black shoe, one sock) snored beneath the dining booth. As it dried out, his hair turned fair and curly. Polly scowled at him. She scowled at Jasper too, and slammed a plate of chicken pie in front of him.

Whenever Jasper asked a question it turned out to be the wrong time. He thought this was probably so with any boys, bright or dim. But he didn't much care about that, because he was still on a pitch of happiness about his family being safe.

"How does the ship sail when nobody's in the wheelhouse?" he asked.

"We use a fly-by-night," said Dr. Rocket. "We're sailing downwind. One large sail will keep us steady."

It was nice to get an answer for a change. "What about the engine?" Jasper asked.

"There are many tricks on Old Ocean," the captain said.

So, no (magic), just luck, clever seamanship or back-up equipment. Jasper had known as much really, because of Polly worrying about the baggy-wrinkles. But though he had the usual pang that there was no (that thing), at the same time he felt there was more hope in this little world than he would have said a week ago. He ate a bite of pie. It was very good. When he'd found his family, he'd ask Polly to make a huge pie and …

A shadow fell across the *Restaurant*. A deep voice, magnified by a megaphone, boomed out: "Heave to!"

Through the porthole was a black-painted pirate ship.

"The *Double Cross*!" whispered Polly. She and the captain stared at each other. Their shoulders slumped.

"Heave to!" boomed out again.

The captain lurched from the table up to the wheelhouse.

"For goodness sake, stay quiet," Polly snapped, then she darted on deck.

Even from where he sat, Jasper could see cannon trained directly at the *Restaurant*. At last he understood why rescuing the man had not been wise. They should have sailed on as fast as possible and not turned back for any reason, even a good one.

He went to shake the man awake, but he lay face down, unmoving. So: an old man, a young woman, a boy with one small dagger at the bottom of his pack, and a dozen pirates leaping down on deck.

What had Lady Gall said to the officer? Dr. Ludlow only pretends his son is not intelligent.

~

By the time Dr. Rocket and Polly were dragged into the dining room by two hefty pirates, Jasper, standing ramrod straight, was wearing an apron. He held out menus.

"Will you take a seat?" he offered.

"Death to the brat!" A pirate in a bandana started toward Jasper, cutlass raised.

Jasper kept his chin high. "Your friends will be more comfortable if they let go of the head waiter. And it would pay to let go of the cook."

The doorway darkened. Jasper could tell it was the pirate chief. His hat was one that would be laughed at in the high street, but at sea it made Jasper's knees buckle. Still, he ducked under the cutlass and placed a menu in the pirate chief's fist. It was crumpled up at once.

"What are you worth!" roared the pirate chief.

"Very little," replied Dr. Rocket.

The pirate chief flung himself down at the table and grabbed a chunk of pie. "Explain it to them, Murgott!"

"Aye aye, Captain Darkblood." The pirate lowered his cutlass and touched his disreputable bandana. "Three choices," he said to Dr. Rocket. "One: hand over your money and treasure. Two: we ransom you. Three: we toss you overboard."

"One," said Dr. Rocket. "We have three pounds and a few odd dolleros and two pennies which you are welcome to. We have no treasure."

"Two," said Polly. "Nobody is likely to pay a ransom for us."

Captain Darkblood had eaten half of Jasper's pie by now.

Murgott laid hold of Jasper. Another pirate hauled the unconscious man half out from under the booth. "Overboard, then. And we keep the ship."

"Four!" Jasper wriggled from Murgott's grip. "Let us go, and I guarantee Polly will give you the best pie you've ever tasted."

"He's brave as well as stupid," Murgott wheezed, "but it's no good." He twisted Jasper's collar, which choked him and made spots dance in his eyes.

"Wait!" Captain Darkblood held up the second half of Jasper's pie and grinned. "You mean there is a better pie than this?"

~

Jasper glanced at Polly, who glared at him.

Murgott loosened his hold. Jasper took a deep breath and rubbed his throat. "We've got cheese pie, chicken pie, beef pie, pork pie, and lamb."

"Lamb!" Murgott didn't look impressed. He yanked Jasper to the door.

"Correct, sir," Jasper yelled. "If anything gets stuck between your teeth, we've plenty of toothpicks!"

"Don't push your luck," growled Captain Darkblood. But he gestured to Murgott to let Jasper go.

Polly was already behind the counter, banging pots as cooks do when they're furious. The pirates shoved the unconscious man back under the booth. With rough guffaws, they began to shout what kind of pie they wanted.

Polly's jaw firmed. "Stop! You can have any sort of pie you want …"

Phew, thought Jasper.

"But wash your hands first!" continued Polly. "Then sit down and be quiet. Wait for the waiter to take your order. That's why we call them waiters. They wait upon you, but you also have to wait for them. Politely!"

She returned to banging pots. Half the pirates jeered, the other half glanced at Captain Darkblood. He gave a chilling laugh but let Polly have her way. Jasper showed the pirates where the bathroom was. They looked sideways at Polly, then lined up. Jasper and Dr. Rocket were very busy for a while, scribbling orders on their notepads.

Polly set plates of pie and salad on the counter. Dr. Rocket and Jasper ferried them to the tables. For some time the only sound was chewing (many pirates, disgustingly, with mouths open). Some of them demanded seconds. "Only," said Polly, "if your plate is clean, if you've eaten all your salad, and ask nicely." With his eyebrows, Dr. Rocket signalled her to be careful. She glowered. "And after second helpings," Polly said, "you keep your side of the bargain and clear off."

Darkblood's eyes were cold as the hours after midnight. He rose to his feet, a hand on the hilt of his sword. "I've decided I want meals this delicious three times a day. Young woman, bring your recipes. You're sailing with us!"

Murgott waved his fingers as if he were as wary of Polly as he was of Darkblood. "To explain, Miss, our own cook can barely boil water."

"There is no honor in your deals," rumbled Dr. Rocket.

Captain Darkblood let out a hard laugh. "What did you expect?"

"You're as bad as Lady Gall!" Jasper shouted.

Darkblood took a step back.

"We can make another deal," Jasper continued, "but you must keep this one. If Polly shows your cook some tricks, you let her go."

~

"I will not make a deal with a cheat." Polly's voice was as strong and steely as a slotted spoon.

"My dear," Dr. Rocket whispered.

"I'll do it!" Jasper cried.

Darkblood roared again and gestured to the pirates to grab Polly.

"I'll show them how to cook!" Jasper repeated. He might make a mess of it. They might all end up murdered by cutlass, pistol, drowning, or having their own pies shoved down their throats until they smothered. But he had to have a chance to find his family.

Captain Darkblood stared at him with those cold eyes, then grinned and jerked his head at Murgott. The pirates went to fetch their cook. When the man arrived, his hands were far from clean. His nose was runny.

Jasper chose Murgott, the cook, and one other pirate. He prayed he would remember everything he had seen Emily doing at home in the little palace. He rolled up his sleeves and scrubbed his hands and arms up to the elbows.

"Look and learn. The first rule of cooking is wash your hands."

Darkblood—laughing—told the pirates to obey.

Jasper gave them aprons. He showed them how to measure flour without spilling it. He demonstrated how much a pinch of salt actually is. He showed them how to keep the sifter low and in the bowl so flour wouldn't snow all over the floor. He showed them how to mix milk (or water, depending) into the flour. The pirates slapped the mixture onto floured boards and rolled it out. Murgott, with the biggest and hairiest hands, was surprisingly neat.

Jasper somehow felt uplifted, as if a whiff of (magic) really was about. More likely it was the memory of helping Emily and his mother in his own kitchen. But the risky part of a pie is in the baking. Jasper watched the pirate cook as he greased a pie dish and lined it with a pastry shell. The cook dolloped in some mincemeat which, luckily, Polly had prepared earlier.

"Now put a pastry lid on top," he told the cook. "And stab three holes for steam to escape while the pie bakes."

He organised Murgott to spread chopped bacon on the bottom of a pastry shell, break six eggs in, then put a pastry lid on that as well.

"That man's a natural at cooking," Polly murmured.

Murgott turned a little pink around the eyes. It suited him, but Jasper didn't comment.

He showed the third pirate the simplest way of all to make a pie. The burly fellow rolled the pastry into a rectangle-oval-it-didn't-matter. Over half of it, Jasper told him to spread grated cheese, chopped parsley, and cut-up tomato. The next step was to fold the other half on top and press down the edges. Onto a baking tray with it, and the pirate slid it into the oven with a crash.

The man beneath the bench had woken up. He stayed there and eased a notebook out of the bundle of black cloth.

Murgott gnawed scraps of uncooked pastry off his forearm. "I enjoyed that so far," he said.

"The thing is, I never asked to be a cook," mumbled the cook.

Darkblood removed his hat and bashed it on the table. Dust and dirt rose in a cloud.

"True, Captain," said Murgott quickly. "You captured him and forced him to it."

"I used to be an accountant," said the cook.

Darkblood's eyes narrowed. "Dealing with money!"

"Not real money," the cook explained. "It was totting up numbers in a ledger—for Lady Gall." The atmosphere seemed to shrink and creak. The cook flinched. "The country's accounts never added up. She made me put money that should have gone on roads and schools in an account called 'Sundries'. She used that on hats, nail files, and vats of beauteen."

"Cheating," Murgott muttered. The word trickled around the cabin.

Polly looked as she often did, sarcastic. "You could help Captain Darkblood with his accounts," she said to the cook.

Darkblood's mouth twitched in a dangerous smile, but he and the cook shook hands. It was a strangely gruesome moment. But here was another chance for Jasper.

"Do you have any prisoners now?" he asked. "Anyone you rescued after the storm?"

Captain Darkblood scowled. "Another mistake. I thought he might be wealthy, but he's useless. And he's limping."

"Only one?" Jasper's voice wobbled, but he managed a bold smile. "Back in Little Skirmish we heard the *Blue Swan* went down. It must have been full of good prizes."

Murgott shrugged and picked his teeth, staring at the oven where the pies baked.

"We argued with the Navy over the ragtags." Darkblood flicked his fingers in disgust.

"Did you capture any children?" Jasper asked.

"Children on a pirate ship? Disaster!" said Captain Darkblood. "The *Red Wolf* took that rubbish, I believe." He caught sight of the shipwrecked man. "What's this?" he roared. "Eavesdropper!"

The man tried to tuck his notebook into his jacket.

"A spy for Lady Gall!" Murgott shouted. "Keel haul him!"

"Not in front of the boy!" Polly cried.

"The boy can look the other way," growled Darkblood.

But by now a delicious smell wreathed through the air. Polly opened the oven. The pies were golden brown. "Jasper has kept his side of the deal. You keep yours," she said. "Take these pies to the *Double Cross* and have them for dinner. Have this scribbler too, for all we care."

"How do you do?" the scribbler said. "The name's Kent. Crispin Kent."

"Would anyone pay a ransom for you?" Murgott asked.

The scribbler shrugged and shook his head.

"No more useless prisoners." Darkblood was about to stride out on deck when he turned back, grabbed the notebook and read what Kent had written. His eyebrows rose for a moment under his hat brim. He glanced at Jasper. With a laugh he flung the notebook to the floor.

"It's lucky that sometimes I keep a deal," he said.

~

Murgott carried the pies away in one of Polly's baskets. The dining cabin emptied of pirates. Dr. Rocket went on deck to make sure they didn't damage the *Restaurant* when they untied her from the *Double Cross*.

"That's the last I'll see of my best basket," Polly said. "But we got away with our lives." She gave Jasper's arm a gentle punch. It told him she was grateful for his quick thinking and the way he'd taught pie-making. It also showed him that she knew he hoped his parents were aboard one of the naval vessels, in disguise, alive. It told him she knew how worried he was about Sibilla.

Surely a toddler would have been noticed? Lady Helen or Dr. Ludlow would have been carrying her. But what if they'd handed her to Trump! In that case Jasper couldn't bear to think what might have happened.

Crispin Kent had not said another word, not even *thank you*. Jasper suspected he'd been awake longer than he'd let on. He was in a booth now, smoothing the notebook's crumpled pages. Jasper dampened a cloth, pretended to wipe down the tables, and tried to sneak a look.

Kent huddled sideways and put an arm over the open book. But Jasper had been able to read three lines.

The first was: He has the royal dagger.

The second was: He is the most dangerous boy at present on Old Ocean.

The third was: No wonder the parents left him behind on purpose.

~

Jasper was blinded by a wing of horror and sadness. The man couldn't mean Jasper—many other boys had daggers. The man couldn't mean his parents—they'd left him by accident. But ... Trump might have left him deliberately—or perhaps his parents had even plotted with Trump to leave him on purpose!

Kent glanced out a porthole at the *Double Cross*, still lashed to the *Restaurant*'s side. He gathered up his book and the black bundle, and hobbled in his one shoe and one sock to the far end of the dining cabin. There, he shook the bundle out and draped it on a chair. It was a thin black cape.

And then Jasper remembered the day of his birthday, and the man who claimed to be a journalist and who Emily wouldn't let in. He remembered the day the *Blue Swan* sailed without him, the tall man strolling past with a notebook and a thin black cloak. The same man? He had to be a spy for Lady Gall.

~

Jasper wiped his face with the cleaning cloth (yuck, very bad idea) and went on deck. On the port side, Dr. Rocket was seeing the pirates up the ladders to the *Double Cross*.

Waves flurried like feathers around the hull. Jasper tried

to settle his churning thoughts. Do spies ever tell the truth? *The most dangerous boy* … And the dagger—was it so very special? He hadn't used it, except to rescue Crispin Kent. He'd tricked his way out of being captured by soldiers— twice, actually. He had tricked the pirates into having lunch on the *Restaurant* instead of robbing them and murdering them all. Then he had shown them how to cook in return for setting the *Restaurant* free. If he was dangerous, it was only by tricking people who were cruel and horribly self-centered.

But he had sometimes been selfish himself—like, being too scared to tell his parents straightaway that Lady Gall had fed his sister poison. He felt so guilty now, he could hardly move. Was that why his parents—or Trump—had left him behind? But why, why would the Provisional Monarch try to murder a little child? Why did Lady Gall want his family dead or captured?

The late afternoon wind was getting up. Spindrift blew into his face. Jasper found that in his worry and confusion he had struggled to the rail near the huge anchor-well aft. He imagined a silver bird in there, growing stronger in its nest, and felt a shred of comfort. At this moment all he hoped was that Sibilla was well. Even now, just thinking of her pixie face and bright blue eyes could make him smile.

He glanced at the pirates' last rope ladder, ready to be drawn back up to the *Double Cross*.

At the railing of the pirate ship, Captain Darkblood in his terrifying hat roared curses that would have made Jasper's pen burst into flames if he'd tried to write them down. He was using the point of his sword to prod a ragged figure in a long-tailed coat and a hat with a bent feather at the brim. It looked very much like Uncle Trump. He was even clutching a satchel.

Jasper's next breath waited in his throat.

Trump was hard against the rail. Darkblood looked about to tip him over or run the sword right through him—probably both. It would serve Trump right for leaving Jasper on the dock—but you can't wish evil on your uncle, not until you're really sure he's wicked. Besides, he might have the answer to why Jasper had been left behind.

Dr. Rocket had disappeared into the wheelhouse. Polly was still in the cabin.

The most dangerous boy (how he wished!) steadied himself. He roared up at Captain Darkblood. "Having trouble with a landlubber, Captain?"

Darkblood's sword was raised high.

Fingers tightly crossed behind his back, Jasper bellowed with pretend laughter. "Chuck the layabout down here! We'll swab the decks with him!"

Darkblood glanced down at Jasper. Trump grabbed for the rope ladder, but slipped in those long-toed boots. Darkblood swiped his sword and missed. Trump clutched the ladder again and, before Darkblood could swipe a second time, slithered halfway down.

Jasper roared again. "Giving us your old rubbish, Captain? You win this one, sir!"

With a final curse, Darkblood cut the ladder. Trump fell on the *Restaurant*'s deck. The rope ladder piled on top of him like a net.

Jasper heard Polly gasp behind him, but she stayed where she was and didn't rush to help. In moments, the waves pushed the ships apart. Dr. Rocket hurried down from the wheelhouse. With a whiskery groan he knelt beside Trump. In his strong old arms, not very gently, he helped Trump up and inside. Trump's eyes were closed. It looked as if he'd hurt a foot or ankle.

Jasper's heart raced as he and Polly followed into the warmth. Crispin Kent started. He stepped forward as Trump collapsed upon a bench, then drew slightly back.

Uncle Trump opened his eyes, saw Kent and frowned. Then he saw Jasper. He gave a little gasp, slowly rubbed his face as if he were tired, and put a finger over his lips.

Polly grabbed Jasper's shoulders and set him aside. "Why did the *Double Cross* toss this rubbish to us?" Her voice dripped scorn.

Uncle Trump had noticed Polly for the first time—his jaw dropped as if he'd seen a frightening angel.

"We've got to reach harbor." Dr. Rocket's old gray eyebrows moved at Polly and Jasper with warning messages. "We'll get rid of both these extras at—er—Battle Island."

Trump closed his eyes and pressed both hands over his brow.

Jasper finished wiping the tables. He hoped—how badly he hoped—he would find a chance to talk to Uncle Trump. He hoped—how desperately and angrily he hoped—his uncle would have news of his family, news that they hadn't been recognized and captured by the troops of Lady Gall.

THE MOST DANGEROUS BOY
AND A DANGEROUS CHOICE

The bright sails of the *Traveling Restaurant* bellied full in the strong breeze. Seagulls screamed and argued. Crispin Kent had found Polly's deckchair. He had done a lot of scribbling, and now seemed to be dozing in the evening sun. Without asking, he had one of Dr. Rocket's caps over his eyes. As far as Jasper knew, the spy and Uncle Trump had still not spoken. Uncle Trump had limped with his sketchbook to the other side of the deck.

Dr. Rocket yelled from the wheelhouse, and Polly nipped up into the rigging. Jasper eased the dagger from the bottom of his backpack, buckled it on and pulled his shirt to cover it. Then he strolled around till he found Uncle Trump. Trump stuck his sketchbook under his arm and leaned on the rail.

Jasper put his hands on the rail too, and swallowed hard. "Uncle …"

"Your mother and father are all right. I'm pretty sure."

"What do you mean, 'all right' and 'pretty sure?'"

Trump didn't answer straight away. "They were taken aboard HPMS *Red Wolf.*"

"Are they still in disguise? Does Lady Gall know?"

His uncle gave a hopeless shrug.

Jasper fiercely blinked back tears. "How was Sibilla's cough?"

Trump's knuckles showed white against the rail.

Jasper grabbed his sleeve. "Is she sick again? Do you mean she isn't with them? You have to tell me what you know!"

Trump put a finger to his lips and looked up at the rigging where Polly's green boots glinted in the last of the sun. Trump kept looking till Polly noticed. She scowled.

In silence, Trump limped with Jasper along the deck aft, to a spot where the wind was not so boisterous. They sat against the railing. Jasper's hand went to the scabbard under his shirt. "Where is my sister?" he said.

"I could have found out, once," said Trump. With a sad little laugh that was more of a sigh, he flipped open his sketchbook and stopped at the last drawing, a half-finished sketch of a baby's face. Trump pulled a pencil from his pocket. As he added a line or two, some shading and cross-hatching, the drawing became a picture of Sibilla. She was waiting for dinner in a high chair, fair hair sticking up in thistledown surprise.

Jasper knelt up to see better, reached out and touched Sibilla's pixie-small hand. Somehow the picture seemed to move. This sometimes happened when he held back tears— things shimmered and seemed to stir.

But now a plate of porridge appeared on the tray of the high chair. Sibilla's face was sad. She took up a spoon and messed her food. As Jasper watched, holding his breath, his baby sister stirred the porridge into a ring, a pool of milk in the middle.

"Good lord ..." Uncle Trump seemed totally astonished.

Jasper's left hand kept hold of the sketchbook while his right hand gripped the scabbard at his side. *Explain it,* he begged silently. *Why is my family separated? Why does Lady Gall hate us? And why does she forbid everyone to talk about magic, when I see things like this that I can't explain in any other way ...*

"... because there is magic in the world," he whispered aloud.

The picture seemed to grow—or Jasper seemed to move into it—and he was no longer looking at a toddler's plate. He was outside, on land, in a warm evening breeze. The moon rose behind a grove of willow trees. In front of Jasper, a lake of pale-blue water bubbled from underground. Around the pool was a gathering of families—parents, grandparents, children playing, babies sitting, crawling, learning to walk.

"It's the Eastern Isle before the Great Accident," breathed Trump. "There is the lake. Those children are the orphans now."

Beside the pool, a young man raised something silver to his mouth—it was a flute. The young man played a melody and laughed. He picked up a dark-haired little girl and played haunting notes of happiness, one-handed. The moon rose higher. A silvery glow filled the glade and shone upon the pool. The lake rippled—something silver, huge and wonderful stirred beside the water—

106

The scene blurred—Sibilla threw her spoon away and started to cry …

The wind nudged the sketchbook out of Jasper's hands. He tried to grab it but the pages fluttered shut.

He was crouched near the stern of the *Traveling Restaurant* again, in strong cold wind. The sun was on the horizon and seagulls screamed. The green sails flapped. The hidden engine roared like a giant heart.

Uncle Trump picked up the sketchbook and held it to his chest. Tears trembled in his eyes. He whispered something that sounded like "Thank you." In a louder voice he said, "She's alive and well. Sibilla is alive."

"But is she with my parents?" Jasper cried.

Trump shook his head.

"Did they leave her behind too?"

"Oh no," Trump said. "Oh, no." He rubbed his face.

Jasper had to ask his next question, though it was hard to get the words out. "Did my parents mean to leave me behind? Did you mean to?"

"That's a tricky one," Trump said in a low voice. "If something is the only choice you have, and it is a hard one, is it deliberate?"

"What are you saying!" Jasper clambered to his feet.

Uncle Trump stood too and gripped the ship's rail. "I'm good at the wrong decisions. I thought you'd be safer left behind. I thought we'd all be safer."

All Jasper could do was close his eyes.

"I don't like adventures any more than you do," said his uncle. "I've always managed to avoid them." He swallowed hard. "But now we have to figure out what to do. Lady Gall must not get hold of you, or me, or Sibilla. The fate of our little world is tied up in it."

This was it, then. This is what Jasper had known from the moment he realized he was on his own, there on the docks of the City of Spires. Big adventures were ahead.

Trump rubbed the deep lines on his forehead. "What choices do we have? What shall we do?"

It seemed to Jasper there were four choices. One was to seek his parents. Another was to seek Sibilla. The third was to run away (maybe the pirates would like a cabin boy!)— and the fourth was to kick and scream in a childish tantrum.

The sun finally dipped below the horizon. Jasper walked a few steps from Trump and stood above the third anchor-well. After a moment he felt steadier. He turned to face his uncle.

"I am going to find Sibilla," Jasper said.

—

SECOND PART

Lunch with the Secret Prince

A NOT VERY
EXCELLENT PLAN

Uncle Trump gripped Jasper's shoulder. "We'll make a plan," he said. He bent closer. "Ah—you still have that dagger?"

"Yes," said Jasper. Was his uncle asking for it back?

"Just keep it hidden," said Trump. He took a limping step and shivered.

"Polly or Dr. Rocket should look at your ankle," Jasper said. "Have you sprained it?"

"Oh—let's not bother them. Especially not—er—Polly," said Trump. "Look, you and I shouldn't seem too friendly at this stage. We'll talk about a plan tomorrow morning."

Jasper felt very like he had on the wharves the day Trump ended up leaving him behind. Was his uncle actually trustworthy? It was not a very nice question to find himself asking.

~

As soon as breakfast was over next morning, Polly disappeared into the rigging. Dr. Rocket was in the wheelhouse, the window open so the breeze slid over his bald head. The spy had taken over a table in the dining room and was scribbling in his notebook again.

Jasper strolled along the deck, pretending to be casual so Trump could meet and talk with him "by accident." When he reached aft, above the anchor-well, he leaned on the railing. Below nestled the enormous bird-like shape. Seeing Sibilla in the picture had made Jasper sure that wonders still existed. For a moment he let himself imagine how astounding it would be if there really was a bird as large and strong as that in the depths of the *Restaurant*.

Uncle Trump limped up and put his satchel down. "One step at a time. Are we agreed?"

"I suppose so," Jasper said.

Trump took his hat off and tried to straighten out the feather. "We can't talk freely with that other chap on board. We must get rid of him."

Jasper stared at Trump. "The spy? You mean, chuck him overboard?"

Trump looked shocked and made the feather worse. "You saved him, didn't you? It would be a rotten thing to do, to chuck him back."

"Exactly," said Jasper.

Trump blew a fat sigh of relief. "But our first step is to put into a harbor as soon as possible and send him ashore. Then we sail off again, quick as a fish."

"Dr. Rocket said they'd drop you both at Battle Island."

"No, no! The *Red Wolf* was heading there!" Trump jammed his hat on, and put both hands on his hips. "Lady Gall had news of the *Wolf* and therefore of your parents. So of course that's where she's going. We can't go near

Battle Island. Use your brain!" He limped off, coat tails swinging.

Jasper noticed that for the first time Trump wasn't carrying his satchel. It was still lying in a corner of the deck. He would have called out, but Trump had just been rude—anyway, Polly was yelling down to him.

"Stop lazing about on deck! Jasper! Give me a hand!"

Jasper checked that Dr. Rocket wasn't watching to haul him back, then scrambled up the rigging. This would be a chance to talk with Polly on her own. By the time he reached her, his foot had slipped twice and his legs were feeling shaky.

"Untie that rope," Polly shouted. Her headband was down about her neck, her hair blowing everywhere, and her apron was covered in ship's grease. "No, not that one! Oh, for heaven's sake! Copy me!"

It was cold up there, and Jasper's fingers weren't as nimble as they should have been. It took a while to get the ropes tied the way Polly wanted.

"You did pretty well," she said at last. She and Jasper hung side by side from the ropes. "Sorry I shouted."

There was no real answer to that, so Jasper smiled without really smiling.

"You're not bad for a first timer," Polly continued. "I'll give you lessons."

"Thank you," said Jasper, not sure if he meant it. "Um—can I ask something?"

Polly looked suspicious.

"Can we just put the first man—Crispin Kent—ashore

as soon as possible? But keep the other one, from the pirate ship?"

"Are you sure?" It was her grimmest voice.

"The thing is," Jasper said, "that second man's my uncle."

Polly looked as if she'd like to say a hundred things, not one of them polite. It also looked as if she'd known all along.

—

THE PLAN IS STILL
PRETTY AWFUL

By late afternoon a large island lay ahead. Dr. Rocket heaved to when the land was still no more than a dark hill upon Old Ocean. The wind was colder. Jasper had just decided to go inside when Trump came by.

"Have you seen my satchel?"

"You left it on the deck this morning," Jasper said.

Trump hurried away, boots thudding like a drumbeat. Of course—he wouldn't want the spy to see his sketchbook with its moving picture of Sibilla.

Jasper raced after him, glancing in through the porthole of the dining cabin as he went. There was Crispin Kent at the table with his notebook—and with Trump's sketchbook, still unopened.

"Trump! Quickly!" Jasper shouted, and rushed in.

Uncle Trump flung into the cabin, hat askew. There were shouts, scuffling, a black notebook, a sketchbook, and a black satchel tossed around, and two grown men wrestling on the floor. All Jasper could think of was how Emily stopped chicken fights. He grabbed a saucepan of water from the galley and tossed it over both of them.

Next thing Polly was in the cabin. "No arguing on my ship! Jasper! Find something to entertain yourself." She smacked her hands together and strode out again. Trump grabbed his satchel and sketchbook, glared at Crispin Kent and hurried after her, boots squelching.

Kent pushed his damp hair off his forehead and looked at Jasper with narrow twinkling eyes.

Jasper stared back at him. "My parents did not leave me behind deliberately."

Kent's mouth worked as if he were chewing a few words to see how they tasted. "I know. Your uncle actually left you. But it's more exciting to blame your parents."

"You're a lying spy!" shouted Jasper.

"No, I just exaggerate." Kent grinned. "I have to tell stories. I'm—um—a sort-of journalist. Some papers like to print dramatic stories. Especially when they're—um— exaggerations that a certain Provisional Monarch wants to have told."

So he did work for Lady Gall. "What's the difference between your sort of journalist and a spy?" Jasper demanded.

Those narrow eyes crinkled with another grin.

"Lies!" Jasper shouted again. "What's more, I saved your life and you didn't say thanks!"

Kent slapped his own forehead. "What kind of man am I!" He kept slapping his forehead and went on deck to go pacing around in his one shoe and one sock. But he still hadn't said thank you.

~

As evening fell, the *Traveling Restaurant* sailed into port. Lights glimmered in the town. Jasper stood between Polly and Trump, watching. Polly glanced at Uncle Trump with a chilly eye. Trump looked like a dog that had been scolded.

Polly murmured to Jasper. "First thing tomorrow, we sail to the south coast and catch the West Wind Drift. We'll reach the Eastern Isle within a week."

"But how will that find Sibilla!" Jasper whispered.

She put a hand on his arm to hush him.

Crispin Kent was near the gangplank as if that would make the *Restaurant* sail faster. His cloak was wrapped around him. Even with only one shoe, he stood with a certain pride.

"So," Polly said loudly to him, "you wanted Battle Island."

"That's what you promised," said Kent.

"Well, you're getting off here," Polly said. "Dogjaw, on the Isle of Bones. And I'd be careful if I were you. Getting off, I mean. The gangplank's tricky."

Kent cleared his throat. "You do know the ocean is full of Lady Gall's ships? That she's searching for certain people? A certain boy needs to be careful."

Trump and Polly stayed silent. So did Jasper.

Kent shrugged. "I might tell a few stories, but that doesn't mean I'm always on the wrong side."

"An honest man wouldn't sneak into my satchel," muttered Trump.

The journalist-spy looked Trump up and down. "An honest man would tell his nephew far more than he's done so far."

"Shut up, the pair of you," said Polly.

The *Restaurant* bumped against the wharf, where workers rushed over to help with the ropes and hawsers. Jasper did the gangplank. He let some of his mood out with bangs and crashes.

Kent glanced along the wharf, and stiffened. He turned back to Jasper. "It would be a very good idea if you were gone by morning, Jasper. Please believe me." Then off he went in the evening shadows, his one shoe thumping on the wharf.

"Clever," said Trump. "Now we can't blame him if things go wrong."

"He's right," called Dr. Rocket softly from the wheelhouse. He climbed down and rubbed his beard. "We must be gone as soon as possible. Look there."

With a shock that made him stagger, Jasper saw that down the wharf were the five masts and three funnels of the *Excellent Hound*. "But Trump said Lady Gall was going to Battle Island!" he cried.

Trump had turned ashen. "Sometimes you get a guess wrong."

"We can't go directly to the Eastern Isle now," Dr. Rocket said, grim-faced. "If she realizes Jasper is on board, she'll be after us at once."

"Ah," said Trump. "Change of plan?"

Polly gave him another icy glance. "When we're buying provisions, I will say we're heading for the southern coast."

"Where will we really go?" asked Jasper.

Polly looked surprised. "I just said. The southern coast.

Everyone else tells lies, but why should I?"

It didn't seem much of a plan.

~

"Guard the *Restaurant*," Dr. Rocket said to Jasper. "But stay out of sight. The rest of us can stock up with provisions. Trump, fetch the handcart. You'll push it."

Trump didn't look at all pleased.

Jasper buttoned his jacket against the cold so he could guard on deck. Dr. Rocket made him tug on a battered captain's cap.

Polly fetched Jasper a wrapped-up piece of pie. "Eat that if you're hungry before we get back."

"I'm not a child," Jasper said.

"Take it!" She stuffed it in one of his pockets.

He sat near the gangplank in the dim light that grew dimmer as evening deepened. He wished he was back home before all this had begun, being bored by his mother's sewing box with all its broken bits and pieces, the list she had about why she wanted to marry the young scientist Hannibal Ludlow, and trying to take apart the circles-and-bead puzzle. He wished Emily was scolding him again for running the cart into the pond. He even wished he was being made to practice the trumpet.

The wharf was empty, and quiet except for the chime of ropes against masts and the rhythm of water. People would be resting after dinner. They might be reading the latest trashy newspaper full of lies. It would be a marvelous world if every newspaper reported the truth. It would be marvelous if uncles didn't leave boys behind on wharves, and if Lady Gall wasn't hunting Jasper's family. He wished he knew why. Was it to do with the Workroom of Knowledge? Was it something to do with Sibilla? Maybe it was to do with the Eastern Isle—Dr. Rocket seemed sure that's where the *Red Wolf* was taking his parents. Maybe Sibilla would be there too—and that was why the moving sketch of her showed the Eastern Lake. Was this somehow all to do with the death of (magic)?

(Magic.) Just before that mist had appeared and hidden the *Restaurant* from the other ships, he had said the word aloud. He'd whispered it when the picture of Sibilla came to life. He wondered if he dared say it now. No. But he breathed it the way Sibilla talked, no sound at all: *Magic.*

Jasper glanced along the wharf again. Still nobody was about. Amid the music of ropes and water was the faint thread of a tune. He wondered if the orphan who'd played the flute would still be on the *Hound*. He pulled Dr. Rocket's old cap over his eyes and stepped onto the gangplank. He timed each step with the slap of waves, so nobody could hear a boy creep from safety into danger.

~

The moon had slid behind streamers of cloud, so its light was fitful. From the darkest shadows Jasper stood and examined the side of the *Excellent Hound*. There were only a few lights, so there must be hardly anyone aboard. Golden chains hung from the hawsers, each glinting with the emblem of Lady Gall (phoenix rising, FOREVER BEAUTIFUL). There were guards at the foot of her gangplank. One of them was biting his fingernails as if he hoped something tasty lurked there. The other was slouching and humming along with the thread of music from a flute.

Sometimes, though you know you're being foolish, you can't stop it. Sometimes, your pocket is heavy with a useful hunk of pie.

THIS IS WHAT HAPPENS WHEN
YOU HAVE NO PLAN AT ALL

Jasper pulled the wrapped pie out of his pocket, held it in both hands as if it were a present, and walked out of the shadows toward the flagship.

"Oi!" The right-hand guard stood straight and glanced round quickly. He would be hoping nobody important had seen him slouch. "What d'you think you're doing!"

"Going aboard, sir," Jasper said.

"Who says?" The left-hand guard had a sneering look.

"I've been told to go aboard, sir," Jasper repeated as if he was a little stupid.

The guard crossed his arms. "Pull the other one," he said.

Jasper blinked as if he was rather more stupid. "Uvver one, sir? Uvver what?"

"Lady Gall is dining in town," said the right-hand guard, slowly, as you do when you're talking to a dumb-nut. "Nobody goes on board till she gets back."

"I'm not nobody," Jasper said. "I'm who she sent. I'm bringing this pie to the orphan." He lifted the package of pie higher. A savoury smell rose from it.

"Why should that brat get pie and we get nothing?"
The left-hand guard snatched out, but the right-hand guard
bumped him off balance.

"Lady Gall would be very angry," said the right-hand
guard, "if she found we'd mucked up what she wanted."

"Oo, she's kind to those orphans," Jasper said.
"Everyone knows that."

"Yeah," jeered the left-hand guard. "And we all get to
wear crowns of feathers 'cause we're bonkers with happiness
and joy."

The other guard kicked him. The melody floated through
the evening air, from a very small porthole near the stern.

"She's—um—sort of kind to that one," muttered the
right-hand guard.

"She's so sort of—um—kind that it's ... oo,
remarkable," agreed the other.

"I know what," said Jasper. "I'll take this pie to the orphan,
then I'll dash back to the dinner party and see if there's any
more. I better be quick. The pie is popular." He didn't want to
give them time to think. With a huge smile, he pointed in the
direction of the music. "There, eh?" They nodded.

Hardly believing his own boldness, up he went into the
Hound.

It was a huge ship, a grand ship, a ship of highly
polished wood and glittering brass. It was a ship where, at
every main stairwell, there stood a guard wearing a uniform
with gleaming buttons.

Jasper had moved in the best of families and been to
several grand occasions. He hadn't enjoyed them. But he

had learned how to behave. Now, carrying the pie before him in both hands, he kept a calm air about himself, though he shook inside. As he reached each guard, he asked in a respectful voice if this was the way to the orphan's cabin.

Each guard, with a surprised but polite nod, pointed him downward.

At last, there were no more guards, no more grand passageways or staircases. There was a dark, narrow corridor and a battered wooden companionway. It was a very different ship below the water line.

A small, hunched sailor stumbled up the companionway, muttering curses. He wiped greasy hands on a smelly rag.

"Excuse me, sir," Jasper began. "Where is the orphan?"

The sailor grumbled. He opened a narrow cupboard that held greasy gray pipes, took out his spanner, jerked it toward the lower level, then began to use it on the plumbing. Jasper didn't like the smell from the deck below, but he remembered the lonely look in that orphan's eye. Holding the pie carefully in one hand, he went backward down the companionway.

There was no light in the stuffy corridor below, except for the faintest glow beneath a door at the far end. From there seeped the music of the flute.

Jasper felt his way along and knocked. The music stopped. Nobody said anything. Jasper knocked again. "Excuse me," he said softly. "I have some pie."

There was a moment of silence.

"Lucky old you," said a husky little voice. "I hope you choke on it."

Jasper nearly grinned. "Actually, it's for you."

"Ha ha. Best laugh I've had for years." The flute started again.

"Excuse me!" Jasper dared to speak louder. "Can you open your door?"

The music stopped. "No."

"Please," said Jasper.

"What?" There was movement as if the child stood up and came closer. "I can't," said the orphan in a testy tone, "because the door is locked and you're the one on the side with the key. So go away."

Jasper couldn't answer for a moment. He felt extremely stupid. Of course the orphan was a prisoner. Then he thought, how dare Lady Gall do this to a child!

He squinted in the dark for a key. Then he ran his hand over the door until he felt an iron bolt. He tried to move it, but it was stiff and heavy. He tucked the pie back into his pocket and worked at the bolt till it squeaked and moved a little.

"I said, go away." The voice was wary.

"I need something strong, a piece of metal or something," Jasper whispered. "To go under the loopy bit to force it up."

Silence.

"I don't trust you. And why should I?"

"I'm the boy who's hopeless at the trumpet."

Again there was silence. Then, under the door, slid something that rattled.

"Blast," the orphan said. "It's stuck."

Jasper felt the bottom of the door and discovered the

handle of a spoon. He wriggled it till it slipped out. "Thank you."

"You're welcome." The child still sounded wary.

Jasper wedged the spoon handle under the loop and wriggled again. It was important not to use too much pressure in case the spoon broke. He spat on the bolt. That helped. With both hands he tugged it open. He pushed the door inward.

The cabin was not much bigger than a cupboard. The orphan wore a grubby cardigan and a skirt, and had her fists up. She blinked at Jasper but didn't put her fists down right away.

"Is there any way we can both get off the ship?" he asked.

"Probably not," said her husky little voice.

~

She looked so hungry when she smelled the pie that it nearly broke Jasper's heart to leave it in his jacket.

"Come with me," he whispered. "Just follow along. Okay?"

The girl glanced round the tiny cabin and grabbed her silver flute with its red cord. She slung the cord around her neck and tucked the flute inside her cardigan.

They bolted the door again so it would take a while for anyone to realize the prisoner had gone. In the gloom they snuck along the corridor and up the companionway. The hunched sailor was still spannering the greasy pipes. Jasper pointed at the sailor's oily jacket and the rag, and held out the pie.

~

In the bowels of the *Excellent Hound*, a bad-tempered sailor was made cheerful with an unexpected feast of Polly's pie.

Down the gangplank of the *Hound* raced an orphan. Her skirt was tucked up to look like trousers. She wore Jasper's jacket, with Dr. Rocket's hat down over her ears. "Back soon wiv pie!" cried the orphan to the guards as she dashed into the shadows of the wharf.

Down the gangplank of the *Hound* stumbled a small hunched figure in a greasy jacket, mopping his face with a greasy rag. "I quit!" growled Jasper, acting like mad. "I hate them greasy pipes an' I ain't going to work for no Lady Anybody. An' I don't blazing care who blazing knows it!" Off he stumbled too into the shadows.

~

Jasper tossed the rag aside and had to chase after the orphan. Luckily, she was not very fit after being in the cabin for so long. She also didn't know which way to go. He caught her up and seized her arm before she'd reached the wharf gates.

"Back this way!" he hissed. She was clever enough not to scream, but she tugged hard. "If you go into town, the hounds will track you," he whispered. "Come with me. I think it's your best chance."

"You think!" The girl stopped tugging. "You don't know?"

Jasper shrugged. "We're making plans one step at a time."

She scowled. "So what's the next step?"

"To sneak back up the wharf, past the guards, to the *Traveling Restaurant*," said Jasper.

She looked at the town, then up the wharf. "You mean there's food?"

Jasper nodded. Quickly, as quietly as they could, the orphan and Jasper crept in shadows. There was the scuffle of rats. A night bird screeched. Jasper and the girl hid under a cart till the bird flew off. While they crept again in the very darkest shadows past the *Hound*, it was a little sad to hear the guards discuss how good their pie would taste, if it ever came.

They kept sneaking for all they were worth till they reached the *Restaurant*. Wind rang the ropes on her masts, and waves rippled against her hull. The orphan followed Jasper up the gangplank, trembling.

"It's all right," he said softly, and beckoned her into the cabin. He nudged the girl toward a door that led below. "Hide till we're safely at sea. Here—I'll make a tray of dinner, and you take it into one of the small cabins. It's much nicer than your last one, and the only lock is on the bathroom door."

The girl had tears in her eyes. But she managed huskily to say, "You promised pie."

~

Dr. Rocket, Polly and Trump didn't appear back till after midnight. They had the cart full of bundles and bottles (for example, of fat green olives). Jasper helped unload. By now he was so tired he was stumbling. Polly and Trump were weary too, and didn't think to ask if anything had happened while they were away.

Further down the wharf a coach with lanterns clattered up to the *Excellent Hound*.

"Dr. Rocket," Jasper asked, "how soon are we leaving?

As soon as possible would be good."

"Why?" Dr. Rocket rubbed his hearth-brush beard.

"Please," said Jasper.

"Hmm," the captain said. "Then fetch your uncle."

Polly and Trump were standing together in the kitchen. When Jasper entered, they jumped. Trump smiled over-brightly as if he'd been scolded again but was trying to make believe he didn't care.

Polly had not looked as cross as this, even when they'd dealt with pirates. She banged drawers and cupboards open. "Did you eat that whole pie, Jasper?"

Jasper had to be honest. "Well," he said, "I did take it."

"Boys," said Polly, "young or old, are nothing but trouble. We're exhausted, we need food, and I want sleep!"

"Cast off!" called Dr. Rocket softly.

Polly's green high heels stalked onto the deck (with Polly in them). "I am not going anywhere tonight! We'll leave first thing in the morning!"

On the night breeze came the sound of barking dogs. Shouts. A trumpet blast.

"Cast off," Dr. Rocket repeated softly. "Now."

Polly tilted her head. A swoop of gulls flew overhead, large dark shapes calling loudly. Polly sighed. "Boys," she said again, and began her climb into the rigging.

⌒

WHO NEEDS PLANS ANYWAY?

It was remarkable how swiftly and silently the *Traveling Restaurant* slipped away from the Dogjaw docks. The moon was bright enough to see by. Dr. Rocket, up in the wheelhouse, was just a dim shadow. There seemed an extra stillness to the harbor, but—as had happened when they sailed through the mist—that stillness hung only about the *Restaurant* herself. Jasper crossed his fingers, saw how skilfully Dr. Rocket steered past the last steamship in the harbor, but let himself give a small prayer of thanks only when he felt the first gentle tossing of Old Ocean.

~

He awoke with a feeling of dread and a sore hand from sleeping with his fingers crossed. He knew that when the others found the orphan, he'd be in big trouble.

What had actually woken him was a wonderful smell.

"There's bacon with this first pancake," Polly called. "With the next, there's banana and honey."

Uncle Trump was already up from the bench where he had slept, and tucking into pancakes. So was the captain.

Polly came and put a hand on Jasper's forehead. "You look pale. Are you all right?"

Dr. Rocket filled his fork with bacon and lifted an eyebrow at Jasper. "From what I remember, boys sleep very deeply when there is nothing on their conscience."

Jasper forced himself to smile. He pushed his blanket off and sat down with his pancakes. He'd better scoff them up before one of the others discovered the orphan.

~

The *Restaurant* sailed herself while they had breakfast. Outside, gulls wheeled around the wheelhouse.

"Today's plan," said Dr. Rocket after a sip of coffee. "A nice easy path south, as if we're going to Herontown at the mouth of the Great South River. But we can reach the West Wind Drift a few miles out. That will take us east along the coast."

"We could sneak up Monkey River," Trump suggested.

"What for? We'd only have to come down again," Polly said. "We're going to the Eastern Isle as fast as we can, while keeping away from Lady Gall. Aren't we? Do you know something you're not telling us?"

Trump shot a funny sour face at Jasper, who found it hard to hide a grin, even though he didn't really trust him.

"Well, it will be nice to have an easy day now we've ditched that Crispin Kent," said Uncle Trump.

Polly sipped her coffee too. "With nobody chasing us, I'll even have time to try new recipes."

Jasper felt he had better speak up. "Um—when we set sail last night, something was going on down by the *Hound.*"

"Lady Gall in a foul mood, as usual." Trump picked up his mug of coffee and wandered about the cabin. He was still limping.

Over his uncle's shoulder, through the window of the dining room, Jasper saw a dark shape on the horizon—behind them. Even though the *Restaurant* was a roundish vessel, you could tell where the stern was by the direction it was traveling.

Dr. Rocket dabbed his beard with a napkin. "Back to work. I want Trump to sort the maps."

The shape on the horizon was growing bigger. It was a ship shape. It belched smoke from all three funnels.

As Dr. Rocket stood up, he glanced out the window and went very still. Polly and Trump looked at him, then followed his gaze.

There was a clatter as the coffee pot toppled to the floor. "The *Excellent Hound*," gasped Trump.

"She's coming as fast as ever I've seen a ship move in all my life!" Polly cried.

Just then there was a cough from the doorway to the lower deck. Jasper squeezed his eyes tight and waited for trouble.

"Good grief," Trump said. "We have a passenger."

Jasper opened his eyes and saw Polly and the captain staring at the orphan. She wasn't as pale as last night, but her hair was a wild snarl and she still looked grubby.

"I hoped I smelled toast," she said in her funny soft voice.

"Not another stray?" cried Dr. Rocket. "Another boy?"

"It's worse each time," Polly said. "This one's a girl."

~

There was no time for explanations or anger, and Jasper couldn't introduce the orphan when he didn't know her name. Dr. Rocket rocketed to the wheelhouse. Trump and Polly trimmed the sails. Jasper was told to mop the puddle of coffee and feed the orphan. With no pancake mixture left, it had to be toast.

The *Traveling Restaurant* sped so fast she almost flew across the surface of the sea. The *Excellent Hound* didn't manage to draw any closer, even though it looked as if she was using steam as well as sail. Both vessels ran with the wind, sun shining and seabirds singing as if danger were no more than a six-letter word.

Dr. Rocket called everyone up to the wheelhouse. It was a squash. The girl brought her fifth slice of toast, and Trump had another mug of coffee.

"Lady Gall guessed we were scarpering to the southern coast. How?" asked Dr. Rocket.

"The sort-of journalist can't have told her. He didn't know," said Jasper. "We're trying to find my little sister," he explained to the orphan. "So is Lady Gall. She's hunting me, too."

The girl licked jam off her last crust of toast. "Why? You said you're no good at the trumpet."

"But who on earth are you?" Polly asked. "How did you get on board!"

"Manners, manners," Trump said. Polly glared at him. He bowed to the orphan, who took a step back and bumped against the map cabinet. "I am Trump, of no surname, Jasper's uncle. This is Polly, and this is Dr. Rocket …"

"Dr. what!" The orphan tried to take another step backward, but had to make do with going sideways. She flung a hand to point at Dr. Rocket. "That's one of the scientists who caused the Accident!"

"Dr. Rocket and the Great Accident?" Jasper looked at Uncle Trump, and Polly, and the captain. "That can't be true!"

"It's complicated," Polly said. "Truth often is."

"Let's finish the introductions." Trump bowed to the orphan again. "As you probably know, this …" He waved his mug at Jasper and spilled more coffee. "Whoops … is Jasper Ludlow. Ah. Actually, no. He's just Jasper."

"Ludlow?" The orphan's cheeks turned blotchy red. "He'd better not be related to Hannibal Ludlow!"

"He's my father," Jasper said.

"Your father made me an orphan!" shouted the girl.

"Girls!" said Polly. "Dreadful creatures! I should know, I used to be one."

Dr. Rocket thumped a fist on the wheel. "Save the arguments till later! Look ahead!"

The southern coast was a rim of cliffs. The blue water of the Old Ocean showed a green fan where a river flowed out into it. The wind was ragged gusts.

"We can't take the Drift now," said Dr. Rocket. "The *Hound* will overtake us in half an hour. We'll head for the river."

"Monkey River?" Trump asked.

"I'll monkey you!" the captain growled.

"That's the Great South River dead ahead," said Polly. "Jasper and girl, go below!"

"Why?" the orphan demanded. "I want to see."

"Go below!" insisted Polly.

"When I'm ready!" said the orphan.

Trump gave a slight grin as if he thought the girl was rather fun. Jasper kept his distance from her, but he stayed in the wheelhouse too. If Lady Gall was going to catch the *Restaurant*, it was no use trying to hide.

The city of Herontown was in sight, ships dotted near its port. Behind the *Restaurant*, the *Excellent Hound* grew larger as if a real dog panted at their backs.

Uncle Trump gave a meaningful cough. "I'm not sure this part of the plan is very good. What is the point of getting to port with Lady Gall so close behind?"

Dr. Rocket's bushy eyebrows drew together. "We're not heading into port. We're hurrying past."

They were?

"The *Excellent Hound* is a great deal bigger than us," said Dr. Rocket. "She'll have to stop at the mouth of the river. She can't sail up because she'd run aground. But we can sail a long way up. Thus," said Dr. Rocket, "we shall escape. I hope."

"For a while," Polly muttered.

Trump had lost his grin. The orphan seemed torn between anger and fear. She glanced at the captain and Jasper with utter dislike.

Jasper couldn't bear it. He'd been hoping that with the

orphan he'd found a friend. He slid down the outside companionway and leaned over the railing at the spot near the third anchor-well. The best plans were not ones you made up as you went along. There was so little hope.

He heard a low groan. Whether it was agreement or despair, he couldn't tell.

A GOOD PLAN MEANS YOU'VE
THOUGHT THINGS THROUGH

How Jasper wished they could have hauled into Herontown, green sails billowing. How he wished they could have tied up at the docks, let the sign clatter down and watched a hungry happy crowd begin to gather. But the *Hound* was so close he could glimpse cannon bristling out along her sides.

Trump came and gripped the rail beside him.

"This is my fault," Jasper said.

Trump gave his half-grin. "It's usually someone's."

The orphan edged up, scowling at Jasper through her black curls. "It's my fault too. Lady Gall is after me."

"That's nice, all share the blame," said Trump.

It looked as if he might have said more, but Dr. Rocket yelled for him, and he swung up into the wheelhouse again. Jasper heard Trump, Polly and the captain start shouting about maps.

Small boats scattered before them as they neared the harbor with the warship at their back. Polly, Dr. Rocket and Trump began yelling louder in the wheelhouse—the muddle about maps was growing worse. From the city came the sound of horns and bells, warning people about the drama out on the water.

Jasper glanced at the orphan. She looked more and more afraid (as Jasper was). She glanced at him too, then swiftly away.

"If I'm going to die," Jasper said, "I'd like to know the reasons. Why did you say my father made you an orphan? I can't believe he and Dr. Rocket had anything to do with the death of … of—" (if he was going die anyway, he may as well say it aloud again) "the death of magic."

She took a step back and her jaw went hard.

He took a gulp of air. "And you're the second person I've saved who hasn't said thanks."

The orphan glanced at the bow of the *Excellent Hound*, so close that if she'd been a real hound they'd have seen drops of water on her whiskers. "You haven't saved me for long," she said huskily. "But fair's fair. I know who you are, so you should know who I am. Don't dare try to shake hands."

"Definitely not," Jasper said.

"Good." The girl pushed her hair behind her ears. "I am Beatrix. My father saw you once in a vision when I was little. I was old enough to remember he thought it amazing and important." She scowled. "It was before your father ruined the Eastern Lake."

Jasper's chest felt hot and choked. "He wouldn't do that!"

Suddenly Polly was with them by the rail. "Hang on tight and argue later. Watch the cannon and be ready to duck.

And, by the way, neither of you knows everything. Nor do I. Nobody does."

"Beatrix said my father …" began Jasper.

Polly frowned. "Hannibal Ludlow did do a terrible thing."

"How dare you say that!" Jasper cried.

Polly had already darted off and grabbed a sail line. She paused to look over her shoulder and shout, "I'll say what I like about my brother! And by the way, just because someone's relative did something terrible does not mean everyone in the family should be clapped in irons!" She hauled herself hand over fist into the rigging.

Polly was his father's sister? Jasper's aunt? Why hadn't she said! He looked at Beatrix. Her cheeks were angry red again.

"My father," Jasper said, "is the nicest man I know. He loves my mother and my sister and me. He only wants to help people."

"So why did he cause the Accident! Why did Lady Gall make him head of the Workroom of Knowledge!"

"For beauteen, of course!" Jasper shouted. "He hates working for Lady …"

"She should have stuffed him in a dungeon, not rewarded him! That's another reason I can't stand Lady Gall!" Beatrix marched off.

Jasper kicked the railing, then turned and punched the cabin door.

"Watch out!" yelled Polly.

The *Hound* had almost drawn level. Deep shouts from officers and sailors came over the water. There was a bang.

A cannonball whizzed sideways and made a harmless splash behind the *Restaurant*. Jasper suspected there'd be trouble for the gun crew who'd fired that one.

He thought of his little dagger with its beautiful etching of dragon-like birds stowed in his backpack. It would be no use today. "Oh please," he whispered, "I just want to find my little sister. Please, please."

The *Restaurant* picked up speed and skimmed into the river mouth. The sails were bright with sun, and it seemed to Jasper as if the bird paintings on the boat's sides moved their wings in an attempt to make her fly over the waves.

It was good luck the great Herontown Bridge was raised so the *Restaurant* could race though, but bad luck it wasn't down to stop the *Hound*. The west bank of the river was crammed with coaches and carriages. People crowded the piers, shuffling. Perhaps they were wondering whether to cheer or not and whether it should be for the *Restaurant* or the *Hound*. Soldiers stood among the crowd—of course, Lady Gall's men always looked awkward. Was the *Restaurant* pulling ahead? Maybe she was.

Dr. Rocket started roaring in the wheelhouse. Jasper heard the crash of the map drawers, and Trump bellowing. Up in the rigging, Polly screamed advice on which way to steer. Other ships were in the way, and sandbanks—all kinds of dangers on which the *Restaurant* could run aground. But she flew full speed up the Great South River.

The shouting from the *Hound* was fainter. Jasper darted up to use the telescope. Trump swiveled it to him, grinning.

He set his eye to it. A blur, a branch of willow tree on the bank, a startled coachman waving his hat with excitement at the *Restaurant*, and Jasper trained the telescope back on the *Excellent Hound*. He gave a yell. She stood on a slant, slewed sideways by a sandbank. A pile of cannonballs toppled overboard like scattered peppercorns.

Polly slid from the rigging and straightened her headband. She leaped into the wheelhouse and hugged Dr. Rocket. Jasper wouldn't have minded a small pat on the shoulder. But Polly ignored both him and Trump, swung down again toward the orphan, and patted her instead.

Dr. Rocket still gripped the wheel. "We're not safe by any means," he grumbled. "As soon as Lady Gall has sorted that out, she'll be after us by land as well as river."

"Can we wait till nightfall and sneak back?" asked Jasper.

"That would be a good plan, if they were not expecting it," the captain replied.

"What won't they be expecting?" Jasper asked.

"If I knew that, we'd possibly be safe," said Dr. Rocket.

That remark was no comfort at all.

~

For the rest of the day, they sailed up river in fine weather. Four black and white gulls followed, circling the masts but not perching. Jasper had thought gulls came inland only when the weather was bad on Old Ocean. Polly glanced at them now and then, and frowned. She kept trying to talk to Beatrix, but didn't seem to have much luck.

Dr. Rocket told Jasper to leave the women to it and to

ponder his mistakes. Jasper's mistakes! Saving Crispin Kent—saving Beatrix—that wasn't too bad compared to Dr. Rocket's mistake, being involved in the Great Accident. Jasper wanted to make a million objections, but that bristly beard was too forbidding.

Trump and Dr. Rocket spread a new map of Old Ocean and the southern coast of Fontania on the cabinet. Jasper tried to nudge between them but the men elbowed him back. He had to squint through the gap. All he could really make out was that the Great South River came from a lake as big as an inland sea. And near the western shore of the lake was a faint sign like a capital D in lazy handwriting.

As the sun dipped toward evening, the river narrowed. The *Restaurant* traveled slowly. Polly and Trump kept their eyes open for snags. Beatrix's back was always turned to Jasper.

With nothing else to do, he thought he may as well make dinner. He examined the chiller cupboard and pantry. He boiled some eggs and arranged a platter with cold sausages, sliced ham, and baby lettuce. He found tomatoes as red and firm as tomatoes out of storybooks, and cucumber as green and firm as cucumber out of more storybooks. He found a loaf of fresh bread and sliced it, not very neatly—but with fresh bread only fussy people minded. He put the chunks and slices into a basket, and set it on the biggest dining table.

For Dr. Rocket, he put out a plate with orange and yellow wild animals painted on it (the captain being very gruff today).

For Uncle Trump, he set out a plate with blue and white fish around the rim (he felt his uncle was rather slippery).

For Polly, he found a plate decorated with a network of pale green leaves (because she was kind, under a prickly outside).

He knew it was self-pitying, but for himself he chose a plate with a red rim and a small red house with yellow flowers. It looked a comfortable, happy place, and he'd probably never live in one.

What about Beatrix? She wouldn't ever be a friend. She still hadn't said thanks for being rescued, she hated the boy who'd saved her, and she was unhappy. Jasper thought she'd probably had her dinner in a grimy bucket when she was Lady Gall's prisoner. He was tempted to find something just as disgusting for her now. But in the back of a cupboard there was a creamy white plate with a rim shaped like a circle of flowers. It reminded him of his vision of the Eastern Lake and the orphans in Trump's sketchbook. Beatrix might like it, though she'd probably still hate him.

~

The *Traveling Restaurant* floated toward a low island in the middle of the river, where sheltering willows grew. The gulls had gone, but night birds began to call. Until now, Dr. Rocket had lowered only the anchors at the bow. If Jasper had known that this time Dr. Rocket was letting down the large anchor at the stern, he would have watched. He only realized the silver anchor had slid into the river when he heard a sound like the contented sigh you make when you lower your weary body into a bath. Nobody else seemed to have noticed.

Jasper announced that dinner was ready. Polly batted his shoulder as she went past, which he decided was meant to be friendly. The others said nothing at all.

The evening was warm. Trump opened all the doors and windows of the cabin to let the breeze sift through, but didn't light a lamp. The moon was enough to see by, and lamps might draw the attention of their enemies. Now and then pale-blue moths flew in. Their wings were luminous, and they hovered over the table. This was helpful. You could see whether you wanted another sausage, mustard or relish, or one more juicy cherry tomato.

"Thank you, Jasper," said Dr. Rocket. "Simple meals are always the best."

Trump chuckled. "The most elaborate meals are best too."

Beatrix hunched over her plate, as if each mouthful were a treasure that might vanish. As a moth drifted by, her cheek seemed to glisten. Finally she mumbled something.

"What?" asked Dr. Rocket.

Polly twisted her mouth at Dr. Rocket.

"Beatrix said 'thank you' to Jasper for making dinner."

"Don't mention it," Jasper said politely.

Tears seeped down Beatrix's face as if someone had left a tap dripping. "I actually said, 'Thank you, but there's not much point.' Lady Gall will grab us up in no time and we'll be dead in a hundred ways."

"What a miserable thought," Trump muttered. "Shall

we have a quiet tune to cheer us up?"

Everyone gave him dark looks, all rather scary in the light from the blue moths. Trump waved his hands. "Beatrix has a flute around her neck. The housekeeper bullied Jasper into bringing his trumpet. Is anything wrong with entertainment?"

Uncles could be embarrassing. This one would end up very sorry if he heard how badly Jasper played. But Beatrix fished her flute out of her cardigan and ran her hands over its small smooth shape. She gave Jasper a sour grin as if she expected him to chicken out. His stomach tried to leave through the soles of his feet, but how could he refuse that kind of dare? He sloped off to fetch the trumpet, and had a trial spit and blow. He'd forgotten all the exercises his tutor had taught him. Wishing he was at the bottom of the river with the great silver anchor, he started playing.

No tunes appeared—rather, no usual kinds of tunes, no melodies. The little trumpet seemed to whisper what it wanted—sounds that suited a calm evening after a dangerous escape. Here were wild but soft sounds like sighs of weariness and relief. Here were small pirrips like a sparrow feeling it was safe to settle down and close her eyes. Here were runs of notes like calm heartbeats. Beatrix didn't join in at once, but when she did it was the same kind of music. Jasper had never played like this before, though he'd always wanted to.

The children lowered their instruments at the same time. The last notes seemed to hover in the air just like the moths.

Jasper glanced at Beatrix. She shook dribble out of the flute and didn't look at him.

Dr. Rocket moved in his chair as if it might be time to do something. Trump nodded as if he was answering a question from the captain.

Polly drew in a deep breath. "I've never agreed with the idea that people should keep secrets from children, especially when those children are so involved. These two are very much involved."

"It's a knotty situation," Dr. Rocket said in his low rumble. "Children don't get told everything while they're too young to understand, because it's tricky knowing if they'll be old enough not to do something stupid."

"Some people are never old enough," Polly muttered.

Uncle Trump lowered his head and thumped it with both hands.

—

NO PLAN COULD HAVE
BEEN MUCH HELP

"I'll turn it into a story," Polly said. "It might be easier all round."

"Thank you," whispered Jasper.

Three luminous moths still drifted in the cabin as she began. "I have to use forbidden words. But I doubt anybody here will run and tell.

"Once upon a time, the world was rich in magic. It was used wisely, not wasted on anything selfish or mean-spirited. It was saved for important things like making sure babies slept safe in their cots, that people had enough to eat, and that the world was peaceful. There were dangers, as there always is with magic. But there was also common sense. Some people began to experiment with science and machines, and that was all right. You see, everyone thought somebody was in charge. The monarch kept a wise eye on the world …"

"Who was the …" Jasper started.

Polly shushed him.

"Some people worried when the monarch, an old king,

fell ill. What would happen if he died? He had one daughter and one son. The daughter was married with a little son nearly five years old. She had no wish to be Queen. The son—" Polly bunched her hands. "He had no interest in royal duties. You see, it was only the royal family that could communicate with the source of magic. That source lay in the Eastern Isle."

Every atom of Jasper's body listened. "Couldn't anyone else at all communicate with it?" he whispered.

"Only the smallest, smallest bit, sometimes," Polly said. "Not even being a prince or princess was enough, sometimes. Like the daughter with the little son—she didn't have much magic, if any at all."

Dr. Rocket spoke up. "Royal children never knew whether they had any powers or not till they turned twelve at least. But they usually had enough to keep the world at peace."

A strange drumming began in Jasper's head, a tingling in his chest.

The bunch of Polly's hands turned into fists of white knuckles. "Nobody believed there would be real problems. Most people thought things would sort themselves out when they had to."

"Things didn't sort out," Jasper guessed. Well, it was obvious.

Polly sighed. "A wise and clever man, a scientist, thought science might help preserve the magic. This was a good idea. If the royal family was not willing or able to control things, somebody should hunt for another way."

Dr. Rocket rubbed his forehead with a wordless rumble.

Polly glanced at him before she went on.

"The scientist thought if he took water from the Eastern Lake and analysed it, it would be a useful start. He took two young assistants with him. One was a brilliant young woman. The other was a clever man who had married a beautiful young lady ..." Here, Polly looked at Jasper. "His wife was the young Lady Helen of the Northern Hills. He was Dr. Hannibal Ludlow. Hannibal's sister also thought he was very clever (and sisters don't always give their brothers a lot of credit). The three scientists sailed off to the Eastern Isle. Lady Helen and Hannibal's sister (and you know, that's me)," said Polly, "and the little boy waved goodbye."

Jasper's heart galloped as if it wanted to run away. His head still thrummed.

Polly continued. "The scientists arrived at the lake and set up their experiments. The young woman scientist went up into the hills behind the lake, and it was then that news came from the City of Spires. The old King was dead. The Prince was on his travels, gallivanting, not to be found." Polly's mouth went thin and cross. "He'd been on his gallivants for months. Years, actually."

Uncle Trump thumped his head again.

"He had left his fiancée behind, and never even sent a note by carrier pigeon!" Polly said.

Trump looked sideways at Jasper. "He was very stupid. That girlfriend is still very annoyed," he muttered.

"Don't say the next bit," Beatrix pleaded in a growl.

"Put your hands over your ears," Polly told her.

Beatrix folded her arms and stuck out her chin.

"So, without a King or Queen to communicate with the source of magic, the two scientists went back to their ship to decide what they should do. It was the young man's job to take the experiments down before they left. He forgot. And nobody was guarding them. Something went wrong— some children toppled the tubs of chemicals. The lake shot up in a tower of spray, rolls of thunder rocked the hills, the lake vanished underground. Most of the people of the lake died in the explosion."

"I'm so sorry." Jasper's voice trembled but he looked straight at Beatrix.

"Hannibal had good intentions," Trump muttered. "He was a good man then. He's a good man now."

Polly tightened her lips. "The third scientist was Lady Gall. She was returning from the hills and saw the accident happen. She saw Hannibal's carelessness. She saw the children spill the chemicals. She saw the deaths, and took control. Well, somebody had to. Because of that, people listened to her when she began weasling her way into being Provisional Monarch. And without a true monarch, nothing can be done about the death of magic. It was too late for the man who should have been King."

"I thought there was plenty of time to swan around and draw my pictures," Trump admitted. "I didn't realize things had grown so problematical."

"I warned you," said Dr. Rocket. "Lady Helen and Hannibal warned you. We sent a hundred messages by post and pigeon. Polly warned you, time and again."

"I'm still a prince," Trump muttered.

"That's not much good when you've lost your magical ability." Dr. Rocket's frown was very severe.

"It's possible that I'm a late developer," said Trump.

"Huh," Polly said. "Too late." She reached out in the dark and put her hand over Beatrix's. "Jasper's father was, and is, an honest man. Misguided maybe, and he was careless. But he's honest. So is Dr. Rocket."

"I'm not misguided anymore, and I hope I'm not careless," said the captain. "I'm doing …" He seemed to think hard what he should say. "I'm doing what I can."

Jasper's mind was like a jigsaw, bits of thoughts trying to fit with other thoughts.

Beatrix pulled her hand away from Polly's. "Lady Gall has dragged me all over Old Ocean. She kept me in that smelly little cabin, and fed me porridge and water in a gray bucket. When she wanted everyone to believe she's kind, she dressed me in a white tunic, and brushed my hair, which I absolutely hate. If I made mistakes on the flute, I got porridge and no water." She looked at Trump. Her huge dark eyes would have made even the innocent feel guilty. "And all the time, you should have been King."

"I'm afraid so," Trump said.

"Right. We're all very sorry about the past," said Dr. Rocket. "But Lady Gall is making a fake crown. She doesn't have to worry about any other royal treasures that might have been lost. A crown will do it. She can have a coronation at the Eastern Lake, send up a few fireworks to celebrate, and everyone will say, 'Oo, lovely Queen. Oo, happy now with feathers on.' They'll be too scared to kick themselves for not stopping her."

Beatrix held the flute so tight she pulled off the mouthpiece. "Nobody can stop her."

"Lady Helen and Hannibal were trying," Polly said.

Beatrix gave a filthy look. "Trying without succeeding is no use."

Trump, Polly and Dr. Rocket glanced at one another. Dr. Rocket nodded at Trump, and so did Polly. Trump coughed.

"The best way to stop Lady Gall will be for the real monarch to get there first," Trump said.

"So?" asked Jasper. "You said it isn't you, even if you are a late developer. Is Polly the real monarch? If she was going to marry you, she would have been Queen."

"I'd have been a hopeless Queen." Polly glared at Trump. "I would have tried, though, since I'd promised. But Jasper, you've missed the point. Only someone born a prince or princess can be the real monarch."

Trump squashed his hat between his hands. "So if it does turn out that I'm too late, Jasper—the real King might be you."

"Me!" Jasper nearly breathed in a luminous moth. His head drummed horribly. This was the bit of jigsaw he'd been desperately ignoring. He'd be an awful monarch. But the old King was his grandfather. Lady Helen would have been Queen if she'd wanted to be, but she'd been busy with a child—and that child was Jasper himself.

"No!" he said. It couldn't be him. He was just ordinary.

"And if the monarch isn't me and isn't you," Trump added, "then I'm afraid it is Sibilla."

The world roared in Jasper's ears. He very deeply didn't want to be the King, but he had seen magic happen with Sibilla. The real monarch must be her.

But probably the last thing Fontania needed was a Queen who still smeared carrot and potato up her nose.

—

GIVE UP PLANS AND HOPE
FOR GOOD ADVICE

"Well," said Jasper shakily. "It explains why Lady Gall wants to capture all my family. And why my mother said I was only ten."

"You're only ten?" Beatrix had found yet another way of looking scornful.

"I'm twelve!" Jasper shouted.

"Then don't behave as if you're ten," Beatrix said in her rough little voice.

"They wanted to keep me home! To keep me safe! They should have told me!" He expected Dr. Rocket, Polly, even Trump to help him out by saying something, but they just sat there in the dark. "I can't remember my grandfather being King. I can't even remember my grandfather!"

"People have two grandfathers, Jasper," Polly said.

Dr. Rocket shook his head in a way that meant everyone had better settle down. But Jasper felt so upset he was afraid he would explode and disappear.

"It explains why Lady Gall tried to poison Sibilla. And she won't stop trying, will she? I have to find my sister!"

His shaking grew worse. "I don't care if she's the real Queen or not. But if Sibilla isn't with my parents she should be with me. I am her brother!" He turned to Trump. "If you drew another sketch we might see more …"

His uncle stood up. "We can't hunt for Sibilla yet. We're still on the run."

And the only way to run from here was up river.

~

Next morning Jasper awoke before anyone else. His backpack was by his sleeping bench. He rummaged in it to feel the dagger with the marvelous creatures etched round the blade, the scabbard crafted to look like feather-scales. But he left it hidden and went on deck. Along the riverbank, wading birds paddled for their breakfast. Flying birds caught flies and any other bugs that flew. Frogs perched on sunny rocks, and flicked sticky tongues to catch the flies and bugs the birds had missed.

When he went back inside the *Restaurant*, there were bowls of hasty porridge and scowls from Beatrix. She was behaving like a six-year-old, if you asked Jasper. He went on deck again as soon as possible.

Dr. Rocket and Trump winched up the anchors. Once again Jasper missed the sight of the large one and felt oddly agitated.

"Can you tell me next time?" he asked as the captain and Trump passed by on their way up to the wheelhouse.

"Pardon?" said Dr. Rocket.

Jasper pointed. "When you use the special anchor. I'd love to see it."

The captain stared at him.

"The bird anchor," Jasper said.

A breeze blew. Dr. Rocket's eyes began to water. "Oh, my boy ..." He gripped Jasper's shoulder. For a moment Jasper thought the old man was going to hug him.

But Trump was yelling down from the wheelhouse. "We have to get moving! What's going on?"

"Nothing!" roared Dr. Rocket. He gave Jasper another pat and hurried off.

Jasper stayed where he was. He'd never felt so sure of anything. There was something very special about the bird anchor. He leaned over—of course he saw nothing—but he stretched a hand as far down as he could.

"I know you're there," he whispered. "You're there, and I'm up here."

Insects darted over the river as it rippled past the hull. Something glided in the breeze, out of the anchor-well. It hovered for a moment till he turned his hand, then it nestled on his palm. He caught his breath. It was a feather, no doubt of it, but it was metal, carved silver, so light and delicate that it floated in the air. Now he knew why people had such a look of loss in their eyes when they remembered the world before the Great Accident and the death of magic. But magic wasn't dead—because something far greater than an anchor lived in the brass cave just beneath him. Heart thudding, he curled his fingers round the feather and bowed his head.

He didn't want to let it go, but he opened his hand. The silver feather lifted in the breeze then rested back upon his palm. He knew he mustn't show anyone. He slipped it into the pocket over his heart.

~

The *Restaurant* moved off. Polly clambered up into the rigging. Dr. Rocket and Trump were grumbling in the wheelhouse. They'd lost the right maps. They needed to know how far up the river they could sail before they might be caught by Lady Gall.

It was astonishing how uncomfortable it felt to be scared and bored at the same time. Ten-year-olds would start to kick things. So would twelve-year-olds. So would anyone, whatever age they were.

"For pity's sake," Polly shouted down. "Stop moping. You and Beatrix, tidy the galley!"

"Why can't it tidy itself!" yelled Jasper.

"Use your brain," roared Trump.

Should Trump talk like that to a boy who might be King? Jasper wondered if Trump might even be jealous. He probably wanted to be King himself after all!

But Beatrix started some tidying, with a fair amount of grumbling and a snarky smile. So Jasper grabbed a broom and bashed it into the corners. He also discovered that if you scrubbed a porridge pot right away, oatmeal didn't set to concrete. Jasper felt much better. If he enjoyed mucking about in the sink so much, it was proof he wasn't King.

But as soon as the galley was done, he was bored again. Jasper thought of having a look at the feather, but it was precious and he might lose it. He just felt it in his pocket and left it there.

Polly took a turn in the wheelhouse. Even from the deck, Jasper heard her nagging Trump, who still hadn't found the right map.

"You should label the blasted drawers!" Trump shouted. He banged them shut, and Jasper heard his limping steps on the outside ladder.

Beatrix nudged Jasper.

"Quit that," he said.

"Can you read?" she asked. "Or can you only play the trumpet not very well?" Before Jasper could answer, she was calling up to the captain. "Since you're all so useless, I'll do the maps. That boy can help me!" She was so full of scorn that Jasper was dumbstruck.

"Good idea!" Dr. Rocket threw rolls and rolls of maps down the inside ladder. "But work together with no arguing." His beard bristled.

Jasper didn't intend to say a single word.

They spread out the maps on the biggest tables, and used all the salt and pepper shakers to hold down the corners. Polly and Trump were quarrelling on deck now, so angry with each other that Jasper had to grin. Beatrix gave a little smile too, and shot a look at Jasper. He pretended not to see.

Finally Jasper had all the northern ocean maps on one table, and Beatrix had all the southern ones on another. They began to sort the southern ones. He found the one with Herontown marked where the Great South River met the sea. A little box of writing down the side explained the signs. There were black arrows for prevailing winds, red arrows for warm surface currents, blue for cold currents. Jasper ran his finger down the blue line of the river.

Beatrix found the map that joined it, and that showed the Great South River coming from the lake as big as a small ocean. There again, near the shore, was the symbol like a capital D, but there was no explanation in the box. Just after it left the lake, the river was full of wiggly lines.

"What does that mean?" he muttered, but just to himself.

Beatrix ran a finger down the box of explanation. Wiggly lines—rapids. She let out a growling wail. "I said there was no point in even trying!"

Jasper grabbed the map and leaped up to the wheelhouse.

~

The captain, Polly, Trump and Jasper huddled around the map spread on the wheelhouse cabinet. Dr. Rocket's blunt fingernail rested on the wiggly lines. Ships cannot sail up rapids.

"Just below the rapids, the road comes closest to the river." Polly's fingernail traced a curving line on the land. "What's the betting Lady Gall's troops are on that road right now."

They might have to leave the *Restaurant* and hide in the forest. Jasper wouldn't be able to find out more about the silver anchor bird. Any chance of finding Sibilla would slip away. He gritted his teeth, kicked every rung on the companionway as he went down to find his backpack, and buckled on the dagger.

He'd just started sorting through his stuff to see what

he could leave behind when a faint noise made him stop. Someone else was crying. It was a lonely sound—Beatrix, crouched in a booth. What should he do?

"Um ... would you like a glass of water?"

"It's your fault!" She rubbed her face, tears turning into anger. "Why did you make me leave the *Hound*? You've made things worse for me! Idiot boy!" Beatrix dripped scorn and tears and rage. It was a tantrum to admire. "Prince Jasper! King Jasper! Oo, not a bit handsome. Not clever at all!"

Jasper's hand gripped the handle of the royal dagger. "I don't blame you for being angry." He turned and walked out on deck as steadily as a prince would do.

Near the stern of the *Restaurant*, he stopped and felt the feather in his pocket—was there a chance? If the royal family could communicate with magic ... He wouldn't have to tell anyone. It wouldn't make him King.

He dashed up into the wheelhouse. "Who says we can't sail up the rapids?" Jasper's brain worked at top speed. "Why can't we try? Dr. Rocket, when does the prevailing wind prevail?"

"What?" asked Dr. Rocket.

"And how strongly does it prevail?"

"What?" asked Polly and Trump.

"Listen ..." Jasper told them how he and his father used to throw flat pebbles into the pond and make them skip. He told them about the little stream that ran down through the garden, into the pond. He told them what his father had said when Jasper tried to skip pebbles up the stream, over the rocks—"Can't be done." And he told them how he had practiced for weeks until he managed. It had made his father very quiet.

Beatrix had come up the ladder while Jasper was talking, and she and the others were silent now. At last, Trump spoke. "Jasper, there is a considerable difference between the *Traveling Restaurant* and a flat pebble."

And that, thought Jasper, is why you can't be the King—you don't hope enough. "The thing is," he said to Trump, "you'll have to be high in the rigging to let me know what's ahead."

"Me!" said Trump.

Beatrix spoke up and made Jasper start. "Salmon travel up river, over rapids."

Trump flung up a hand. "The *Restaurant* is not a fish!"

The orphan jutted her jaw. "Salmon try and try and try until they do it!"

"We've nothing to lose," Polly said.

Dr. Rocket's hand rasped over his beard. He glanced at Jasper, then back down the river. He glanced at Polly and gave a nod.

"It's all in the angle," Jasper said. "You need to think about the angle you throw the pebble, and make it bounce off the rocks in the right direction."

"I have no wish to be on a ship that bounces," said Trump. "I hate adventures. But perhaps now is the time to say that no matter who else might want the blame, it is my fault in the first place that we're here, and I'm sorry. I'll go up the damn rigging if I have to."

Polly seemed surprised. She reached to touch Trump's sleeve but pulled back at the last moment. "Jasper," she said, "you and Dr. Rocket better stand at the helm together. I'll do what I can up the mast. I'll have to call out in plenty of time. Trump?" She gave him a look, as if she were giving a disobedient dog a second chance, but she gave Jasper a quick smile.

A bugle called, deep in the forest. Distant shouts rang out. Soldiers. Trump and Polly began to climb up separate masts. Jasper crossed his fingers.

"Two more things," he said. "Beatrix—can you shelter near the bow and call out dangers? Thank you. And we need the wind to blow really hard. We must get our speed up."

"I never like to say the word 'impossible,'" said Dr. Rocket.

Jasper clasped the hilt of the dagger. *Please, please, please*, he whispered.

On the riverbank, a soldier appeared. He shouted, and more men came running out of the trees. An officer waved a sword. His troops began readying their rifles. Ahead, there was a roaring sound.

"Rapids!" Polly yelled.

Trump clung to the crow's-nest with one hand, and shaded his eyes as he peered forward. The air grew dark with the wings of many gulls, and filled with a whistling and beating of feathers. Behind the *Restaurant* was the roar of wind. The banks of the river were taller now, towering in steep bluffs on either side. A second troop of soldiers appeared on the cliff top. The first shots fired.

Please, thought Jasper. *Please, please.* He pressed the silver feather in his breast pocket, then put both hands upon the wheel. The prevailing wind scooped down on the Great South River and filled the sails with a furious gust. Dr. Rocket stood right behind Jasper, reaching around so his wise hands gripped the helm too. Jasper used all his skill at skipping great pebbles, all his certainty that magic survived, all his confidence that the only way to save Sibilla was for the *Traveling Restaurant* to skim over the river.

"Don't look behind!" he cried to himself. "Think of Sibilla! Keep looking up the river!"

They bashed against a rock, they hurtled over a pile of mossy rubble, the wind lifted into the sails again. The wings of many birds added to the roar of the strong wind and the warning cries from Polly, Trump and Beatrix, and up they swept, hitting rocks, knocking and scraping against the canyon sides. Wind blew in a never-ending blast. Jasper gripped the wheel so hard his arms ached. Dr. Rocket helped hold it steady, but it was Jasper who knew when to swerve the great round ship from one rock to the next to keep it upward and on. One moment they faced backward but spun around again, and still they hurtled up the canyon, scudding and splashing. Behind them the roar of wind was a deep movement like the beat of a pair of mighty wings. Jasper nearly burst with joy. No matter what he and the others were doing or how hard the wind blew, it was the magic creature who dwelt in the *Traveling Restaurant*—a young dragon-eagle disguised as a ship's anchor—that propelled them helter-skelter up the rapids.

The ship lurched, they breached the final shoal, and sailed battered but successful into the wide waters of the lake.

Dr. Rocket steered away from the main current into calm water where Jasper, in a voice hoarse with shouting, called out, "Anchor!"

He heard a groan of pleasure in a job well done, and saw a glimpse—just a glimpse—as the dragon-eagle of living silver loosed its grip inside the anchor-well and slipped down into the water with a sigh.

———

MAP IS ANOTHER WORD
FOR PLAN

Flocks of ducks, geese, and swans floated on the lake, resting after helping the dragon-eagle, who must have called them. Trump seemed almost smug, and he'd certainly helped. But it was embarrassing when the others (even Beatrix) thanked Jasper. The dragon-eagle had saved them, not him. But each time he tried to say, "The dragon-bird did it," or even, "It was actually the anchor," the words didn't come. Each time he tried to ask Polly or Dr. Rocket if they had known the dragon-eagle could help—because surely at least Dr. Rocket was aware of the great creature living in the ship—the words lodged like secret pebbles in his throat.

All Jasper managed to say, at last, was this: "Please, we all helped. It wasn't just me."

Polly must have realized how shy he felt. She dusted her hands. "Right, we'll put things shipshape. Then we'll have a bite of lunch and see if we can make some sort of …"

"Plan," Beatrix and Jasper said in ragged voices.

Before he went to help tidy up, Jasper leaned over the side near the stern. The segments of paint on the *Restaurant* were still as bright as circus colors. Below him, the water of the lake was a deep green swirl. You couldn't see anything—no anchor nor anchor chain, of course. But Jasper hoped the marvelous creature watched him from the lakebed.

"Thank you," he whispered. "We all thank you." The feather was too precious for him to keep. He took it from his pocket and let it drift upward, out of his hand, away.

A few bubbles rose to the surface, as if something down there smiled.

~

When Jasper went inside, there was still plenty to clear up. Chairs had been tossed around on the wild ride up the rapids. Pots and pans had fallen off their hooks and out of cupboards. Latches had burst open with the weight of jostling kitchenware. Thank goodness no windows or portholes had been smashed, but boxes and jars of provisions had flown everywhere. Beatrix had already swept up a pile of rice.

Polly handed Jasper the dustpan and brush. He still wasn't used to the idea that she was his aunt. Families, Jasper realized, could be tricky things.

"What?" Beatrix asked in her gruff voice.

He stopped brushing up bits of a broken cup. "What do you mean, what?"

"You were thinking something difficult," she said.

Jasper checked to see that Polly wasn't in sight. "Just that families are like—um—octopuses."

Beatrix made such a funny expression that he laughed for the first time in a long while. "I mean, each person in a family is like one tentacle. They go in different directions and twist about. But whether they like it or not, something holds them all together."

"I've only got cousins," Beatrix said.

"Sorry," he said. Because, of course, she had lost her parents and his family was to blame.

~

"We can't make any decisions," said Dr. Rocket, "until we know exactly where we are." He spread the chart of the lake out on the cabinet. Its name was Lake Riversea, which Jasper thought was trying to have it three ways.

"The safest thing might be to stay in the middle of the lake," suggested Polly. "If we see anybody coming, scoot fast in the other direction."

That was pretty weak for Polly. It looked as if Beatrix thought so too.

"What?" Polly asked Jasper. "What are you thinking?"

Jasper was saved by a bump on top of the wheelhouse. Trump swung off its roof and through the door. The tail of his coat caught, he tugged it free and bumped his funny-bone. "Ouch!" He rubbed his elbow. "Change of plan."

"Impossible," said Dr. Rocket. "There was no plan in the first place."

"The thing is," Trump said, "one of our masts is cracked."

Polly's face turned red. "I examined the masts myself, Trump. I know more about ships than you."

"Agreed, but I …"

"You've been an idle sketcher! A layabout …"

"Excuse me!" Dr. Rocket held up a hand. "Why don't we have a look?"

So they did. Luckily, the tallest mast of the three was not cracked. Luckily, the second wasn't cracked either. But the third one was. It must have happened coming up the rapids. As for Polly not noticing, it was a small crack, low down, as fine as a (quite thick) pencil mark. Polly looked so angry that Jasper was worried she'd accuse Trump of cracking the mast himself.

"We must rig a new one as soon as possible." Dr. Rocket went back to the map of the lake, passed his old blunt fingers over the shoreline and stopped near the sign like the letter D. He raised his head to see which way the wind was blowing. "Get to work," he said.

It was huge trouble to take down the shreds of the old sails and run a new one halfway up the main mast. Jasper tried to help, and so did Beatrix, but they kept getting in each other's way. Almost everything they did—and absolutely everything Trump did—was scolded by Polly. Trump kept making silly mistakes but laughing them off. Once he almost patted Polly's shoulder, and she looked as if she'd bite him. Dr. Rocket's bald head went patchy with rage and he slid the wheelhouse door shut with a bang.

"You might be right about families," Beatrix muttered.

"Up anchor!" bellowed the captain.

Jasper darted to the railing over the third anchor-well. He was just in time for a brief bright flurry as the silver creature shook water from its feather-scales. Then it disappeared into its cavern. Jasper stood unable to move or even breathe. At last he'd seen the dragon-eagle properly. It was beautiful. It was young. It had a crest of silver-gold.

Something touched his shoulder. "Come along," said Dr. Rocket quietly.

—

BEFORE YOU MAKE A PLAN,
PERHAPS YOU HAVE TO
MAKE ANOTHER PLAN

The wind was warm. Rocked by the waves of the lake, Jasper fell into a half dream … he was standing on the wharf back in the City of Spires, where he'd argued with his parents. They had rushed off to buy medicine for Sibilla and left him behind. In his half-dream, he tried to call out that he understood why they had taken Sibilla instead of him. But they should have known how dangerous it was for her. She was the Queen, because magic still existed. But she was upset and not eating. She needed to be loved and played with. Whether or not she would rule the country, she needed to learn things. Children who learn to count their blocks and build towers, who show pages in their picture books to their blue monkey toys, can be happy children. He loved his little sister beyond all measure. He'd do everything he could to find Sibilla. If only he got the chance. Which, right now, didn't seem likely even if there was a dragon-eagle …

He came awake after his uncomfortable half-nightmare.

A cloud passed over the sun. *Hide the dagger*—the words brushed through his mind like a soft rasp of feather. Lady Gall's troops would be heading toward the lake on the forest road. He didn't know why the dagger was so important, but he stashed it at the bottom of his backpack, and shoved the backpack under his bench, hidden by a pillow.

Beatrix was huddled on deck, head in her arms. They were some distance from the shore, but close enough to see a beach or two, and some rocky places that might be good to explore if soldiers weren't hunting you down.

"Look!" he called to her.

"Not interested," she growled.

A thin trail of smoke rose among the trees. The nearer the *Traveling Restaurant* sailed, the more it looked as if a smoke-pen had scrawled an invitation to the passing vessel: *Come on in.*

~

Beatrix stayed huddled up while the *Restaurant* pulled into a small bay and headed for a pile of rocks. Jasper was afraid the *Restaurant* was going to run aground, but the rocks weren't what they seemed—they were a jetty, cunningly disguised with clever paint of mossy green. Polly tossed out a line. A small man in a brown jerkin appeared from behind a tree. He tugged the rope and slung a loop over a rock. It held tight, creaking.

Dr. Rocket tipped up his bearded chin and scanned the sky.

"Will the *Restaurant* be safe here from wind and currents?" Jasper asked.

Dr. Rocket grumbled and nodded.

"But—only one rope …" began Jasper.

"Yes, yes." The small man clapped his hands. "Welcome—my name is Hartie—come ashore. Your lunch is waiting."

Lunch? It was long past lunchtime. They hadn't felt like food, and had snacked on fruit and biscuits. Jasper wasn't even hungry now.

There was no village on the lake edge, only thick trees. But Hartie and Dr. Rocket headed across the beach and into the forest. Polly followed, high heels sinking in the sand. Trump stuck his satchel under his arm, limped after her and offered his arm. She ignored it.

Beatrix appeared beside Jasper. "How did that little man know we'd be here? I don't trust them. I don't trust anyone."

Jasper wondered if he should let her know there might be hope. He could perhaps try to mention the silver feather. But even if he got the words out, she might not believe him. He sighed and set off. Beatrix could come or not, he didn't care.

Under the trees was the faintest of paths. (And Beatrix did come, lagging behind.) The path finally stopped at a clearing with low bushes either side. Ahead was a long building, cunningly disguised with more clever paint to look like a small hill. Hartie let out a soft yodel. Jasper tried not to laugh. Beatrix gave a hiccup, almost a giggle. She looked slightly interested at last.

The double door of the house opened in the middle (as double doors are meant to, after all) and two other small men emerged. They were dressed like guards, though not in armor and plumed helmets like the cruel and stupid guards of Lady Gall. These ones wore baggy brown trousers and soft hats that looked more like little head-bags.

The guards stood each side of the door. Through it came a tiny lady with a wide full skirt, a wide full hairstyle, and a wide full smile. She looked like a bun.

"Rocket!" she said softly. "Dear Polly. Oh—and Lord Trump." She didn't smile so widely when she spied him. Trump looked put out.

The lady turned to Jasper. "You know who I am? You can't guess? I am the Duchess Donna. You have a look of your father," she said. "It's the nose. And a look of your mama."

Jasper blinked. A look of his mother? But Lady Helen was beautiful, and Jasper certainly was not.

Duchess Donna smiled a soft wise smile. "It is in the eyes," she said. "She was my dearest friend, you know, at school. And you," she said to Beatrix, "oh dear." The Duchess opened her arms, stepped over and gave Beatrix a hug.

Beatrix looked startled. Her arms didn't seem to know what to do. They lifted, stiff at the elbow, waved about, then went back down.

The Duchess let go and patted Beatrix on both shoulders. "You'll learn how to do it when you've learned to trust someone. You're a good girl, I can tell."

Beatrix scowled as if she wasn't sure she'd like to be a good girl.

The Duchess didn't seem offended. She clapped her

hands, and the guards jumped to attention, smiling, not at all like proper guards. "Lunch!"

They trailed inside. In a long low room a table was laden with food. Suddenly Jasper felt starved. The small men held a chair out for the Duchess, another for Polly, and one for Beatrix. Beatrix looked even more startled. Trump, the captain, and Jasper found their own chairs. Trump set his satchel down beside his leg.

"Let's play grace," the Duchess said.

From a side table, Hartie whisked up a slender set of silver pipes and played a merry tune. It seemed to sing, "Dig in!" Politely, Jasper waited until the Duchess picked up her fork before picking up his own. Duchess Donna nodded at him, smiling.

"I believe in healthy food like this," she said, waving at the bowls of salad and platters of roast vegetables. "I also believe very much in cake."

Jasper had already noticed the side table with its enticing cake-like mounds covered with a white lace net to keep bugs off. He saw Beatrix had an eye on it as well.

"Over the last sad years," said Duchess Donna, "the *Traveling Restaurant* has brought such well-concealed joy to people that it is a pleasure to return some of your kindness."

"People pay us," Polly said.

"That's not what I'm talking about, Polly dear, as you well know." Duchess Donna's smile was mischievous. She turned to Trump and looked stern. "So, Trump. I also believe in interesting conversation over a meal. What was your excuse?"

"Er," said Trump in a surprised, embarrassed voice. "Do you think we should, in front of the children?"

The Duchess put down her fork and looked at him severely. "Since the children are very much involved, I certainly think so. You may begin."

"What can I say?" asked Trump.

"The truth is a good place to start," Polly said.

Trump's jaw went knotty for a moment. He even squeezed his eyes shut as if he might cry.

"Please," said Jasper.

Trump glanced at his own clasped hands upon the table. "I assume you're asking about what happened after the *Blue Swan* was wrecked. Well. Er." He was certainly not as smug now as he'd been earlier. "We landed in a lifeboat on a very nasty, rocky, windy beach. I promised to take care of Sibilla if Lady Helen and Hannibal were captured. Hannibal was not keen. I'd already—er—left Jasper behind, after all. I'm afraid I shouted. I said if they hadn't been such bad parents, I'd never have had to look after their son in the first place." Trump beat his forehead with his clasped fists. It was a wonder he had a brain at all, he did that so often. "The main thing was to keep Sibilla safe. She's far too young to show any magic yet, and Jasper is barely twelve. If either of them has ... er ... ever does, the magic may not be powerful and lasting. But Lady Gall obviously plans to get rid of both the royal children, just in case."

Sibilla did have powers already. Jasper knew. He'd seen it in Trump's sketch.

"The truth," said Duchess Donna.

"Of course," said Trump. "Lady Helen and I had to get to the Eastern Isle to stop the false coronation. What a terrible choice—to try and save Fontania from Lady Gall, or protect the children. I'm afraid it made Helen's hair become so excited her scarf fell off. The captain of the *Red Wolf* recognized her. She handed Sibilla to me just before she and Hannibal were captured. The *Red Wolf* is going full speed to the Eastern Isle. I—er—hot-footed it, just in time. The *Sea Terrier* and the *Double Cross* were bearing down …"

Jasper stood up, fists clenched. "You knew Lady Gall had my parents all along! You didn't tell me! Where is Sibilla? Have you lied about …"

"She's safe!" said Trump. "I promise she's safe. In Monkey River. At least—I hope so."

Dr. Rocket shoved his chair back, and Trump flinched.

"What about the picture in your sketchbook!" Jasper pointed to Trump's satchel.

"Jasper, this is the truth," Trump said. "Captain Darkblood's ruffians were pounding along the beach toward me and Sibilla … Well, as you see …" He wiggled the leg that made him limp. Of course, his uncle couldn't run fast with a painful leg. "Some of Lady Gall's men do not support her, though they must pretend they do. The captain of the *Sea Terrier* recognized me. This was my chance. 'Here is a child who might save Fontania,' I told him. 'Keep her away from Lady Gall.' I wasn't sure if he believed me." Trump was talking to the whole group now, not just Jasper. "But in a sketch I drew, Jasper and I saw …"

Trump suddenly stood up. His chair fell over. Though he was pale and grubby, for a moment he looked like a prince. "I drew a sketch that came to life. Jasper and I both saw it. Sibilla was alive. It seems I may have come into some power very late and very little. I have to go to the Eastern Isle to stop the false coronation. Jasper, you'd better give me back the dagger."

If Jasper had been wearing the little weapon, he'd have passed it to his uncle right away. But it was hidden on the *Restaurant*. He was about to say so, but Duchess Donna held up her hand. Silence hung like wings about them. Then the Duchess craned her neck, just a little, to see the artist's satchel. She gave Uncle Trump a stern stare.

Hartie frowned too, pattered across, picked up the satchel and carried it to the side table. He pushed the cakes together to make room for it.

Trump swallowed. He limped over to the table, opened his satchel and took the sketchbook out. His eyes closed for a moment. Then he opened his eyes, and the sketchbook.

The others left their places and gathered around.

"Draw the moment when Lady Helen asked you to look after Sibilla," murmured the Duchess.

Hartie held out a pencil. After a moment, Trump accepted it. On the page before them, Trump sketched Lady Helen and Dr. Hannibal. Jasper couldn't stop himself from reaching out to touch the margin of the page. The scene seemed to widen. His parents huddled together on a rocky beach. A fierce wind blew the scarf off his mother's hair—Sibilla wasn't in her arms. Around them were soldiers.

In the background was the *Double Cross* and one of Lady Gall's ships ... clouds scudded ... a seagull flew across the page and screamed ...

In the clamour of waves and wind and shouting, Sibilla's toy monkey sprawled on the rocky beach. Jasper heard his mother's voice: *Did you give him enough money?* His father replied: *Don't say his name ...*

Polly nudged Jasper aside. Once again the picture was no more than pencil lines and shading.

"The pirates told us you had no money," Polly said to Trump.

"I gave it to the captain of the *Terrier.*" Trump tucked his injured leg behind the other. "To go and hide in Monkey River. To take care of Sibilla."

"You trusted a man you had to bribe?" Dr. Rocket was as fierce as a great old warrior.

Trump closed the sketchbook. He was pale, so pale. Jasper understood. Because of the moving sketch, his uncle realized he must be King after all, and he hated the idea just as much as Jasper did. But it did mean that Trump had a chance to defeat Lady Gall.

~

Duchess Donna was the perfect person to take charge. "A rested mind comes up with better plans. Now, a late lunch means a later supper, so we will rest till supper time. There are newspapers to read, though they are a week old. The carrier eagle comes on Thursdays, so it will be later on today. Something to look forward to, like cake."

With her own hands, she cut a wedge for Beatrix first,

then Jasper, and told them they could sit with their cake outside. That meant the grown-ups wanted to talk in private.

Jasper didn't feel like sitting with Beatrix. She didn't like him and he couldn't blame her. He needed time to himself anyway. He carried his plate outside to a stone bench in a small sheltered courtyard with tumbled flowerbeds. Chocolate cake is at its best when it's moist and thick with cream topping and silver balls you can crunch with your back teeth. If you're upset, you feel a little better while the taste of cake is on your tongue.

He was very relieved that he was not the secret Prince. But if Trump was definitely the real King, Sibilla couldn't be Queen—and Jasper felt anxious about that. It was ridiculous of him. A baby who still had tantrums when she couldn't find her favorite toy could not be a better monarch than a grown man. Perhaps it was Jasper who was jealous. Perhaps he just wanted to keep the marvelous dagger.

He looked up at the low green roof. A black gull perched near the chimney (which was disguised as a little pile of rocks). Birds had been appearing in his life for many days now. The seagull on the wharf had stabbed his hand when he'd tried to feed it. In Dogjaw, black and white gulls had chased the white chicken as if they knew he'd try to save it and be caught by Lady Gall's men. Not all birds were bad, though. He was sure that Polly talked to birds, at least a bit. Birds had helped their impossible dash over the rapids. And, of course, there was the dragon-eagle.

Beatrix came into the courtyard and stopped when she

saw Jasper. He put his empty plate down and clasped his hands on his knees to wait until she went away. But she came and sat beside him. The breeze made fallen leaves flick around their feet like brave little sparrows. After a while Beatrix said something so softly Jasper didn't catch it.

"Pardon?" he asked.

"I'm sorry about your little sister," she said huskily.

"Thank you," Jasper said.

They sat in awkward silence.

At last Beatrix spoke quietly again. "When we came up the rapids, I remembered something. The day of the Great Accident, when the lake was ruined, I heard the sound of wings. Very large wings. So much about that day was frightening, but I wasn't afraid of the wings. I was very, very sorry that—" she frowned, as if she was trying to remember how she'd felt when she was so small, "—that they had to fly away with broken wings. They gave the saddest cries. But I was also—I don't know—happy that they might have escaped."

It was like having another piece of an enormous jigsaw puzzle but no idea what the final picture ought to look like.

"I just thought you might be interested." She stood up quickly.

Jasper reached out and stopped her. After a moment he spoke softly too. "I saw a feather made of silver. It was like a dragon's scale."

He didn't know if she believed him, but her eyes widened, and she smiled. He couldn't help but smile back.

She began to say something, but a beating in the air made them glance up.

Toward the roof, a large bird was descending. It had something in its claws. For a heart-stopping second Jasper thought it might be his little sister. But it was the carrier eagle with the week's newspapers.

~

The eagle perched on a stone table and ruffled its golden-brown feathers. It turned a proud head as Hartie came running from the house. Hartie bowed to the eagle and said thank you, then took the bundle of papers the bird had dropped at its feet.

The great bird blinked at Jasper. Jasper was glad he didn't have to go too close to that yellow curved beak, and offered to help cart the papers inside. Beatrix stayed to watch a guard feed the eagle, though Jasper noticed she stood behind a very tall plant pot.

In the front hall, Hartie took a knife from a drawer and cut the strings around the bundle. He and Jasper began to unfold them and lay them out in order of when they were published. There was the paper Jasper's parents subscribed to at home, *Fontanian Daily Watch*. Some were from other towns and islands. One was called *Watch Out!* Another, that seemed very low class, was *The Two-Daily Blast*. Its headline said: "`TRUTH OUT ABOUT LOVING PARENTS!`" The sub-heading said: "`Noted noble-woman and scientist husband sell their children!`"

Jasper opened his mouth to gasp *How awful*. It stayed open as he read on:

> Lady Helen, famous for her beauty and kindness
> to strangers, has shown an ugly heart and great
> unkindness to her own children. She and her
> husband, Hannibal Ludlow (Head of the Workroom
> of Knowledge), were seen selling their baby
> daughter to a gypsy. This horrifying exchange
> took place in the town square of Battle Island's
> major city.
>
> The parents have also sold their son to
> work in a kitchen. He is a plain-faced boy,
> not handsome enough for Lady Helen to keep
> beside her. He shows no sign of a good
> brain.
>
> This news has shocked our little world. Lady
> Helen is no longer the most popular of the
> minor noble-women. There is great public pressure
> on Lady Gall to take the title of Queen, but
> she insists she is far too humble.

Jasper read it through twice before it sank in. At the end of this passage of lies and half-truths was the journalist's name: Crispin Kent.

The small man was at Jasper's elbow, reading with his mouth open as well. "Wickedness," he said. "Thorough selfishness, head to toe. Or it would be, if it were true."

Jasper's hands shook as he carried the newspaper inside. Trump, the Duchess, Polly and Dr. Rocket looked up from their unsmiling conversation. He laid the paper on his uncle's knee.

Dr. Rocket again moved very fast for an old man, and read over Trump's shoulder. Trump had turned as white as the margins, and worry was scribbled on his brow.

The captain grabbed up the paper and thrust it at Polly. She and the Duchess read it together.

Jasper had to speak. "It's a lie that they sold me to work in a kitchen. It's a lie that my parents sold Sibilla to a gypsy. They gave her to her own uncle. We know Crispin Kent tells terrible lies. But his lies have bits of truth in them! Has Uncle Trump told the truth about Sibilla?"

The Duchess came toward Jasper. He threw her hand off. He didn't want comfort. Tears blinded him. Someone took his arm again, and he let himself be led out into the courtyard. When his eyes cleared, he found Polly sitting at his side. Beatrix was nearby. She'd seen him crying. He buried his head in his arms.

Polly patted Jasper's back. "Tomorrow, the captain will find a good strong tree for a new mast. It won't take long. We must be off as soon as possible."

Off where? It was all so hopeless that Jasper wanted to lie down and never get up.

"The true monarch is either your uncle, or you, or Sibilla," Polly said. "There are jobs to do. One step at a time. As usual, it's the best way to walk."

Beatrix came closer, grinning a little grimly through her tangled hair. "So far each step has been the first in another disaster. But we're still here, I suppose."

Jasper sat up. If she had toughened up again, then so could he.

A PLAN THAT
ACTUALLY SUCCEEDS

Next morning, they found a tall straight tree.

They suggested to any birds, mice, squirrels and insects living in it that it was time to move out, and said "Excuse me" to the trees around it.

Hartie, the guards and Dr. Rocket took turns to hew with axes. They kept telling Trump to stay out of the way because he was already injured and he was hopeless at this sort of thing anyway. Trump limped off into the forest, muttering curses.

The Duchess shouted after him, "Buck yourself up!"

Jasper took a hammer from Beatrix to show her how to use it. But his hand slid and he dropped it and scattered all the nails.

"You're a prince but you're thick as a brick!" she yelled at him.

Jasper went to fetch Trump, and found him putting his boot back on. "If that ankle's bad, put a bandage on it," said Jasper.

Trump swore at him, so this was not the time for Jasper

to find out if his uncle was honest and true.

They set the new mast up on the *Traveling Restaurant* with only one spanner lost overboard, two bruised knuckles, one sore elbow, and countless more curses.

—

SO THAT'S GOOD, BUT ...

Two nights later, Duchess Donna and her household stood on the camouflaged jetty and helped the *Restaurant* cast off. Jasper wondered if the way they lived under that long green roof, with everything disguised as part of the forest, and the fact that they were all ... well, rather short, meant they were dwarfs or perhaps pixies. Dwarfs, as he had read in those forbidden books hidden in the attic of the little palace, were pleasant creatures with pouchy faces and large axes—not quite like Duchess Donna and her servants. Pixies, as far as Jasper knew, were dainty and annoying, like Sibilla when she was in a mood. Well, whatever the Duchess and her people were, they were wise to stay hidden unless there was a return of magic. But that wouldn't happen till Lady Gall was stopped.

The *Restaurant* floated away from the jetty, and soon the little beach seemed deserted. Jasper hung about near the third anchor-well, but the dragon-eagle was probably asleep. It needed rest, he knew that. Dangerous times were ahead.

He went into the galley and found Beatrix puzzling over recipes for cake. He turned to go out, but—

"What's this word?" She pointed.

He turned and stared. She'd taunted him before, as if she was brilliant at reading. "It says 'ingredients.'"

She frowned at the page. "If I want to make a cake, I have to get it right. What's the point of baking a bad cake?"

"None, I suppose." Jasper shrugged. "You know, you could have stayed with Duchess Donna," he said. "She liked you. You liked her. You could have had a hundred cakes baked for you. We might be captured and killed where we're going."

Beatrix tugged her hair so it covered her eyes even more. "Shut up."

The insides of Jasper's ears went prickly. Why was she so rude when he'd tried to be nice!

A shout from Trump gave him an excuse to dive out on deck. A far-off bugle call was sounding, another bugle answered it, and shots rang out. From the trees—from the low green house of dwarfs or pixies—rose a faint scrawl of smoke, then a flare of fire. It was a terrible message that Lady Gall's troops had come upon the house of Duchess Donna. The crack of rifles came again.

There was nothing the *Restaurant* could do but sail on. Beatrix stood at the rail, crying. Jasper didn't weep, but felt his fury and determination rising.

~

Lake Riversea was so wide that it was the second day before they saw the shore on the other side. If only there was a faster way to travel. Like birds did. But that raised a scary question. The *Traveling Restaurant*, in the middle of the huge lake, would easily be spotted if Lady Gall used spy-birds.

"Would spy-birds be magical or not?" Jasper said to Beatrix in the galley.

"Probably both," she answered.

"But Lady Gall's the enemy of magic."

"She's the kind of person who says one thing while she does another." Beatrix gripped a mixing bowl and beat hard and very noisily with a wooden spoon.

Jasper waited until Beatrix had gingerbread biscuits in the oven and the cabin was empty. Then he sat with his backpack and emptied out his belongings. He refolded his clothes and replaced everything—except the dagger—tidily back into the backpack. It took a couple of goes to get right, but Jasper didn't think of it as time-wasting—it wasn't easy trying to decide whether to give the dagger back to Uncle Trump.

He heard Polly's light steps clatter in, pause, then continue up into the wheelhouse. Dr. Rocket's heavy tread came down.

Jasper felt a tap on his shoulder.

"I'd buckle it on, if I were you," the captain said. He waited while Jasper did so. "Now, come up and give me your opinion."

~

A chart of Lake Riversea lay on the cabinet. There was the start of the Great South River. And there, many miles from it, was a mountain range between the Lake and Old

Ocean. On the other side of those mountains lay Monkey River. Almost by itself, one of Jasper's hands moved to the far side of the mountains where a faint dotted line joined the river. He frowned. He traced the dotted line back to the mountains and back to Lake Riversea.

"I remember more and more about boys," the captain murmured, and there was a grumbling that might have been a chuckle. Jasper edged away. "Sometimes," said Dr. Rocket, "it isn't so much someone laughing at you, as them recognising they used to be like you when they were young." He gave Jasper a light punch on the shoulder. "You are very like your father, you know. He would get an idea into his head. You'd tell him if it was a good or bad one, but he wouldn't listen. He'd continue to wrestle with it till he was certain for himself."

"You mean, he never took your advice?"

"I would never say that to a man's son." Dr. Rocket had a wheezing fit, which took a while to settle.

The scent of gingerbread wafted from the galley.

"What is our plan?" Jasper asked.

Dr. Rocket glanced out to where Trump sat in a deck chair looking glum, boots up on the rail. "Sibilla is in Monkey River, on the *Sea Terrier*, if your uncle is telling the truth."

"If?" Jasper looked at Dr. Rocket.

"If so," continued the captain, "we must get there as fast as possible."

"How?" Jasper asked. "It's over the mountains."

The captain drew in a great breath and blew it out slowly. "We'll have to leave the *Restaurant* after all."

"But we can't leave the dr…" Jasper stopped. The captain had never mentioned the dragon-eagle. That probably meant nobody should.

Jasper looked at the map again. Something about it bothered him. The thing was, lots of rivers run into lakes, which was how you got lakes in the first place. Then water had to flow out, so there was another river at the weakest spot or lowest spot. The Great South River was the weakest spot on Lake Riversea.

"What's the matter?" asked Dr. Rocket.

"Well," said Jasper, which gave him time to keep on thinking. "What's that?"

The captain kept one hand on the helm and leaned to see where Jasper pointed. "A bit of the lake," said the captain.

"It looks almost the same as the bit where the Great South River flows out, over the rapids."

"Any geographer will tell you that two rivers can't flow out of the same lake," said Dr. Rocket.

"I know that. But what are those circles?"

"A whirlpool," said the captain.

"Oh," said Jasper.

"Things get dragged down and don't come up."

Jasper put his nose closer to the map. To reach Sibilla as quickly as possible, over the mountains to Monkey River, they would have to go dangerously near the whirlpool.

A RECIPE IS A PLAN
OF SORTS

How many days had Jasper been escaping Lady Gall? Where was she now, with her stiff face and stabbing nails? He mooched into the cabin, where Trump doodled in his sketchbook. The galley counter was heaped with plates of gingerbread men, gingerbread women, and gingerbread children. Polly handed Beatrix a piping bag. Beatrix squeezed icing to make buttons and smiles. Her tongue stuck out as if it helped her concentrate.

No matter how delicious it smelled, when Jasper tapped the gingerbread it felt like concrete. "It keeps well, doesn't it?" Jasper said. "We could store it carefully, and sell it for a huge profit next time the *Restaurant*'s open."

Beatrix looked suspiciously at him and handed Trump a gingerbread man. Trump nodded thank you, but set it on the table. Beatrix frowned and gave Jasper a gingerbread baby. He tried nibbling its toes. Rock hard. Weren't there times when it had to be okay to tell small lies?

"Mmm! Really good enough to sell next time we stop," Jasper said.

She blushed, and almost looked pretty. Anyone could look pretty when they were happy, because prettiness was a state of mind, or so his mother always told him. But then Lady Helen was very beautiful and he was plain. So he knew she only tried to make him feel better, as mothers are meant to. Still, Beatrix was almost pretty.

Polly looked over Trump's shoulder at his sketch. "And?" she asked coldly.

Trump glanced up. "See for yourself. Nothing." There was a sharp note in his voice.

Thankful for an excuse to leave the gingerbread, Jasper hopped off the stool. In the pencil drawing of Sibilla in a high chair, her face looked dirty and her clothes shabby. It was just a sketch. No magic.

But they absolutely had to know if she was safe. "Put your hand on it," said Jasper.

"What?" asked Trump.

Jasper picked up Trump's hand and showed him what he meant. Jasper left his hand there too. The magic happened.

Sibilla scowled at a plate of beans and cabbage, and you could smell it—stinky. With one hand she pulled her own hair, as toddlers do when they're close to cranky tears. She pushed the plate away.

Trump let out a low, slow breath. He raised his head and looked at Jasper.

If Jasper had gazed at the picture any longer, his heart would have grown too sore to let him move. But he was saved from that by ...

"Trouble!" the captain shouted from the wheelhouse.

Jasper rushed to the porthole. Trump scrambled from the table and ran outside, followed by Polly. Beatrix seemed frozen to the spot, there in the galley.

Out from a gentle-looking bay sailed a fleet of small dark ships with purple sails. They sped toward the *Traveling Restaurant*. The sky was gray with cloud, and there was a pattering like rain. Tiny black fish dived in the waves.

Jasper realized the black fish were actually arrows. And each of the swift ships flew a pennant with the sign of Lady Gall.

Polly was already strapping herself into thick clothing to protect herself up the rigging. She threw some at Beatrix and Jasper. Neither of them dared grizzle about how silly they would look all bundled up. They scrambled into it.

As Jasper tumbled out on deck, Trump grabbed him. "Do you have the dagger?" His voice was low and quick.

Jasper glanced at his backpack. Then he remembered he had the dagger strapped on—it felt so much part of him he'd forgotten. But Trump had shoved past into the cabin.

A flock of screaming birds flew overhead. It was clear that the arrow-ships were forcing the *Restaurant* further and further north, closer and closer to the whirlpool. Now, too, the enemy schooners were closing in. Arrows thudded onto the deck and hull, and bristled from the wheelhouse wall.

Trump had Jasper's stuff all strewn over the floor. "Typical boy!" he cried. "No brains worth a bean!" Trump flung the empty backpack aside and rushed from the cabin. "Keep under cover!" he yelled back to Jasper. "Polly, get down from there at once!"

"We're not stupid!" shouted Polly. But it was pretty dumb to be up the rigging in an onslaught of arrows.

An arrow pinned the tail of Trump's jacket to the wheelhouse ladder. He wrenched free, but slipped across the deck so that his injured ankle stuck under the railing. He tugged and his boot fell off. Jasper darted to grab it, rolled with it, and out of the boot rattled some coin. Disbelieving, he put his hand into the boot and pulled out a wad of banknotes.

"You said you had no money!" Polly shrieked. Yes—Trump had said he'd given Hannibal's money to the captain who was hiding Sibilla.

"I can explain!" Trump yelled.

"Save your lying breath!" screamed Polly.

The deadly ships bore down upon the *Restaurant*.

Jasper rushed into the galley and swept an armload of gingerbread into a basket. He was acting without thinking—though really he was relying on what he knew about the world. It was not as much as a grown-up might know, but it was something. Besides, one of the main grown-ups in his life was a self-serving cheat who didn't deserve to be King. He raced back on deck and flipped a gingerbread man toward the nearest enemy schooner. It fell short, but (amazingly) floated. He tossed another. A bird snatched it out of the air, carried it over the enemy deck and let it fall. Jasper tossed a third. A gust of wind whisked it up and across. It hit the enemy sail and dropped to the deck.

Beatrix appeared with another basket. "You could have

just said you didn't like them!" She started throwing gingerbread as well.

Jasper didn't know if the plan worked for the right reasons. What would the right reasons have been, anyway? At first the enemy archers were so surprised they fell about laughing. They lowered their bows, tried some gingerbread and—laughing—beckoned for more.

Clouds thickened. They were moving further from the enemy—but the wind was blowing from behind Jasper. Why had the enemy stopped firing? Why were they continuing to laugh? Surely not just because of the gingerbread. The air was full of rain ... no, it was spray.

With a terrible understanding, Jasper turned around. The *Restaurant* was being drawn toward the whirlpool.

"Trump! What are you doing?" Polly screamed.

He was wrestling with the davits of an orange dinghy. It was obvious he didn't know how to do it properly. The dinghy crashed off the side of the ship. A wave splashed up over Trump. He wrestled to release another dinghy. Did he think he could escape in that? No chance!

—

THE BEST PLAN,
FOR NOW

Enemy ships on one side, whirlpool on the other—Jasper thought it didn't matter if he died, but it would matter very much if Sibilla wasn't saved. He tumbled to the rail and begged silently for help from the dragon-eagle. There was no answer.

"Everyone get inside!" Dr. Rocket bellowed from the wheelhouse. "Shut the doors and portholes!"

"Take your own advice, you daft old man!" yelled Polly.

In growing darkness and spray from the whirlpool, Jasper fought his way along the deck. At last his fingers came upon the door. He slid it open and tumbled in. Polly was lashing Beatrix to one of the brass poles for safety. She also showed Beatrix how to undo the knot, if she needed. Beatrix's eyes were dark with angry fear.

Where was Trump? Still outside?

The *Restaurant* tipped violently. The first circle of the whirlpool had her in its grasp. Trump struggled past a porthole, but didn't come in.

"Rope up!" Polly shouted to Jasper.

He did as he was told, lashing himself to the nearest pole while she tied herself to another. But the ship swerved sharply, and Polly fell to the floor. Swearing, she picked herself up and finished the job just before another terrifying swing.

The swerving grew worse—one moment darkness, the next a flash of daylight, then darkness again. The ship jerked and the door crashed open. Jasper saw Trump out on deck, not safely tied, and struggling to release another dinghy. The tail of his coat flapped in the wind and caught in the mechanism. He tried to wrench himself out of the coat, but it simply tangled tighter.

Jasper wriggled from his ropes and dived for the door. He slid the dagger from his belt.

"You do have it!" his uncle cried with wild joy.

Jasper slashed at Trump's jacket. The fabric came free, and his uncle staggered, grabbing Jasper's shoulder.

"Get inside!" he shouted. He threw Jasper in front of him.

The cabin door slammed shut. Jasper slid the dagger back in the scabbard and flung himself at the brass pole to rope up again.

But Trump was still outside. Round and round the vessel whirled. A flash of orange passed a porthole—a glimpse of Trump fighting to hold onto the ship with one hand, while he pushed another dinghy off with the other— then the *Restaurant* plunged into darkness. Jasper tried not to cry out, just to think fiercely: *dragon-eagle—my sister— dragon-eagle* ...

The ordeal was a nightmare of roaring darkness. It was a fever dream but cold, whirling, and spinning till Jasper didn't care what happened next. It was hours, perhaps a whole day. Time didn't matter. Perhaps time didn't even work. At last he realized the whirling was not as violent. It was more like a fast ride in one direction; though the ship still swerved, there were bumps and bangs, the boom of vast quantities of water thundered on.

~

The roaring had stopped. The *Traveling Restaurant* was bobbing—it seemed—in one place. The darkness was a little less intense. Outside was a glimmer like moonlight.

The knots that had kept Jasper tied to the pole had tightened with the bashing about, and he struggled to loosen them. Polly was having trouble with hers too. At last he managed to free himself and to help her out. She looked awful, and muttered that she wanted to throw up. Jasper backed away just in case she did. Beatrix called out, and Jasper waded through puddles where water had leaked in to help with her ropes. Then he clambered over a heap of wet cushions and broken chairs to find the door. He and Beatrix pushed and banged till it creaked and slid open. They stumbled outside.

In fresh air and soft moonlight, Jasper saw the damage. On this side of the ship, one dinghy hung from a broken davit. The rest were gone. There was no sign of Trump. The masts were cast down in a tangle of canvas and ropes. Up in the wheelhouse, through a cracked window, he could make out Dr. Rocket slumped over the wheel.

Behind them were the mountains. But Jasper knew the *Restaurant* was no longer in Lake Riversea. This was a stream. Jasper caught his breath as a sudden gush of water pushed the little ship on further, and she bumped against a bank. There was only one explanation. The whirlpool had sucked them down to an underground river. That river had carried them under the mountains and up to the surface again. With the help, perhaps, of the dragon-eagle.

Jasper trembled, and staggered against Beatrix. They had to cling to each other, which was a bit awkward, and slid down to sit on the deck. He ached all over. If this little river joined up to Monkey River ... if Trump had told the truth after all, and the *Sea Terrier* with Sibilla on had sailed into Monkey River ... how soon could the *Restaurant* sail on to find his sister?

But one thing must be done, before anything else. As soon as he had a little strength, Jasper crawled along the deck toward the anchor-well. "Are you all right?" he whispered.

There was a faint shuffle, like feathers moving when a bird took a shallow breath.

"Thank goodness," Jasper murmured. "And thank you."

NO LOOPHOLE IN THE
BEST-LAID PLAN

For a long hour Polly stood on deck weeping for Trump, with Dr. Rocket beside her. "He was a layabout, a slacker. A liar and cheat!"

Jasper hovered nearby, not knowing what to say.

"At the end, he was a good man," the captain rumbled. "Getting rid of the dinghies made the boat lighter. It gave us more chance of escaping the whirlpool."

"But he died! So he was stupid!" Polly's voice was clogged with tears.

"My dear," said Dr. Rocket, "all men are stupid now and then. Many women are as well."

Polly buried her head in the captain's jacket. He let out a yelp, and staggered.

"You broke an arm and didn't say anything?" Polly cried. "Men are such idiots!"

"It's only bruised," the captain said.

She bullied him inside to strap it and make up a sling. "Jasper, come lend a hand!" she yelled.

But Jasper couldn't move. "You go," he said to Beatrix,

though he supposed she would sneer. She didn't. She seemed to realize how complicated he felt about his cheating uncle being drowned—the secret Prince who was too lazy to be King but not afraid to release the dinghies in the whirlpool. His uncle, who had saved Jasper by throwing him into the cabin and died himself. His uncle, who might have been a good King in the end.

He crept off to find a quiet corner on deck. Moths as large as hats flickered in the moonlight. The night was soft and still. Behind them, steep cliffs framed the stream where it emerged from under the mountain. Somewhere down Monkey River as it flowed on to meet Old Ocean was a vessel at rest. A military vessel with one unhappy toddler on board. Jasper had to make the best plan of his life so far.

~

One thing about Dr. Rocket with an arm in a sling was that he couldn't do many repairs to the masts and sails. One thing about Polly in tears was that she worked more furiously than ever, and made Jasper and Beatrix work more furiously than furiously. The *Restaurant* was battered and rusty now. Her once-bright paint was scuffed and flaked. It took two days to make the ship shipshape. But now she was riverworthy. And one thing about being on a river was they didn't have to sail down. They could let the little river do the job. All Dr. Rocket had to do was steer.

So they came to Monkey River. Jasper hadn't seen a monkey yet, but names could be misleading. He hadn't seen a heron near Herontown, either.

Floating (and steering) downriver was uneventful and gave him lots of time to think. When he had a break from helping in the wheelhouse, he looked again at the dagger, turning it over and over in his hands. He'd only used it for rescuing people: first, Crispin Kent, then Trump (though Trump had died anyway). He must have been meant to keep it, because if he'd given it back to his uncle it would be at the bottom of the whirlpool now. Jasper's breath began to shudder. It was three days since the disaster. But you didn't stop grieving in only three days. Jasper let his tears fall, and the sun and wind dried them on his cheeks.

A flock of birds soared overhead, a sign of evening closing in. Dr. Rocket waved his good arm to show he was heading for safe anchor, and the *Restaurant* nestled near some willows. Jasper clambered up the rigging, in case he could see anything useful.

He saw a rope bridge. Beyond it, on the far bank of Monkey River, lay a sloop-of-war.

~

Jasper figured Dr. Rocket, with his bruised arm, should not be told of new developments. Nor should Polly, with a broken heart and high green heels, because this part of the riverbank was mostly swamp. Beatrix was the help he needed, but he couldn't ask her. His family had already wrecked her life. What Jasper had for help—he hoped—was luck.

It was very lucky the river had a rope bridge over it, just five minutes' trudge from the *Restaurant*. He trusted the bridge wouldn't sway too much and wouldn't break. Oh— and he hoped that the naval vessel was not a pirate ship well disguised, and that it was, after all, the *Sea Terrier*.

Step one in his plan was: wait till morning.

~

In the silvery light of dawn, Jasper made sure the scabbard was buckled tight. He slipped into his woollen jacket, now filthy from adventure, and tugged on one of Dr. Rocket's hats. He let a rope ladder over the side and slid down. The only sounds were the rippling of the river, a chuckle of ducks as they dreamed of worms, and his heartbeat in his ears. He crept over swamp and through brambles till he came within sight of the rope bridge.

A bramble branch swished behind him.

"Ouch," said a throaty voice. It was Beatrix, sucking a scratched hand. She wore the grubby little sailor's jacket from the *Hound* and another of Dr. Rocket's caps.

"Go back," Jasper hissed.

"Just as I thought, you're being dumb," she whispered back.

"Go back," he hissed again.

She crept closer. "You can't smuggle your sister out of the *Terrier* by yourself."

"If it is the *Terrier*," he said. "And how did you know?"

She rolled her eyes. "I can climb rigging too, and I've got a brain."

"Sibilla's not your sister. You hate my family."

"It's hardly her fault," Beatrix said. "She's only little."

"For heaven's sake, be quiet then," said Jasper. This was actually pretty close to having a friend.

He told her the next steps of his plan, and they crept on.

It was slippery, scrambling up the bank to the rope bridge. The swaying bridge made Jasper feel sick, though Beatrix didn't seem to mind it. On the other side, mud stuck to Jasper's boots but Beatrix discovered a knack of walking from one dry fallen branch to a sticking-up bit of rock. He copied her.

As they came closer to the ship, Beatrix pointed to the name. Thank goodness—it was the *Sea Terrier*.

Early morning crickets began to chirrup in the reeds. A frog or two grumbled about having to get up and set to work. A few birds coasted overhead, too high for Jasper to tell if they were seagulls. Two small green finches zoomed along. A goose gave a honk. But when the children reached the ship there was no movement on board. The two guards on deck were dozing.

"Excuse us," whispered Jasper. "Excuse us!"

One of the men straightened up immediately. His cheeks fired red, and his eyes moved fast from side to side.

"Ahoy!" Jasper said. "Down here."

The guard looked around again, then leaned over the railing.

Jasper didn't want anyone to ask an awkward question in the middle of his plan, so he spoke fast. "How's the kid? That awful baby?"

The guard made a face. "Grizzling all night. Don't think it's been to sleep at all. It's no wonder me and—" he jerked his thumb at the other guard, still dozing "—have awful headaches."

"I can imagine!" whispered Beatrix, smiling up at him. She elbowed Jasper. Now they knew a little child was on the ship. It must be Sibilla.

Jasper gave what he hoped was a mischievous grin. "That's why we thought we'd sleep off ship. It wuz no fun. We wuz bit all over by gnats."

"Suppose you want to come aboard now," said the guard.

Jasper nodded. "Better get down to the galley before we get uz in trouble."

He'd hoped the guard would lower the gangplank, but the man fetched out a rope ladder. "Hang on," he said. "Blasted loops never want to fit on these blasted hooks …" He wrenched hard. "There we go."

The ladder unrolled down the *Terrier*'s side.

They scrambled up, and Jasper said thanks. Before the guard had time to wonder why he hadn't seen them before, they scuttled off along the deck. The other guard was unhooking the ladder and rolling it up, yawning.

Now what? Which way? Jasper stood and listened.

There was a clank of far-off machinery in the ship's insides. That was all. He beckoned Beatrix, and tried an unimportant-looking door. It ought to lead to the galley— everyone knew Lady Gall thought soldiers and sailors should be fed plenty but not well. He sniffed the air in the passageway: stale cabbage.

With Beatrix behind him keeping watch, he listened at every door. Behind one, there was snoring. Behind another, a ringing alarm clock. Someone bashed it quiet, and there was the muffled heaving of blankets being pulled over a mumbling head. Far-off there was still the sound of machinery, but now the sound of something nearer, a small *clank-quack*. His heart leaped. It was the sound a child makes when it's starting to cry.

He closed his eyes, thought of the dragon-eagle, opened his eyes and pushed the door.

The room was a musty mess. In one corner was a child's cot, the blankets tangled. In another corner was a chair where a sailor sat, head in his hands. In the middle of the room a table was heaped in mugs and dirty dishes. With its back to the door was a high chair, and in it sat a child in stripy leggings and a tunic with dirty frilled cuffs. She had a sticking-up quiff of fine blonde hair.

As he stood there in that first gasp of relief, Sibilla dropped a spoon on the floor and grizzled again. *Clank-quack.*

The sailor lifted his head, and saw Jasper and Beatrix.

"How's the brat?" Jasper mouthed. He scanned the room but couldn't see Sibilla's stuffed monkey. "Still not eating?"

With a groan the sailor dropped his head back into his hands. "If this kid ain't kept healthy, Captain Brickle will have my guts for garters." He groaned again. "First Mate Scruggs will have what's left!"

Sibilla sounded snuffly. Her nose would be running. She stretched her arms out, fingers wiggling desperately. *Clank-quack* ... The man stuck another spoon into the porridge and offered it to her. She whacked it to the floor and tried to twist out of the high chair.

"You have a break," Jasper mouthed. "I'll try."

"Be my guest," the sailor said. "I'll be back in five minutes—or never, if I have my way." He made for the door so quickly, Beatrix had to dodge aside to let him through.

Sibilla rubbed her eyes with the backs of her hands. Jasper stepped to the table, took a clean spoon, put a tiny morsel on it and danced it in the air. He bent down a little, so when she saw him she wouldn't get too big a fright. Her mouth was opening to let out an almighty roar.

"Hello," he said softly. "Hello, Sibilla."

Her mouth stayed open, she looked up and her eyes widened. She lurched at him with both arms and nearly toppled the high chair. Firmly and gently Jasper hugged her. "Hush," he said. "Hush, Sibilla."

~

So far, the plan had been dangerous. From now on, it was perilous.

Beatrix helped Jasper unlatch the tray of the chair so he could lift his sister out.

Next step: Beatrix pulled out a packet of matches, crumpled a piece of paper, and put it on the table. She put the matches next to it.

It was too risky to really light a fire. What if it took hold and they couldn't get off the ship themselves? What if someone actually died? But if they put matches and paper on the table, yelled "Fire!" and they were caught, they could truthfully say somebody could have lit a fire. Grown-ups usually thought children were idiotic, so Jasper and Beatrix hoped they'd get away with it.

Down the passageway they went, Jasper carrying Sibilla. She wriggled. He put a finger over his lips, then over hers, and she seemed to realize she must be quiet. Whether or not she was the Queen, she was a clever toddler. Give them half a chance, as Emily said, all toddlers are.

On deck, Sibilla squinted as if she hadn't seen daylight for days, and hid her eyes.

They neared the gangplank. Jasper nodded and ducked down while Beatrix ran toward the guards.

"Fire!" she cried. "Fire in the kid's room! Fire!"

One guard sped away at once. "Fire!"

The other jumped on the spot as if he couldn't make his mind up. At last he raced off. "Fire!" he yelled. "Fire! Fire!"

Beatrix found the rolled-up ladder and dragged it to the side. "You first!"

"No, you!" said Jasper.

"You're carrying the baby!" Beatrix said.

"If you go first, you can catch her if I drop her," Jasper explained.

Beatrix had fitted one loop of the ladder to the first hook, but struggled with the other. "The blasted thing won't stretch!" she cried.

Doors began to bang inside the ship. "Fire! Fire!" Sailors in pyjamas came running out with buckets, lowered them over the side and formed a line to pass them inside to douse the … where was the fire supposed to be?

"No fire!" came a shout inside the *Terrier*. "False alarm! All clear!"

"Hurry!" Jasper tried to shove Beatrix onto the ladder. The tricky loop slipped free. "Stupid girl hands!" he shouted.

"You do it, princey smarty-pants!" she screamed.

"Dozy orphan!" he yelled back. "I wish I'd left you on the *Excellent Hound*!"

There was the tramp of boots and the shuffling of naval slippers. Large naval hands took hold of the rope ladder, unhooked it and rolled it up. Men in uniforms and dressing gowns surrounded the children. There was nothing at all funny about a naval bathrobe when the pockets bore the emblem of Lady Gall.

A sailor took Jasper's sister from him. Sibilla burst into tears, and who could blame her? More sailors hauled the children's arms behind their backs. Jasper struggled and his jacket slipped half off.

"Sir!" A sailor pointed to the scabbard at Jasper's waist.

An officer with a First Mate's cap strode up and stared. "Aha." He grinned, showing very strong square teeth. "A princey smarty-pants, all right. And now we've got him."

THIRD PART

Barbecue with the True Crown

CHANCE MEANS LUCK
MEANS MAYBE

"Take the children to Captain Brickle's cabin! On the double!" ordered the First Mate.

Sailors bundled them along the deck. Beatrix looked furious with Jasper. But this was her fault! If her hands hadn't been so feeble! If she hadn't shouted so rudely that he was a prince!

The First Mate knocked on the door of a cabin. A voice calmly said, "Come in."

The door opened. Jasper thought there might be hope. Trump had said this was the captain who did not support Lady Gall, and Trump had sometimes told the truth. There was a vase of river grasses on the captain's desk. There was a sketch of a monkey in a frame on the wall. Sibilla pointed to it. The sailor dumped her on the floor and brushed nose-run off his sleeve (Sibilla's nose-run, not his own).

The First Mate saluted. "Two extra children, sir."

Captain Brickle put his hands in his dressing-gown pockets. His eyebrows moved only a little. "So I see, First Mate Scruggs. Where did they come from?"

"Sir," the First Mate said, "that is a mystery. But sir, the boy carries the royal dagger."

Captain Brickle continued to look calm. "May I see this article?"

The First Mate gestured to the sailors. Fairly gently, they wrenched Jasper's coat back off his shoulders. Everyone stared at the scabbard.

"Am I permitted to examine it more closely?" asked Captain Brickle.

Jasper expected Scruggs to rip the dagger off him. Instead, a sailor pushed him nearer the desk. The captain leaned forward, hands folded over his stomach, and looked at the scabbard. In the silence, his calm face was no longer quite so calm. Was he going to let them go? Jasper's heart raced faster and faster.

"You're right," said Brickle at last. "I am prepared to bet it is the dagger."

"Is everyone scared to touch it?" Beatrix asked in her huskiest cross voice.

Captain Brickle glanced at her. "What's that around her neck?"

A sailor tugged the red cord, and of course it showed the flute.

"She's not allowed to play it." Captain Brickle wrinkled his forehead. "It will make our heads ache."

The First Mate's eyes gleamed. "This girl's the stolen orphan! We have the baby Princess, the Prince, the royal dagger and, to cap it off, we have this brat! Well done, Captain! Shall we clap them in irons now?"

"That sounds noisy." Captain Brickle put a hand over his eyes.

"Do something!" Beatrix hissed at Jasper.

He hissed back. "What? Whip the dagger out and stab the Mate? What use would that be? There're dozens of them! It's going to be all right. Wait and see."

"You're dreaming," muttered Beatrix.

"Sir," said First Mate Scruggs. "It was top brain power to look after the little Princess and make her more presentable before we took her to Lady Gall. Top thinking, sir, even if it didn't work."

Sibilla blinked at the First Mate. Her nose was running again.

"But sir," continued Scruggs. "The royal dagger changes things. Permission to suggest we send an urgent message to Lady Gall. Permission to suggest we set off to meet the *Hound* this very hour."

Captain Brickle tapped his fingers on the desk. "Where's my morning pot of tea? Where is my toast? For goodness sake, Scruggs, think it through—children need fresh air. Let them muck about on deck. We need rosy cheeks, bright eyes, bright smiles. We can't have them pasty-faced when we present them to the Commander-in-Chief, soon to be Queen. As soon as I've had my tea and toast, I'll be up on the bridge. Then we'll set off. Does that suit you?"

First Mate Scruggs looked humbled. Brickle shooed everyone out. Behind his closed door came a long bored sigh.

Jasper was sure that Captain Brickle was friends with

Uncle Trump. Somehow, they'd soon be free.

~

Fresh air on deck meant having to sit on a bench in a corner, penned up by eight sailors and an officer. Some of the sailors showed off their Lady Gall tattoos. It seemed the best ones were done with purple ink. It was taking ages to prepare the Captain's toast. Nobody brought the children anything. And strangely, nobody had taken the dagger from Jasper. Why would Lady Gall want it? Her usual greed, Jasper supposed.

Sibilla had fallen asleep on his lap. Time seemed to wriggle backward. Beatrix gave a sour whistle through her teeth, and eased the flute to her lips. At the first line of melody, the officer opened his mouth to say stop, then grinned instead.

A tuft of grass moved on the riverbank. Another tuft rustled, and another. A group of ground monkeys popped up from some burrows: *whoo-oop?* The flute gave a squeak, then Beatrix played more loudly. Sibilla sat up and stared at the monkeys as if the world was mad.

"Monkeys," Jasper whispered. "Like your toy."

She gave him a disapproving look and thumped her head back on his chest. The officer chuckled. Jasper realized the man must like children. He must have known that any music would attract the monkeys. So, some of the sailors were on Brickle's side, they weren't all slaves to Lady Gall. Jasper's hope grew stronger.

All the guards were chuckling now. As Beatrix played on, the monkeys draped leaves over their heads and tried to grab them off each other. With a scream, a fat one bounded off into the swamp. Jasper laughed, but Sibilla still refused to look.

Then the officer stood up and craned his neck. He shaded his eyes. Suddenly serious, he beckoned another officer, who opened a small telescope.

Jasper climbed on the bench. There was a patch of reeds, a fallen tree, a glimpse of orange. It was the same orange as the dinghies from the *Restaurant*—though more probably it was a patch of wild pumpkins. Jasper rubbed his eyes. The fat ground monkey danced back along the riverbank, wearing a battered shred of hat—like Uncle Trump's (minus the feather). A shout went up from the officer with the telescope.

Beatrix stopped playing.

The gangplank rattled down, and a squad of sailors marched out and squelched over to surround the wild pumpkins—except that the sailors heaved up a plank or two of orange-colored wood. When they marched out again, they were carrying a body on a stretcher.

Beatrix put a hand on Jasper's arm while the stretcher came on board. The body was covered in bruises, mud, and cuts. Beneath the mud and bruises, it was pale. It wore a tail coat cut to shreds.

"I'm so sorry," Beatrix whispered.

The body groaned.

As the sailors set the stretcher down on deck, Captain Brickle emerged in his brightly buttoned uniform, holding a cup with his last sip of tea. He looked at the stretcher.

Jasper nudged Beatrix. Any moment, they'd be all right.

"Trump?" the captain said. "You're in a worse state than ever."

Trump's eyes opened. He looked up at Captain Brickle. He let out a faint sigh and closed his eyes again.

Captain Brickle turned to Jasper and set down the tea cup. For a moment, Jasper still hoped—but the Captain's eyebrows moved in the slightest sneer.

"Your uncle has had his chance, I think." He raised a fist above his head, and his sleeve slid down to show a purple tattoo. A bird with its wings out. FOREVER BEAUTIFUL.

"Lady Gall!" cried Captain Brickle. "Forever Queen!"

The officers and crew all saluted with one hand and raised the other in a fist. "Lady Gall!" they roared together. "Lady Gall!"

~

Jasper reeled with the mistakes he'd made.

"What a coronation gift!" said Captain Brickle. "Lady Gall can have the layabout Prince, the dagger, and the brats as a multiple present."

"Not all of us!" Jasper said.

"No?" Captain Brickle tipped his head.

"You don't need Beatrix. Let her go. She's not important."

Beatrix punched Jasper on the arm, then punched him again.

"You're a little gentleman-hero," said Captain Brickle. "But we'll carry the motley lot of you to the Eastern Isle. Give the dagger to your uncle, boy. Then, Scruggs, take them all below!" He sauntered off, up to the bridge.

With an ugly scowl and grinning square teeth, Scruggs grabbed Jasper and shoved him toward the stretcher.

Jasper knelt by Trump. His uncle let out a gasp that pretended it was a laugh. "I said there'd be adventures," he murmured. "They're not over yet."

"Here," said Jasper, beginning to unbuckle the scabbard. "Because you're the King."

"No, no. I was afraid I might be, but I'm not," Trump whispered. "But Jasper—there is still magic, so there's still hope. Pretend to tuck the dagger into my belt, but keep tight hold of it. Don't try to save me. Just tell Polly that I know I messed up horribly. And I'm sorry to ask you this, Jasper, but please say I always told the truth when I said I loved her. Now, is the dagger hidden? Good. Then grab your chance to get away."

"What chance?" Jasper's eyes had blurred.

Trump flicked a glance at Jasper's cap. "Hats," he muttered. "That wretched monkey ran off with my hat. They're keen on hats." His eyes closed. Soldiers bent to lift the stretcher, but Trump raised a hand. "Too dangerous to move me. Let me lie on deck …" Once again he seemed unconscious, but a finger beckoned Jasper with one weak flick. "Lady Gall must never get hold of the dagger. Monkeys, Jasper. Hats. Any moment."

With his jacket covering the dagger, Jasper backed away to Beatrix and Sibilla. He told Beatrix quietly what Trump had said. "But what did he mean?"

On the riverbank, the monkey in Trump's hat was still

the center of jabbering attention. The other monkeys wanted it, but he (or she) kept bouncing out of reach. What a show-off! Still, it was hard to take your eyes off Trump's hat bobbing between tufts of river grass …

"Ah," said Beatrix. She touched the cap she wore.

"Ah," agreed Jasper. "Carefully then, okay?"

"I realize that!" She rolled her eyes in her best scornful look.

The order was given to raise the gangplank. Two sailors saluted and stepped up to obey.

Trump suddenly cried out. Moaning horribly, he flailed his arms and legs.

"A fit!" Scruggs cried. "He's having a fit!" Soldiers rushed forward.

Jasper and Beatrix took hold of Sibilla, one arm each, and edged aside. The sailors kept winching up the gangplank, but their eyes were on Trump.

Trump moaned more loudly. Jasper and Beatrix edged further along the deck toward the rising gangplank.

"Fetch the doctor!" ordered Scruggs.

The children reached the gangplank. "The doctor's here!" a sailor said.

"I've no idea what's wrong," said someone who must have been the naval doctor. The sailors crowded even closer. "What happens if I press your tum like this?"

Trump gave an incredible moan. Jasper couldn't tell if it was fake or not. He scrambled to the end of the gangplank, held Sibilla tight and dropped down onto the riverbank. Beatrix landed next to him. The gangplank continued to rise.

Beatrix hurled her cap at the monkeys, grabbed Jasper's and hurled that too. Then they ducked under brambles, and slunk away as swiftly and as carefully as they could.

Jasper glanced back. Their caps dived and darted among tufts of grass. It looked exactly as if some children were trying to hide.

—

ONE FAINT CHANCE

Then it was through the swamp again as fast as possible.

"Don't hurry," Beatrix gasped. "We mustn't draw attention to ourselves."

"Hurry!" Jasper panted. "They'll be after us." Already, there were shouts and orders.

At the rope bridge, Jasper held on with one hand and with the other gripped Sibilla's clothing tightly. They swayed and lurched across. He tried not to panic. But he knew that when the sun was high enough, the shadows hiding the *Traveling Restaurant* would disappear.

Back at the *Restaurant*, Dr. Rocket and Polly hurtled down the gangplank ready to scold—they stopped as soon as they saw what the bundle was in Jasper's arms. Thank goodness they were more sensible than many grown-ups. They didn't grab Sibilla and squeal, "Hello sweetie, aren't you cute." She'd have screamed loud enough to bring a thousand Scruggs and Brickles.

"That child needs a thorough wash and food," said Polly. "Then more food and a good long sleep."

"First, we have to summon up what magic there might

be." Jasper tried to get his breath back. "We need mist!"

"Aye!" Dr. Rocket's arm was still in the sling. "But the second 'aye' is up to …"

Carrying Sibilla, Jasper ran aft. "Please," he whispered as he stood above the brass anchor-well. "Please find the strength. It's for Sibilla. She's here. She's only small. And she's the Queen."

There was a moment of stillness when air and water seemed to shimmer. A silvery mist began to drift around the ship. Within moments, the curls and coils had woven a pearly cocoon. Jasper set his grimy and hungry sister on the deck.

"Sibilla," he said, "do you want breakfast?"

She clutched his pants leg with both hands and looked down through the rail. *Big chicken*, she breathed.

Jasper hoped the dragon-eagle wouldn't mind that the true Queen had called it a big chicken. It was probably her way of saying thank you.

~

They didn't dare begin sailing. They had to wait, moored in the bubble of mist. Polly and Jasper fed Sibilla. Then they bathed her, and Polly scrubbed and rinsed her tunic and leggings. Jasper had to dress her in one of Polly's blouses. It was gigantic on her. Before he'd even done up the buttons, she sprawled asleep on a rug, very still.

The river chuckled past in silver ripples. At last, Dr. Rocket wrestled his arm out of its sling, tested his grip and tossed the sling into the laundry basket.

"We must be silent if we pass the *Sea Terrier*," he said.

"Let's hope the mist holds, because we might run into a search party at any moment. They might even be outside this very second." He climbed up to take the helm.

The ship began floating downstream. Mist brushed against the portholes. Surely someone on the *Terrier* would notice the floating patch of fog. Surely the search party would see it. What a slender chance they would escape!

Sibilla woke up. Jasper found a wooden spoon and popped a dish towel over it to play quiet *peep-oh*. But she just sat swamped in Polly's blouse. When he dressed her in the dried tunic and leggings, he had to move her arms and legs as if she were a rag doll. "Peep-oh!" he tried again. She turned away. He didn't know what to do. Toddlers are meant to dart like moths and pop up in unexpected places. They're meant to burble and squeak, and leave a trail of toys behind. Emily always said the mess and zooming showed how happy and healthy they were. Sibilla hadn't stopped moving since she'd taken her first breath. Even when she was asleep, her pixie fingers had fluttered without stopping. But now—being whisked from home, then from her parents, tossed to Uncle Trump who gave her to Brickle, and the sailors not knowing how to look after a small child …

Beatrix tried playing with Sibilla too. No smiles. No interest at all.

~

The *Restaurant* continued to slip downstream in its shell of mist. How strange and terrible it was to be with his baby sister, possibly the promise of a good new world, while on the same ship traveled possibly the last creature of deep magic.

If only they could all travel somewhere safe from every danger while the dragon-eagle and Sibilla gained strength. The world needed his little sister to grow well again, to grow old enough to be a good Queen.

Light through the door darkened with a long shadow as they passed the *Terrier*. Through the mist came shouts and orders. "We can't set off before the search party is back!" "We have to leave now, sir!" "I'll blazing sir you!" There was a clatter like a metal bucket, and lots of cursing.

From the rigging came a slight scream, and a gasp from Polly. Jasper clutched up Sibilla, darted on deck, and saw Beatrix hanging from the rigging by one hand.

Dr. Rocket stuck his head out of the wheelhouse. "Quiet," he hissed. "What are you doing!"

"I want to see …" Beatrix slipped and screamed again. Polly scrambled over and wrapped her tight to the rigging with both arms.

For a moment there was utter silence on the river.

A puzzled voice came from the *Sea Terrier*. "Who said that?"

From somewhere came a deafening *quack quack!*

"Only a swamp goose," said the voice. "Loud, though, for this time of year."

"Do you think the search party might be in trouble?"

"Should we send a search party to find the search party? Sir?"

The bucket clattered again, and the cursing continued, just as shocking. The *Traveling Restaurant* glided on.

Gradually the mist thinned and vanished. Jasper knew

the young dragon-eagle had done more than it should. "Thank you," he whispered. "I promise not to ask for any more help unless I'm desperate."

He heard a faint clatter of silver feathers, and felt an answering *thank you* in his mind.

~

They were alone on the river now, except for a multitude of birds all sizes, shapes, and colors, wading, swimming, diving, and perching in the rigging. The sun was overhead. Lunchtime, if anyone had an appetite.

Polly and Beatrix clambered down to the deck, Polly growling—softly, but still growling. "If you could see them, silly girl, they could see you!" She disappeared into the galley.

Jasper followed. It was time Sibilla had a drink of milk. He found Polly crying into a dish towel.

"I'm sorry," said Jasper.

"For what!" Polly snapped.

What he wanted to reply was, *For you being in love with my uncle, for not telling you yet that Trump's still alive and he loves you, because Lady Gall is going to kill him anyway, and you'd scream so much that the* Sea Terrier *would hear.*

"For what I've just thought of," he said instead. "We're going downriver."

Polly snapped again. "So?"

"It's just that downriver is the only way we can go," Jasper explained. "When the search party gives up, the *Terrier* will come downriver too. They've got guns. They haven't got useless torn sails and a very old engine like us. Captain Brickle and Scruggs will be wondering where we came from, and where we went. We can't let the *Restaurant* be noticed."

"Blast," said Polly. She tipped her head back, and Jasper copied her. High above circled three black and white seagulls. "Blast and damn," she said.

———

A SHAKY CHANCE

More and more gulls circled above, calling to each other, forever spying.

With only two ways to travel, it was either back into certain danger or onward to possible danger. Jasper made a playpen out of chairs on their sides, and set Sibilla in it with more wooden spoons, clothespins, and a set of bowls that she could use for drums. She still wouldn't touch anything he put out for her, but Jasper wasn't ready to give up. Then he hauled himself to the wheelhouse to open the map cabinet.

Dr. Rocket glanced at him. "Don't you trust the captain?"

"Would you?" It had popped out. Jasper felt himself redden.

Dr. Rocket's beard twitched. He grunted like a large dog and stared downriver, hands steadfast on the wheel. He was keeping in the shade of trees as much as possible (which wasn't much, in fact, but there you are). The map was not encouraging either. The mouth of the river would be hard to navigate. It spread into channels like a frayed end of string. Just before it began to fray, one town was marked. Its name was Stumbledon. It sounded like those awful circus clowns that grown-ups think children love but that actually give lots of them bad dreams. The *Restaurant* couldn't sail faster than the *Terrier*, so she'd have to pretend to be a restaurant. Stumbledon was the only place to do it.

Traveling there, they were gnawed by mosquitoes. Beatrix made a doll out of spoons and a dish towel. Sibilla refused to look it. Beatrix sulked. A family of hippo-geese with beaks as big as suitcases swarmed around. Jasper was afraid one would flop on board and gulp Sibilla up. When the hippo-geese splashed away, Beatrix went out on deck and played her flute. She should have known better. She knew how Monkey River got its name.

Through a porthole, Jasper noticed grass rustle on the banks. There was a *whoo-oop,* and up popped a monkey. It showed its teeth and leaped at Beatrix. The flute squealed. In the next beats of sunshine, a tribe of ground monkeys scrambled onto the *Restaurant* and began dancing on the wheelhouse roof. A fat one gibbered at Beatrix and she backed away along the deck.

"It loves your music," Jasper called.

With a filthy look at him, Beatrix stopped playing, rushed in, slammed the door and hid her flute under her cardigan. The monkey grinned in through a porthole. Sibilla's top-knot quivered. She glanced at Jasper as if to say, *Not my toy—take it away!* But her being horrified was far better than her being sad and limp.

There was a warning shout from the wheelhouse and

the *Restaurant* veered sideways. Tree branches brushed the portholes. The river echoed with the churn of a large ship's engine.

One heartbeat of shock, and Jasper saw the *Sea Terrier* sail past the portholes, her funnels spitting smoke. Another heartbeat, and he realized the *Restaurant* had not been seen. She bobbed calmly in the *Terrier*'s wake. He glanced at Beatrix. Her dark eyes showed she'd seen—as he had—the bound man between armed guards. Uncle Trump. He had a leaf crown on his head. Captain Brickle and First Mate Scruggs were bowing to him, jeering. Trump's head hung very low.

"Did Polly and Dr. Rocket see him?" Beatrix whispered.

"There'd be yelling if they had," said Jasper.

"Well, I won't be the one who tells them," Beatrix said.

~

Dr. Rocket let out another shout. "Stumbledon ahead!"

Jasper ran up the companionway. "Let's hurry past!"

"We're popular here," replied the captain. "Besides, we should stock up. But the biggest 'besides' ..."

Jasper glanced at the sky. The circle of spy birds had grown bigger. The ship definitely had to pretend to be a restaurant and nothing more.

They moored at a rickety jetty. Half a dozen ground monkeys scampered from the crow's-nest, ran over Beatrix (who shrieked) and Polly (who cursed), leaped off the rail, and ran whooping off along the dock. They leaped over garbage cans (clatters), market stalls (shouts of "Oi, my bananas!"), and stole all the colorful hats.

On the jetty, townsfolk crowded about with anxious chatter. "It's so faded and scratched! Is it the *Traveling Restaurant* or not?"

Sibilla's eyes were big and worried. Jasper and Beatrix set her high chair near the galley, where she'd be close to Jasper while he worked. Dr. Rocket began setting tables. Outside was the clank and bang of Polly letting down the sign.

Gasps rippled through the crowd. Jasper noticed everyone staring up. Dr. Rocket dropped what he was doing and hurried on deck, Beatrix with him. Tying on his apron, Jasper followed.

In silvery new lettering the sign read:

THE TRAVELING RESTAURANT
ALL-AFTERNOON AFTERNOON TEA
TRUE ROYALTY LOVES US
(OTHER FOLK SAY WE'RE TOPS)

Beatrix nudged Jasper. "What's going on?"

"I told you ages ago about … the silver feather," he managed to whisper. "I think the wonderful thing is growing stronger after all."

A cheer started in the crowd, but a huge black and white gull swooped down to the railing. It squinted at the sign with a spying eye. Silence fell again at once.

There was no time to think. "Blazing customers!" Jasper yelled. "They're my worst nightmare! Running a restaurant is hard enough without having to serve customers as well!"

Dr. Rocket stared at him, then grinned. He winked at the crowd. "I suppose these people want the blasted gangplank next!" he roared, and crashed it on the jetty.

People nudged each other and erupted into silliness—thank goodness, they understood! Everyone scrambled up into the dining cabin, shouting and shoving for good seats. "Where's the menu? Is there enough for me and you?" They dropped knives on the floor, demanded fresh ones—whoops!—dropped those as well. The afternoon tea consisted of scones, berry jam, and dollops of cream. There were cupcakes of every decoration. There were cream cakes, cream pies, and creamy milk shakes. There was runny cream in jugs, and bowls of whipped cream. The customers dripped it on the tables, off the tables, and trod on it with big shoes. Sibilla's eyes grew wider every minute. By now, nine black and white gulls were perched on the rail, spying with yellow eyes.

"I don't want cake!" bellowed a customer. "I want an omelette bigger than my face!"

"Nobody's having omelette! It's afternoon tea!" Dr. Rocket bellowed back. "Nothing in the world upsets me as much as rude customers!"

"But we always smile at them, no matter what!" shrieked Polly.

"Our faces ache from smiling!" Beatrix wailed.

The captain gave another wink. "Especially when we're being watched."

Sibilla gave a shriek as if suddenly she'd got the idea, bashed the tray of her high chair, and scowled at the spy birds.

Beatrix kept shouting and mopping up cream. Polly was so red in the face that Jasper knew she wanted to storm out of the galley and throw saucepans at the birds. But you can't do that to spies—it lets them know that you know what they are.

A new customer turned up with a copy of the *Fontanian Daily Watch*. "Is that the latest?" someone asked.

The new man looked exactly like the others, apart from not being covered in cream and cake. Dr. Rocket wiped the only spare table and offered a menu. The man said "no thank you," sat back and opened the newspaper. Things settled a bit. Other customers leaned forward, trying to read the front page. A laughing toddler was hushed by its big brother: the boy glanced at Jasper, and mouthed "pies," which was weird till Jasper realized of course he meant "spies." He also noticed how Sibilla eyed the other toddler. At last she looked more like her usual self.

"Ah!" The new customer put a finger on a front-page paragraph. "The Provisional Monarch is speeding east on the *Excellent Hound*. She has stocked up on fresh cannonballs. The ... um, wicked pirates who ... er ... stole Lady Gall's niece—" the speaker paused, and an *Oo, 'orrible!* rippled through the crowd—"escaped only a short distance."

Lady Gall's niece? Did that mean Beatrix? It was amazing what lies some papers printed. The toddler's brother grinned at Jasper.

The man read aloud. "The wicked pirates were led by a villainous old man. The crew included a nimble and bossy young woman and a nasty, skinny, mouse-haired, very plain boy. They all drowned in the rapids. (*Hoorah*, said the customers.) Their vessel was completely smashed into kindling." (*Hooray, rah rah*, said the crowd.)

"However!" The man's finger traced the next line. "If anyone should see that wicked pirate ship, man, woman, or very plain boy, information must immediately be sent by pigeon post to the nearest military depot. Search parties are searching every port."

"What a relief," said a woman, "to know that Lady Gall will save us all from wicked pirates. Oo, Lady Gall's the one!"

The black and white gulls stretched their wings and flew away. The river rocked the *Restaurant* gently.

"Phew!" said the toddler's big brother.

"*Hoo-blazing-rah*," muttered the crowd.

"Ain't it interesting," another woman said, "that Lady Gall suddenly has a niece. She never had a niece before."

"Ain't it interesting," said someone else, "how careful you have to be in case there's a spy?"

"Tweet tweet!" said another person—and everyone pretended to duck from bird droppings.

"*Some birds good*," sang a mother to her children, "*Some birds bad. Nod politely, say excuse me …*" She fluttered her fingers above her ears, drooped them down as if it was some sort of game, then scooted the children off their chairs and out the door.

"Thank you for helping, everyone," called Dr. Rocket. "Now we'd better clear up and clear off."

"Right!" said one of the men. "It will do us no good if dear kind adorable Lady Gall decides we've sat and had a slice of cake from ... oo! such wicked pirates."

"Her dear kind royal temper would turn—just as we never use the word that starts with m, we never use the word that sounds like 'ugly,'" added another.

A small boy laughed. "Oo! Sounds like, because it is!"

The man who'd been reading began folding the newspaper, but stopped. "I missed the last page. Engagements and weddings ... oh, blast. Oh blast and blazes." With a desperate look at Polly, he scrunched the paper.

Dr. Rocket reached the paper at the same time as Jasper and flapped it open. They both read the crumpled words— silently, thank goodness: `The engagement is announced between Lady Gall, Provisional Monarch, and Lord Trump of the Northern Hills. The wedding will take place in three days' time, along with the coronation.`

"This is utter nonsense, Trump di—" began the captain, but Jasper tugged him to the corner near the high chair. There, he whispered that Trump was alive, that Trump had saved them on the *Sea Terrier*, that Jasper and Beatrix had seen him sailing past, a prisoner.

"My boy, you've done very well. I'm proud of you," muttered the captain. "But we have reached disaster point. Don't tell Polly. Not yet. Leave it to me." He tore the page from the paper and stuffed it down his shirt front. There were tears in the old man's eyes. "This might be the last afternoon tea we ever serve," he said, then raised his voice. "We must cast off!"

~

The customers disappeared in a whispering rush. Dr. Rocket climbed back into the wheelhouse.

Polly rattled the last dishes into the sink. "What was that about?" she asked Jasper.

He couldn't tell her so he pulled his dumb-nut face.

"Gangplank, Jasper!" roared Dr. Rocket.

"Annoying boy!" Polly swung out on deck and up the rigging.

In her high chair, Sibilla stretched toward the door and wiggled her fingers.

Jasper hurried over. "The other children had to go home. Sorry, Sibilla."

She was huffing and puffing, fighting to let him know something important.

"I don't understand," he said.

She blinked, then closed her mouth and puffed her cheeks. The monkey-bum face!

He burst out laughing. "You want a monkey!"

Sibilla clapped her hands. *Monkey!* she breathed. *Yes!*

"But ..." Was there time for Jasper to catch one ground monkey for his sister? They'd stolen all the bananas, so how would he tempt them? But he couldn't disappoint Sibilla when she seemed so much better. He rushed to his backpack, fished out the trumpet and hurried on deck. He put the trumpet to his lips and blew three notes. Some bushes rustled. A bonnet and two hats came hurtling out, but only one monkey scampered to the dock and onto the deck. That was all right—they only needed one. Jasper tossed his trumpet over to Beatrix.

As smoothly as he could, Jasper cast the *Restaurant* off from Stumbledon while Beatrix coaxed the monkey on into the cabin with a quiet *toot, toot*.

~

Sibilla and the ground monkey sat and stared shyly at one another. Jasper gave them each a little bowl of cut-up apple.

~

Finally the *Restaurant* had threaded through the river channels for the open sea. Polly hopped down from the rigging and called to the wheelhouse. "I've been patient. Alarmingly patient. My patience has run out! What on earth was in the newspaper?"

Dr. Rocket beckoned them all up and pulled the page from his shirt front. Polly grabbed it.

"Engagements and weddings … Lady Gall and Trump? But he …"

Dr. Rocket explained in a gentle voice.

"He's alive?" said Polly.

"And he said he truly loves you," Jasper muttered.

"Of course he does!" said Polly. "But he's going to marry …" She screamed and thumped both fists on the map cabinet.

"Think, Polly!" said Dr. Rocket. "Nobody could imagine that Trump wants to marry the ghastly Gall. It's part of her plan to become Queen, to marry the man who should once have been the King … Polly!" He grabbed her fists. "We have three days to get to the Eastern Isle and stop her."

FAT CHANCE

Three days! Could they stop the wedding and coronation? Rescue Jasper's parents and Trump from under the noses of Lady Gall's men? No chance!

Jasper swept the galley floor. He wiped the tables, again. Beatrix was teaching Sibilla and the monkey a finger game: *Ten little chimpanzees standing in a row—Bow, little chimpanzees, bow down low* .... The monkey wasn't very good at copying. Nor was Sibilla. Everyone looked worried and frustrated. The heart of the most dangerous boy on Old Ocean (and Monkey River) squeezed until it hurt. He had to come up with a plan.

Dr. Rocket called down for a mug of tea. Jasper carried it up. "Captain, Trump said not to rescue him ..."

The captain gave him that look that said I don't want to understand boys. "Jasper. I'm too old to figure out the rights and wrongs of everything. All I know is that we must get to the Eastern Isle." Dr. Rocket glanced up at a pair of furious green boots high up the mast. "Apart from anything else, if Trump marries Lady Gall none of us will want to live with Polly."

"Do you have to live with her?" asked Jasper. "You could travel on without her."

Dr. Rocket rasped his beard. "It would be unkind to abandon your daughter when she's so unhappy in romance."

Jasper's jaw dropped. "Polly is your daughter? Then you're my …" Grandfather! It was a few moments before he could speak again. "I wish people would be more honest about things in this world."

"It is to achieve that," said Dr. Rocket's angry muffled voice, "that we are putting ourselves, and the future King or Queen, into great danger."

"It's the future Queen," said Jasper.

"Go below," said Dr. Rocket. "I'm not in the mood."

~

Jasper stood near the anchor-well of the dragon-eagle and tried to work out what to do. If they took Beatrix to the Eastern Isle, Lady Gall would capture her and she'd be punished, even killed. Jasper himself would be captured and killed. So would Sibilla. Actually, Lady Gall would hunt them down wherever they went.

He turned round, eyes damp, and found Beatrix coming toward him with Sibilla in her arms. The monkey followed.

"Where's the next port?" Beatrix muttered.

He looked into her eyes, and knew she understood. Dr. Rocket was a useless grandfather. Polly was a useless aunt. Of all the grown-ups they'd been dealing with, only Duchess Donna had shown any common sense, and her home had been burned to the ground. He hoped she and her little people had had time to get away ...

"What I think," Beatrix whispered, "is that you and I should take Sibilla somewhere safe. We have to hide till you and Sibilla are old enough to fight Lady Gall."

"By then, she'll be Queen Gall." He pretended to throw up.

"Only till you stop her," Beatrix said. "I'll help."

He stood very still. Did Beatrix believe in him that much? Could he really save his sister and Fontania?

———

A CHANCE GOES WRONG

Next morning, under a gloomy sky on a gloomy sea, the *Traveling Restaurant* sailed into the City of Much Glass. There were gloomy faces on Polly and the captain. Milk had gone sour in the chiller-cupboard. The bread was stale. Not even the monkey wanted a lunch of spotty apples.

The men who helped them tie up gave pale grins. "Nice to see you. It's time we 'ad a treat."

The captain didn't answer, beyond giving a small smile and friendly salute.

It was all Jasper could do to be polite to Dr. Rocket and Polly while they organised themselves to go shopping for provisions. He and Beatrix had their own plans. Once again, he'd found maps useful. The countryside behind the city was full of caves and forests where three children could hide while they grew up—he hoped. He and Beatrix pretended to be grumpy with each other, kicking the rail and not talking.

"Will we be serving lunch? Or dinner?" Beatrix asked with an innocent blink at Dr. Rocket.

Dr. Rocket shook his head. "Too dangerous. Now, Polly

and I are off into town. Don't either of you leave the ship. Do you hear?"

Jasper was impressed with the way Beatrix let her mouth drop open and her lip curl, as if running off was a stupid idea that would exist only in the brain of a brainless boy. He made his eyes wide with virtue. "When will the *Restaurant* cast off?"

Dr. Rocket glanced at sky and tide. "Within two hours. Stay in the cabin. And don't fight. We can't risk being noticed at this late stage."

For a moment Jasper saw a truly worried grandfatherly frown in the captain's eyes. From the odd look on Beatrix's face, he thought she'd seen it too. But they couldn't change their plans.

The captain and Polly took the handcart and hurried off. Jasper hung over the railing near the anchor-well. He hoped the young dragon-eagle might send him some comforting feelings. But still he heard and felt nothing. He leaned over even further and glimpsed the silver point of a folded wing.

"You kept us safe as long as you could," he whispered. "Forgive me for exhausting you. You've done wonderful things for my sister. I know you're stronger now, but you're like us—you're too young to fight this battle yet. I hope you can stay hidden till we're all ready."

He could have said more, but it would have been soppy.

~

His backpack was fastened. Beatrix had a small bag Polly

had given her, and stuffed into it two spare cardigans (also from Polly). The trouble was, Sibilla refused to move without the monkey.

~

They borrowed another handcart. It wasn't stealing because they were only going to use it on the wharf. Nobody took much notice of them trundling Sibilla between the stacks of goods from other ships. Jasper glanced back once. Some segments of the *Traveling Restaurant*'s hull seemed brighter again, but most of it was sadly shabby. Soldiers were about, and lots of naval uniforms. Beatrix whined and grizzled, which was a brilliant trick. It made everyone avoid them, and kept attention off the monkey. Jasper had begun to like Beatrix a bit. This was good, because when they escaped he would have to spend a lot of years with her.

They left the cart at the wharf gates. Jasper had a note already scribbled, which he wrapped around the handle: *We really needed it. Thank you. Sorry for the inconvenience.*

"That's a long word," Beatrix said.

"It means 'bother'."

"I know that!"

The monkey joined in the jabber, and they shut up.

Now they had to travel through the crowded city. Beatrix looked uneasy.

"Let's make Sibilla walk," Jasper said. "One hand each, okay? The monkey can grab on wherever it likes." (It actually grabbed the handle of Beatrix's bag.)

The City of Much Glass was named for a good reason. The shop fronts were like mirrors. Now and then Sibilla and the monkey whimpered with shock when they saw the reflections of other monkeys and other little children with surprised hair. Beatrix and Jasper acted jolly, as if they were heading off to school for show and tell. Jasper kept seeing men who looked like pirates off the *Double Cross*. Beatrix kept seeing search parties of soldiers. Actually, Jasper saw them too. Once, he saw Dr. Rocket in the distance buying cheese. In the circumstances it was very hard to look jolly. The further they went, the harder it was. It was even harder when the wind began to blow and it was cold.

In front of a magazine shop was a newspaper hoarding: "Royal Marriage Two Days Off. Bridegroom Blissfully Excited." There was a large picture of Uncle Trump in a ruffled collar, with a fake smile that showed clenched teeth.

Jasper stopped and used his sleeve to wipe Sibilla's nose.

"Do all little kids have runny noses?" Beatrix asked. "Or is it just her?"

"They all do!" Jasper snapped. "Shut up. Act normal."

"With a monkey helping carry my bag?" Beatrix showed her own clenched teeth. So did the monkey.

A squad of soldiers marched into view and headed toward them. The children ducked around a corner and into a doorway, where a sign said: "Associated Newspapers of Old Ocean. Editorial offices, second floor." The soldiers marched past outside, and Jasper dragged Beatrix and Sibilla further into the big foyer. A crowd of people hurried up and down a flight of stairs.

Sibilla sat plump on her bottom and started to cry.

The monkey copied. Sibilla hit it. The monkey screamed.

A woman who looked like a kind young grandmother bustled over. Without even asking, she scooped up Sibilla, who gave a hiccup and stared at the woman as if she'd never seen a grandmother before (actually, she probably hadn't, so that made sense).

"Why aren't you at school?" said the woman, looking at Jasper and Beatrix while she juggled Sibilla and a large handbag. "This one's too little for school, isn't she? Is this your monkey? Where do you live?" She didn't wait for any answers. "Are you cold, sweetie? Would you like a sip of warm milk? I wonder if we'll find a banana for your furry friend?"

The woman swept up the stairs, an astonished Sibilla looking back over her shoulder. All Beatrix and Jasper could do was follow with the monkey, right into the newspaper office.

~

The warm milk pleased Sibilla, so that was good. The monkey sat on top of a pile of the day's papers, and asked for some milk too: *Whoo-oop?* The woman kept up her nosy questions. She reminded Jasper too much of Crispin Kent. Beatrix pretended she was bored and didn't reply. Jasper pretended he didn't understand. "Different language," he kept saying. "Different language."

"You're new in town?" the woman asked. "Are you lost? I'll fetch a policeman! Oh, there are lots of Lady Gall's troops around today. Shall I ask them …"

"Not lost!" Jasper grabbed a *Fontanian Daily Watch* from

under the monkey. "Newspaper! Buy! For parents!"

"What a good story!" The woman rang a bell and scribbled a note. "Newcomers to City of Much Glass, can't speak the language, send children and family pet to buy local paper!" A messenger came running in, and out. "We're chock full of stories about the royal wedding, but there's room for a short piece about children and pets. Let's wipe the little girl's nose, shall we?"

She mopped Sibilla, straightened Beatrix's cardigan, and made a dive at Jasper. He leaned back quickly, dropped the paper on the table, and tidied his own collar.

"I want an article about the *Traveling Restaurant* too!" the woman said. "Do you know it? It's always so exciting when … Oh, here is the artist. And is this our new reporter? Yes, it is! I'll leave them to it." She gathered up her bag and hurried off.

In came a young woman with a sketch pad. She sat down at a desk, threw open her pad and began drawing Beatrix and Sibilla. A man came in behind her—sandy-haired, in a thin black cloak. It took a moment for Jasper to realize it was Crispin Kent. Kent's eyes twinkled at Jasper with surprise. He glanced at Sibilla for a moment, then gave her a tiny salute. She copied him exactly. Beatrix hadn't seen Kent before, but she frowned at Jasper and drummed her fingers on the desk top: *Let's get away.* Kent pulled a chair up to the desk. The artist tore the sketch from her pad, slid it across to Crispin Kent, and stumped out of the office.

Kent closed the door. "Hello, Jasper. What a good story you'll tell," he said with a grin. "Will it be as good as the one about when we were heading to Battle Island but you dumped me instead on the miserable little Isle of Bones?"

Beatrix glanced from him to Jasper.

"It's the journalist who writes lies," hissed Jasper.

"Damn," said Beatrix.

In the silence, the monkey put the trash can on its head and covered itself completely. Sibilla dragged the sketch toward her, upside down. She put grubby fingerprints on the margins.

Crispin Kent grinned more widely. "Are you on your way to someone's wedding, Jasper?"

In a cold hard voice Jasper answered him. "Please thank the lady for the milk." He stood up and beckoned Beatrix.

"I never expected Trump to marry Lady Gall," said Crispin Kent. "He's mad keen on that aunt of yours, Polly of the green high heels."

"We know that," Beatrix muttered.

Kent cocked his head. "I've seen you with Lady Gall. 'Lady Gall's niece.' Ha! That wasn't one of my inventions. It was a good one, though."

"We're going," Jasper repeated.

"The papers say Trump and Lady Gall will have a happy marriage," said Crispin Kent. "But you know better than to believe everything in every paper. Right, Jasper?"

Sibilla was still studying the sketch of herself with Beatrix and Jasper. Gently, Jasper pushed it out of her reach in case she touched it properly and Kent realized she had magic. She pulled the newspaper toward herself instead. Her fingers butterflied onto the picture of Uncle Trump.

Jasper put his hand on hers, to stop her …

… and the image of Trump trembled. His white ruffled collar grew crumpled and grubby. His hand came into view and tugged the ruff as if it strangled him. He rubbed the hand over his forehead, raised his head and gazed straight at Jasper. Jasper felt Beatrix and Kent leaning close behind him.

Trump gasped. "Jasper, is that you? Where are you? Do you have the dagger? Are you … yes, you've got Sibilla!"

Crispin Kent leaned over Jasper's shoulder. "Trump? Good heavens, if this is what I think it is—it changes everything!"

"Yes," said Trump. "Magic, better late than never. Kent, you're a side-winding scoundrel but you've got a good heart."

"I haven't," said Crispin Kent.

"Kent, keep the children safe," urged Trump. "Lock 'em up if you have to, till it's over. It's the little world's only chance. And tell Polly to stay away. Make Rocket understand that Lady Gall will kill them all. They must stay away from the Eastern Isle!"

"What's in it for me?" Kent asked.

"It's the best story of your life," answered Trump.

"This will be the end of you, Trump," said Crispin Kent. "The very end. Full stop."

Trump grimaced again. "Kent, promise …" The vision broke up. On the table was just a picture of the "blissful" bridegroom and the heading about the wedding in two days' time.

RIDICULOUS CHANCE

It was absolutely clear to Jasper now. The magic only happened when Sibilla was involved. The country depended on her. And toddlers didn't know about telling lies. If she grew up surrounded by honest people who truly cared for her and helped her learn, she had a good chance of staying honest. Jasper supposed that once upon a time Lady Gall might have been a true-hearted toddler, but that was another story.

"We're on our way," he said to Crispin Kent.

"You'll get lost without a guide," said Kent. "I'm coming too. I promised Trump."

"He asked you to, but you didn't get around to it," Jasper said.

Kent grabbed a sheet of paper and scribbled a note: *News of big story. Don't look for me. Wait for scoop.*

"Right," he said. "We're off."

~

The afternoon was darker and colder, and Sibilla hated being carried. She didn't want to be not carried either, and stood absolutely rigid. *Monkey*, she insisted in her wordless way. *Monkey monkey now!*

They'd lost the monkey? "We'll get a monkey later." Jasper hitched up his pack.

No-no-no-no-no, Sibilla mouthed. She flung herself on the pavement and started kicking. The only way to get her moving would be pick her up bodily and carry her screaming to warn Polly and Dr. Rocket.

"I am not playing my flute here to tempt the monkey!" Beatrix said.

"Monkey?" said Kent. "I know where it is. Wait!" He bought a banana from a nearby stall and ran back into the office.

Jasper knelt down beside Sibilla. "Please," he said earnestly, and pointed to a shop window which reflected the naughty screaming child with hair like hers. She stopped her embarrassing display and sat up. Tears still dripped down her cheeks.

"Quick!" Jasper hoisted Sibilla into his arms, and Beatrix grabbed her bag. They ran. He had to stop several times to put Sibilla down, take a breath and hitch his backpack again. Despite the bitter wind, Jasper was hot and sweaty by the time he and Sibilla and Beatrix arrived at the wharf gates. Jasper started to sigh with relief …

But there, along the dock, at the gangplank of the *Restaurant*, was a search party of Lady Gall's guards, swords drawn and rifles cocked.

Running steps sounded behind Jasper. He looked round … It was Crispin Kent, with the monkey wrapped in his cloak. He was holding up a bitten hand.

"Well, Jasper, you can't win everything," he gasped.

IMPROVING YOUR CHANCES

"You think that's it?" asked Beatrix. "You think the *Restaurant* won't get away again?"

Kent pulled Jasper and the others into a hidey-hole behind a stack of crates. "Jasper, I've never thanked you for saving my life. This seems the time to do it."

"We don't trust you!" Beatrix cried.

"Wise girl. Don't trust anyone," said Crispin Kent. "Trust luck, that's what I do." He grinned, and Jasper hoped it was a true and friendly one. "The question is," said Kent, "what's the best way I can say thank you?"

There was a squawk and a flutter. A big black gull with yellow eyes circled Jasper's head, then whirred away. Jasper stole a look between the crates at the search party. The gull had landed near the officer's feet and was cawing at him loudly.

"Hey!" The officer pointed his sword at Jasper. "Boy! Wait there!"

Jasper touched his cap, and stepped back behind the crates. He had noticed a large ship nearby. It seemed familiar.

"I must trust you," Jasper said to Crispin Kent. "And

there's how to say thank you." He jerked his head toward the ship he'd spotted, and picked up Sibilla.

"Allow me," said Crispin Kent. He stuffed the monkey into his jacket, and spread his cloak wide. Jasper and Beatrix sheltered beneath its billows and they all strode out. They marched straight for the big black ship. There were no cries or rifle shots from the search party.

Through Jasper's awful adventures, he had often remembered what his mother said about good manners. He didn't think this was natural for boys, or girls for that matter. But sometimes they had paid off. The particular ship he had noted was called the *Double Star*. He was ninety-nine percent sure she used to be the *Double Cross*. High near her stern was a tiny skull and crossbones the pirates had forgotten to paint out.

Jasper rapped a knuckle on the railing of the gangplank. "Excuse me?" he called. "Ahoy?"

A head that used to be a pirate's head popped into view wearing a smart cap and a pleasant smile. "Ahoy and sorry, mates. But we're full up."

"We don't want to join the crew," Jasper began.

"Don't need supplies, either." The ex-pirate craned his neck and saw the monkey in Kent's jacket. "Nor entertainment. Stand back, please!"

The gangplank creaked and lifted an inch.

"Stop!" cried Jasper.

The gangplank lifted another inch.

"Stop—please!" Jasper shouted.

It creaked, and halted. The ex-pirate's head reappeared.

Peep-oh, Sibilla breathed, and did one.

"Cute baby," said the ex-pirate.

Jasper smiled with all possible friendliness to make sure he got exactly what he wanted. "Have you plenty of milk aboard?" he asked.

The ex-pirate nodded.

"Thank you so much!" Jasper glanced behind him—still no search party. With great care, he stepped up over the gap onto the gangplank and hurried aboard. The others followed.

"It will be wonderful to see Captain Darkblood again," cried Jasper. "We've just time for a chat before you sail!"

~

It was a large, comfortable and clean captain's cabin. The ex-pirate chief was just as tall and broad about the shoulder, just as black-bearded as before. But his face was brighter. His skin glowed with health. His smile showed very clean teeth. He wore a sensible black cap like Dr. Rocket's.

"I apologize for dropping in at short notice," Jasper said. "My—er—friend here is a journalist. We thought you'd make a fascinating story."

"Indeed?" The captain nodded to Crispin Kent. He offered a plate of savoury nibbles to Beatrix and Sibilla, and sat down. The ground monkey climbed on his lap and admired his earring (the only remaining touch of dramatic dress).

"I owe this boy a lot," Darkblood told Kent. "A well-fed ship is a happy ship. A ship that carries a good accountant is a good business venture." He made kissing noises to the monkey (whose ears went flat against its skull).

The men began chatting. Jasper kept an eye on the harbor. In failing light, he saw a ship with a round hull glide toward the headland. Good news: the *Restaurant* had escaped from Lady Gall. For a few minutes he knew things would be all right. Then a rocking motion brought him to his feet. He raced to a porthole.

Bad news: the *Double Star* was under sail.

~

It should have been exciting to spend a day or so under full sail on a black ex-pirate ship. Delicious aromas of pie (bacon and egg, chicken and corn), orange cake, and lemon slice floated through the air. By now, Beatrix was in the galley, helping prepare the day's lunch with Murgott, the one whose hairy hands had been so good at pastry. Crispin Kent was there too, interviewing Murgott.

But Jasper hadn't been able to warn Dr. Rocket not to go to the Eastern Isle. And he still had to get Sibilla into hiding. He sat on the floor of the captain's cabin and handed her biscuits, which she fed into Darkblood's money box.

The captain stretched out in his armchair. "It was high time I gave up piracy," he said.

"Really?" Jasper asked.

"Fighting the sailors of Lady Gall? It's amazing how friendly one feels, with a well-fed stomach. I don't think I or any of my crew would do well in battle these days."

"Er," said Jasper. "What port are you putting into next? How soon?"

"I'm not saying we wouldn't fight," Darkblood mused

on. "But I wouldn't bet on us the way I used to. It's best to be honest."

"Well—can you let us off as soon as possible?" asked Jasper. "But you keep the journalist?"

"And the monkey," Darkblood said.

My monkey, breathed Sibilla, and she hit the captain's knee. Luckily, being well fed, the ex-pirate chief laughed (showing several teeth, both gold and black).

———

A NOSE FOR A CHANCE

At least they'd escaped the search party. It might have continued to be all right if the hounds of Lady Gall had been properly fed. But the next afternoon Murgott began to prepare a veal casserole, and the breeze wafted the scent across the waves to the deck of the *Excellent Hound*, into the nostrils of the hungry animals—and probably the nostrils of Lady Gall's men. So much for Jasper's brilliant idea, of teaching the pirates to cook. A few days ago, it had helped the *Traveling Restaurant* escape the pirates. Now, it went like this:

An ex-pirate poked his head into the captain's cabin. "The *Excellent Hound* is bearing down on us. Shall we run up the skull and crossbones? Oh right—we used it for dish towels."

"We'll be fine," said Captain Darkblood. "We have extra muffins."

"I like sharing," said the ex-pirate.

"But," said Jasper, "we don't actually want to be captured."

"I did warn you we weren't keen on fighting now," said the ex-fierce ex-pirate chief. "Oh, hello, lassie, you've something to say?"

"Lady Gall will have you hanged!" yelled Beatrix. "She does that to pirates. She does it to anyone if she can think up an excuse!"

"Look on the bright side," said the ex-ferocious ex-pirate chief, "you want to go ashore. The *Hound* will take you to the Isle. You might get a chance to see the wedding. You're too young to be at sea. I ran away to sea when I was ten, but these days it's different."

"Ahoy!" cried a sailor through a megaphone on the *Excellent Hound*. "Dinner smells good! May we come aboard? Goodness me, you used to be the *Double Cross*. Darkblood is under arrest!"

Darkblood put on his sensible hat and ran out on deck. "But I've reformed!" he called.

"You have to tell the Admiral!" shouted an officer on the *Hound*. "Come over! He'll give you a certificate!"

"Just the Admiral?" said an ex-pirate. "Not Lady Gall? We thought we heard a dog or two. But if she's on a faster vessel speeding to the wedding, then we'd be very happy to come across!"

~

It was fair enough that they couldn't expect the Admiral to come to them. And the ex-pirates and the naval officers were convinced the children would find the flagship interesting. So unless they made a noticeable and dangerous fuss, Beatrix, Jasper, and Sibilla had to go with everyone else to the *Excellent Hound*. The monkey perched on Crispin Kent's shoulder, and they all scrambled into the longboat.

After a few notes on a bugle and some saluting, they

were shown into the presence of the Admiral. He was up on the quarterdeck, the clean bit away from ordinary sailors. Jasper couldn't see or hear any dogs, which was a relief. The Admiral saluted and smiled. Now that he was not with Lady Gall, he seemed much nicer. Some of the scars under his nose from her fingernails were healing, but there were several fresh ones. Beatrix kept her head down, hair over her face, and Jasper tried to stand in front of her. It would be terrible if a sailor recognized her. Sibilla kept a grip on the knee of Jasper's pants.

Captain Darkblood unbuckled his sword and placed it on a special table set out ready. That was polite.

The monkey jabbered and tugged Kent's ear. The Admiral chuckled. "Your friend thinks you should put your sword down too."

Crispin Kent's eyes twinkled. He emptied a pocket knife and three pencils from his jacket, and gave them to the monkey. The monkey rattled them down beside the sword.

"Anything else?" asked an officer. "Handkerchief? Picture of your mom? A box of matches?"

There was general laughter before a gesture from the Admiral made everyone hush. Except the monkey. It dashed to Jasper and tugged his jacket. There was another ripple of laughter.

Jasper figured he'd better take the dagger from his scabbard before it attracted too much notice. He slid it next to Darkblood's sword. If he stood near the table, perhaps nobody would see the dagger clearly. Beatrix huddled so close, he felt her trembling. Sibilla looked up, worried.

The monkey tugged her topknot.

"Bad animal!" cried Crispin Kent.

The monkey jumped on the table and let out a scream as Kent grabbed for it. Even the Admiral flinched at the sound and looked scared, which was surprising in an Admiral.

Behind him, the door to his state room opened. A woman stood there, a sleeping mask dangling from a sharp purple fingernail. Jasper shuddered even before he recognized her properly. Another finger was pressed on that place between her eyes where normal people have a frown line. He bet she was wondering how long before she could have another injection of beauteen. A snarling hound stood either side of her.

She spotted the monkey first. "Kill it!" she said.

Kent shoved the monkey down his jacket, though it wriggled and probably bit. "I'm a journalist!" he said. "Pet stories are popular!"

The hounds leaped at him, sniffing.

Lady Gall gestured and there were handcuffs on Crispin Kent in seven seconds. (The soldiers left the monkey in his jacket.) A hound, sniffing and dribbling, paced toward Jasper. He put Sibilla behind him, but Lady Gall had caught sight of Beatrix. With a shriek of rage, she slashed out with her sharp nails. Beatrix ducked. Lady Gall swung to the table, snatched Darkblood's sword in both hands, raised it to slice at Beatrix—and stopped with the sword held high. She turned back. She had seen the royal dagger.

"Stop!" she cried. Even the hounds were motionless.

Lady Gall let Darkblood's sword clatter to the deck.

Slowly she flexed her hands as if what she was about to do was dangerous. She reached out and took the dagger in utter silence. She held the weapon up. Light glinted from the points of her nails, off the blade and from the etching of dragon-birds. Lady Gall didn't smile. But when she turned back to Jasper and Sibilla, she looked as smug as a slug in a lettuce.

—

NO CHANCE AT ALL

Lady Gall cast a sly glance at Crispin Kent, who winced as if he had indigestion. She cast a scary glance at Beatrix. Beatrix's jaw went stubborn as she stared back at Lady Gall.

The Provisional Monarch pushed her hounds back into the state room, made a swift hand gesture, and suddenly the soldiers and Admiral were more warlike. They whisked Jasper and his sister into a corridor leading to the nearest cabin, shoved them in, and locked the door from the outside.

There was a narrow bunk, a chair, a pile of books, a small telescope, and a First Mate's hat. Through the porthole, Jasper could see part of the quarterdeck. He heard the shouts of sailors clambering up the rigging, of full sail being deployed … all the clamour and bustle of a warship readying for full speed ahead for a wedding and coronation.

He knelt and put his arms around Sibilla. "If I have anything to do with it, you will be monarch," he said. "You might hate it, though. I would."

His little sister smiled at him. *Jasper*, she said in her soundless whisper. *Splash!*

He had to laugh. She'd remembered their last day back home when they rode the cart into the pond and he got in such trouble.

More splash! Sibilla said.

"A huge splash one day, I hope." He hugged Sibilla even more tightly and breathed in her grubby toddler scent.

The *Excellent Hound* scudded along. In the stateroom next door, the hounds of Lady Gall bayed in full voice. Jasper climbed on the bunk and peered through the porthole again. Beyond the quarterdeck on the gray waves of a dirty ocean was exactly what he didn't want to see. The *Traveling Restaurant*.

~

Lady Gall didn't give many orders. From what Jasper could make out, all she did was point, and soldiers and sailors sped about. There was the flap of stout-bellied sails, the roar of thick strong smoke from all the funnels. The many cannon of the *Excellent Hound* had been frightening when they'd fired at the *Traveling Restaurant* and chased it into the Great South River. From aboard the *Hound* they looked even more threatening now they were going to attack his grandfather and aunt. At each huge cannon a dozen burly sailors had stacks of ammunition, things to stuff the gunpowder in with, and burning braziers to light the fuses. All this for a small round restaurant that had no weapons and relied on tattered sails and shreds of magic. Jasper's heart was sore at the thought of the young dragon-eagle. "Please be safe," he whispered.

Sibilla looked up from where she sat making a tower

with the books. *Bird*, she breathed. She lifted her arms like wings and flickered her fingers. He smiled and she turned back to playing.

The door crashed open. Two sailors pushed Beatrix and Crispin Kent inside. One of the soldiers entered too and stayed, very official, his back against the door and hands behind him.

"Beatrix?" Jasper asked. "When they start firing, keep your head down."

"I'm not stupid." She sat on the bed.

"I'll keep the monkey's head down," said Crispin Kent. It peered from his jacket.

The *Hound* scudded on after the *Traveling Restaurant*, and the view through the porthole grew worse and worse. Sometimes they couldn't see the *Restaurant* at all. When they did, she seemed closer—then more distant—closer again … How blue the ocean was. How the waves rippled in the sun and dazzled the eyes. How swiftly the *Excellent Hound* raced on, her cannon ready.

Jasper used the small telescope to get a better view of the *Restaurant*. Her brass was dull, her paintwork faded. The sails flapped and hung askew.

"They can't kill Polly and Dr. Rocket," said Beatrix. "Not if all the family has to attend the wedding."

The soldier at their door gave a small cough.

"What?" asked Jasper.

The soldier muttered from the corner of his mouth. "I'm afraid they don't really count, 'cause they're not royal."

~

The first shot fired. Sibilla let out a cry. Jasper dropped the telescope and wrapped his arms around her head to save her eardrums from the explosion. The next minutes clamoured with shouts and orders, the boom of cannon, the laughing shrieks of Lady Gall as splinters flew from the hull of the *Restaurant*. Jasper snatched up the telescope again and glimpsed Polly dashing to the wheelhouse. Dr. Rocket seemed to have collapsed over the wheel. Polly grabbed hold of it. Cannon continued to fire, cannonballs splashed around the *Restaurant*.

Please, Jasper thought with all his might, *please, dragon-eagle, find the strength to carry Polly and Dr. Rocket on—please!*

Wind filled the *Restaurant*'s tattered sails and she moved out of the line of fire.

"Give chase!" shrieked Lady Gall, and for an hour the *Hound* pursued. For an hour the *Restaurant* swung out of range again and again. It was an agony to watch. Jasper knew the dragon-eagle with its failing energy, its frail young store of magic, was trying its best.

He saw Lady Gall turn from the quarterdeck and disappear—into her stateroom, most likely. The soldier, Crispin Kent and Beatrix tried to see through the porthole, and jostled for the telescope.

A sob blocked Jasper's throat. He picked Sibilla up and hid his face so the others wouldn't see him weep. He had to get as far as possible from the sound of the *Hound*'s cruel hunt. He tried the handle of the door. Unlocked. Into the corridor and down he went with Sibilla, past the grand staircases and formal areas. There was the passageway that led to the dungeon where Beatrix had been prisoner—

Down another dark passageway, he heard Lady Gall's voice. He shuddered. He laid a finger over his sister's lips, and hunched in the darkness.

"You will obey me," said Lady Gall's syrupy voice.

A voice that was no voice gave a great sigh. It meant: ~ I will not ~

"I have sheltered you for seven years," said Lady Gall.

~ You've kept me in darkness ~ said the voice. ~ It was your fault that I was wounded ~

"You've been able to grow stronger," said Lady Gall. "You owe me gratitude."

~ You ruined my home and you blamed others. You blamed the young scientist for leaving the experiment unguarded. You blamed the dead children for knocking over the experiment, when it was you who set it up again and did the deed ~

"And I will be Queen," said Lady Gall.

~ You are not the true monarch ~ said the voice that was no voice. ~ You have no magic ~

"You owe me thanks for giving you shelter," repeated Lady Gall. "And I command you."

There was silence.

Lady Gall gave a small triumphant laugh. "You cannot refuse. Because I have this!" There was a rustling sound, then a faint clink of metal as she showed something she must have had hidden to the owner of the great voice.

There was a sigh, like leaves in a forest when a bird descends upon a branch.

"Thank you." Lady Gall's voice was as cold as rock in ice. "So you will obey. You have gained enough strength to perform the very small task I ask of you. The rebels must die. Crush the *Traveling Restaurant* entirely!"

A dim light appeared beneath a heavy door. It opened, and out Lady Gall glided with a lantern. She doused the light, swept past Jasper and Sibilla, and disappeared to the upper decks.

Jasper held his little sister in the dark. She patted his shoulder as he groaned with fury and disgust. Lady Gall, who called magic the Great Nonsense, had her own secret creature. And she had caused the Great Accident. She had blamed his father and grandfather. She had ruined the lake herself, and blamed the dead children! No wonder she became Provisional Monarch. She had cheated all along. It was lies, more lies, and wicked cheating.

Behind the heavy wooden door the voice that was no voice began a groan no human or animal throat could have uttered. It was loud but somehow soundless, like the roar of air. Even in the belly of the ship Jasper felt the vessel turn. The *Excellent Hound* was gathering speed to ride right over the *Traveling Restaurant* and crush it to the bottom of the sea.

ALWAYS WORTH A CHANCE

Sibilla wriggled in his arms. In the dim light she pointed at the heavy door.

Should Jasper do what Sibilla wanted or hurry her to safety? But where would she ever be safe? Once Lady Gall was Queen, she wouldn't let Jasper, Sibilla or their parents live longer than a day. Jasper said a silent message to the young dragon-eagle—*Be as strong as you can be, please save yourself*—then stepped forward and gave a little knock.

"Excuse me?" he said.

There was a pause in the powerful breathing. Jasper took that as a sign he could enter the creature's lair. Holding Sibilla, he stepped in.

The belly of the *Excellent Hound* was a huge dark cavern. The only light came from a cold green eye and a green glow in the shape of a coronet.

~ Don't stop me ~ said the voice ~ until I have finished ~

"Please, if you crush the *Restaurant*, you'll kill it," Jasper said.

~ Kill what? ~ the creature asked.

Bird, said Sibilla soundlessly. She pointed to the coronet.

~ Birds can fly away ~ the creature said ~ I cannot, until the monarch has a crown ~

"I am very sorry," said Jasper. "I am sorry for anyone who has to do what Lady Gall demands."

~ She bowed to me ~ the creature said.

Jasper realized the rustling sound had been Lady Gall curtseying to the creature. He was astonished. She didn't usually show respect to anyone or anything unless she got something out of it.

~ And ~ added the creature ~ she showed me that she owns this ~

In front of the creature, just visible in the shadows on the floor, glinted the dagger.

"Actually," Jasper said, "she took that from me. It was my uncle's. Now it probably belongs to my little sister. See—here's the scabbard on my belt."

Suddenly he knew what he must do. He set his sister down. "Copy me, Sibilla," he said. Then he put a hand over his heart and bowed, the most courteous bow he could manage, one foot before the other, bending his knee to the floor. "Please, do not chase the ship where my aunt and grandfather are in trouble. They are good people. Please, do not make them die. Please, show mercy."

He glanced at Sibilla. Could she manage it? She was only two. But up came her hand, over her heart. She looked at the terrible creature, and with her other hand pointed to its glowing coronet. *Please*, she said soundlessly, *please please*.

Then she took a step toward the creature. Before Jasper could stop her, she reached out and stroked its great scale-feathered paw.

"No sad," she said.

They were soft but the first words in her young life that she'd said aloud.

The frightening light in the creature's eyes became warmer, silvery-gold. Jasper saw more clearly. Slowly it dipped its head, and the cold glowing green seemed to flow like wax from a candle from its crest of feathers, down its silver-feathered neck, to the floor of the hold and through cracks in the boards. The cold green light disappeared.

Its curved beak moved as if the great creature smiled. ~ Take your princely sign ~ it said.

Jasper took up the dagger.

~ Let me see you wear it ~ said the creature.

Jasper slid the dagger into its scabbard, and bowed again. The creature turned its head, examining him, then closed its eyes. The huge head lowered to the paws covered in silver feather-scales.

Jasper tried to back out with Sibilla. But she tugged free, looked up smiling at the giant creature, and touched its paw again.

"Two birds," Sibilla whispered.

One warm green eye opened. The dragon-eagle raised its head. It let out a long sigh that made the whole ship shudder.

Jasper whisked up Sibilla and ran.

~

Nobody had missed them. Not that it mattered. Lady Gall shouted in her sickly cold voice that after the wedding everybody, crew and prisoners, would be punished. She'd wanted the *Restaurant* wrecked, not simply captured. In the meantime, could they kindly (oh, what poison was in the way she said "kindly") lash the *Restaurant* to the *Hound* with the stoutest of ropes, and sail direct to the Eastern Isle with no talking. The wedding was tomorrow. She would need her beauty sleep.

"As well as your beauteen," muttered Jasper. He was not altogether surprised when a sailor let out a laugh but said pardon me as if all he'd done was belch.

—

A CHANCE WOULD BE
A FINE THING

Next morning, Jasper knew they'd all be thrown into a dungeon as soon as the *Excellent Hound* reached shore. He was right. Soldiers hustled him, Sibilla and Beatrix onto the deck of the *Hound*. The *Restaurant* was moored behind her. Another troop of soldiers was wrestling Dr. Rocket and Polly down the gangplank. Jasper had time to see the sweet green curve of the valley of the Eastern Isle and a flash of blue from the lake before soldiers rushed him along the pier toward a fine brick building. They dragged him through the manor-house gate, past guards at the door, through a spacious entrance hall and down a flight of steps into the dungeons.

A jailer unlocked a door and thrust him through. Beatrix and Sibilla followed in a tumble. Luckily, Sibilla was on top. The door clanged and the key grated in the lock.

Jasper had a moment to think *I still have the dagger* before he heard his mother gasp. Back home, he'd heard it when he complained her leek and potato pie tasted like worms. He'd heard it when he hurtled down a step and bloodied his knee. He'd heard it when he drew a picture of Lady Gall being pecked by their chickens. Annoyed gasps. Worried gasps. He'd never wanted to hear the gasp that meant she was terribly upset in a dungeon and they were in trouble.

It was still wonderful to have her hug him. It was wonderful to have her fold Sibilla in her arms and stroke her tuft of hair. Wonderful to hear her say, "Jasper, I missed you both so much I thought my heart would shrink to nothing."

It was good, too, to have his father hug him till his ribs almost cracked and say, "We're in a mess. My dear son, I am sorry. But at least we're all together."

By now, Jasper could see in the gloom. He introduced Beatrix to his parents. For a moment, he thought she'd yell curses, but she shook hands. When she turned away, she rolled her eyes at him. He didn't mind. He understood. He had something to tell them all, anyway.

Large boots tramped along the corridor. The door crashed open, and Polly and Dr. Rocket were shoved in. The door banged shut.

Dr. Rocket had a bandage round his head. Polly's arm was in a sling, and her headband was a gag around her mouth. She tore it off. There were more gasps, and careful hugs. Dr. Ludlow hugged his father (Dr. Rocket). Dr. Rocket hugged his daughter-in-law (Lady Helen, whose red hair was curling with emotion). Polly and Lady Helen (two sisters-in-law) hugged each other, and so on. Beatrix was starting to look left out, which Jasper knew felt horrible.

"Hey," he said.

She shuffled as though she'd like to say "Get lost."

Instead, she said, "Welcome home, me."

Jasper cleared his throat and spoke to his father. "There's an awful lot you didn't tell me."

His father groaned and rubbed his big nose. "Jasper, it was a problem. When you were very young, should we have told you things you couldn't understand? When you were a little older, should we have told you things that were frightening? The very night your mother decided it was wrong to wait any longer, Trump turned up. He always had rotten timing."

There was a bump, a clatter. Outside?

"Hannibal," said Dr. Rocket, "there's something I kept from you and Helen for the same sort of reason. It might have given you hope. But if it came to nothing, it would have been false hope. A parent never knows what's right."

"Very comforting," Beatrix muttered. Polly reached out with the arm that wasn't injured. Though Beatrix flounced, she still somehow edged nearer to her.

Dr. Rocket beckoned everyone close so he could whisper. "But I must tell you now. The night after the Great Accident, I found—" he lowered his voice even more—"a young dragon-eagle. The last trace of magic. It was close to dead. It needed shelter. I didn't dare trust anyone. I've looked after it ever since …"

"You should have let me know!" Hannibal cried.

"You still trusted Lady Gall at that stage," muttered Dr. Rocket. "The dragon-eagle needed somewhere safe. It needed time. After a few months, Polly and I realized that the *Restaurant* too seemed to have a faint touch of magic—

very faint. The best thing was to keep the dragon-eagle secret. The *Restaurant* had become a nest of magic where the young one could grow in its own way." Dr. Rocket cleared his throat. "When I realized Jasper was my grandson, I wondered if the dragon-eagle would grow stronger with him near. And it seemed to, for a while."

Jasper's chest felt hollow with guilt. "I asked it to do too much. Every time I try to do the right thing, it turns out to be wrong. I'm sorry ..." But he must tell them about the other dragon-eagle, the older one, which had given him back the princely dagger. It hung at his waist. Only he and Sibilla knew. And there was more—the news that Dr. Rocket and his father had not caused the accident. That the children of the Isle had not caused it. That it was Lady Gall herself. "Mother ..."

But Sibilla wriggled out of Lady Helen's arms and pointed to the door. "Monkey!"

"She's talking? She's talking!" Lady Helen's hair was a mad red tangle. "Oh, sweetheart, I'm afraid that monkey's lost."

Sibilla looked puzzled. "Man."

Jasper explained. "She doesn't mean her mangy toy. She means the journalist has the monkey. Mother ..."

"That journalist?" cried Polly. "He's not a real one, he's a lying wretch! Is he here to report on the coronation?"

"Monkey!" Sibilla paddled her feet.

"Find her something else to play with," said Dr. Ludlow.

Jasper gave up for now at least. Lady Helen hunted for her bag, the one Emily had shoved stuff into when they left home. Jasper searched in it, and found a stale bun wrapped in a napkin. That kept Sibilla busy while she crumbled it and offered it around. There was a brush, so she tried doing Jasper's hair. He didn't like it, but only reminded her not to thump his head with it.

When he tried again to tell his parents about the second great dragon-bird and Lady Gall's greatest cheat, there was another clatter.

"Someone's listening," whispered Dr. Ludlow. "We won't mention the …" he fluttered his hands, "… on the *Restaurant* again. Agreed?"

"Right!" Dr. Rocket might have thought he was whispering, but he was an old man who'd had a whack on the head in a sea battle. "It won't matter to us. After the coronation, we'll have to take the secret to our graves."

"Will the wedding or the coronation be first?" Lady Helen's hair was a tight red tousle now. "Will she do both together? It's not the wedding my poor hopeless brother wanted."

Polly moaned and burst into tears.

Dr. Ludlow thrust both hands into his own hair and gave a tug. "Poor Trump! As soon as Lady Gall has married him, she'll feed the useless wretch to the unlucky fishes."

A shaky voice spoke out of nowhere. "Do you mind? Choose your words carefully."

"Trump?" Polly rushed to the wall and pressed an ear against it. "Trump!"

"I'm in the next cell. Polly, it's too late to say I'm sorry."

Polly sniffed hard and slapped the wall. "Say it anyway!"

Jasper pointed to a small air vent at the top of the wall. Dr. Ludlow knelt down, and Jasper climbed on his shoulders.

"Good lord, you've grown heavy." His father straightened up as best he could. "Can you see anything?"

"Well?" said Polly. "Well?"

Jasper pulled himself to the vent and peered through. "He's tied to a chair. In handcuffs. He's had a gag on, but it's slipped. He doesn't look much like a bridegroom. Isn't the wedding meant to be today?"

"Don't remind me!" shouted Trump.

"I'd like to know one thing." Jasper gripped the edge of the vent and tried to balance on his father's shoulders. "You lied about the money."

"I didn't! I gave half to Captain Brickle. What a waste of trust that was. I kept the rest for another emergency."

"It's an emergency right here," said Polly in a cool strong voice. "What use is money now?"

Jasper saw Trump sigh. "I wanted to bribe any other troops who caught me. It was only a matter of time before they did, and I knew Lady Gall would think of a wedding to make it certain she'd be called the Queen. A wedding to me, Jasper, not to you. Hell's bells, you're too young to marry anyone."

The thought was so appalling that Jasper nearly fell off his father's shoulders.

"But it didn't work, so forget it," muttered Trump. "Brickle and Scruggs got it all in the end and spent it on fresh tattoos."

"Sorry," Jasper said. "We all get things wrong sometimes."

"And I'm better at that than most people." Trump lifted his head and grinned (rather ghastly, but still a grin). "It was fun sometimes, nephew, while it lasted."

"My back's giving out!" warned Jasper's father.

They toppled down.

"Trump?" Lady Helen called softly. "You and I each had a crumb of magic once, but let it go. Trump—do you still hope that Jasper or Sibilla …?"

Just as softly, Trump called back. "I hope like blazes. It's one of them, or both—and it could be magnificent. But they're so young! And no magic has come back to the lake. I'm sorry, everyone. I know it's the end of me, but with a bit of luck it won't do the … er … the bride much good either. I plan to yell my head off at the wedding."

A growl of tears from Polly, and Lady Helen and Beatrix put arms around her.

Jasper saw that Dr. Rocket was watching him with a grandfatherly eye. No magic in the lake—because the dragon-eagle was too young and hadn't got there? Because the monarch had not been crowned? He edged nearer to the captain and tugged his sleeve.

"I suppose it's all right to hope," murmured Jasper. "Captain, listen—on the *Hound*, Sibilla and I …" And he whispered all about the second dragon-eagle.

Dr. Rocket smiled, with a finger to his lips. He edged the side of Jasper's jacket up and gave a small nod when he saw the dagger and scabbard. "My boy, the less said at this moment the better."

"Aye aye, Granddad," Jasper answered.

~

Everyone felt silent, except for a sigh or sniff or groan. They knew it must be lunchtime, but there was no lunch.

Sibilla took turns to sit on everyone's lap till even Dr. Rocket's prickly beard seemed boring. Then she searched in her mother's bag again, and pulled out a soft pouch full of knobbles. Lady Helen's jewels. Sibilla liked the bangles best, and put three on each arm. Jasper, sitting beside her, sorted through the sewing things till he found the puzzle of wire and beads. He still couldn't pull it into two, though it sort of expanded and contracted. Sibilla took it off him and jammed it onto his arm. She rummaged deeper in the bag. There was another scone, and three oranges. Jasper tossed an orange at Beatrix. She caught it and was surprised into a grin.

"I think we will be summoned very soon," said Lady Helen. "Oh—Beatrix." Beatrix, with a mouthful of orange, looked alarmed. "Thank you for being a friend to my son. In this he has been lucky. You're a strong and sweet girl. I'm glad to have met you."

Jasper and Beatrix blinked at each other.

Lady Helen took the brush and tried to tame her hair. "I hope Lady Gall will let us wash our faces. If there's a journalist present, we must look dignified, whatever happens. After all, we are the royal family."

There was a short silence. Trump's voice came through the grille, a little shaky. "Dignified. I'll see what I can do."

Outside the cells was the tramp of marching feet.

~

For wedding guests, they were shamefully grubby. They tidied themselves as well as they could with the tiny bowl of water the jailer brought them. They shared the brush (Emily would have scolded them about that) and tucked the jewelry into hiding under their sleeves or collars. Jasper left the wire and bead puzzle on his arm. They had no hope that Lady Gall would release them after the ceremony, but it was best to have their valuables, just in case (so that was a little hope, even though things seemed most hopeless).

Jasper hung his little trumpet around his neck. "We might have another chance for a duet," he whispered to Beatrix. She didn't smile. He didn't blame her. But he intended to blow very rude noises as soon as Lady Gall ordered them all murdered.

"Stop mucking about!" said a guard. "Time to go. Quick march!"

Dr. Hannibal stood up. "I expected Lady Gall to demand a last injection of beauteen."

"Don't know about that," said the guard. "Rumor is, the lake will make her beautiful. There'll be no more need of that beauteen."

After a moment of stillness, Lady Helen lifted up Sibilla and nodded to the officer politely. Dr. Hannibal Ludlow held out his arm. His wife took it. They walked out as if they led a grand procession.

~

It was a perfect afternoon for a royal wedding. In the tiny harbor, ships bobbed at anchor. The golden beach gave onto soft lawns and curving paths edged with silvery-blue flowers. In the center of the small valley lay the lake. It was like a place you would see only in a dream. Of course, Jasper had seen it in a sort of dream, but this was real. In the circlet of trees around the lake, birds piped and sang. They darted and wheeled in the soft warm air. On the lake, birds swam and dived. Every bird around seemed more beautiful than any Jasper had ever seen, their plumage more glossy, eyes bright and alert.

On the lawn a long golden carpet led to a small platform at the edge of the lake, and halfway along it was an archway of white roses. There stood the altar with vases of more white roses. It actually looked simple and pretty, if only you really wanted to be married.

How boring it was waiting for the bride and soon-to-be-Queen. Between Dr. Rocket and his father, Jasper put the horn to his lips and puffed a scrap of tune. Lady Helen looked around with a brave smile. So did Polly. Beatrix turned her head away. Jasper played another line of melody, then lowered the trumpet. He stared at his feet. His shoes were as dirty as he'd seen them.

Then there came a third line of melody—from Beatrix's flute. He raised his head. She glanced at him with her small smile. Jasper played the fourth line, Beatrix the fifth, then they played together, soft as sparrows. Birds began to flock toward the lake. Shadows gathered under the trees—curious shadows, as if they were ghostly shapes of wistful people.

From the manor house marched a squad of soldiers with a pair of drummers rat-a-tatting. Jasper and Beatrix, side by side now, stayed with their own rhythm. From another direction came the townsfolk of the Eastern Isle, such as they were. A few grown-ups, a lot of children—the rest of the orphans, Jasper supposed. Horses pulled small carts. There were carts full of cushions. Some of the people were on foot, others in wheelchairs.

There was also Crispin Kent, notebook in hand. He looked as if he'd eaten too much sweet stuff, which probably meant he'd been interviewing Lady Gall. The ground monkey sat on his shoulder and clung to his hair.

Beatrix played her next line with more oomph. The monkey's ears perked. The shadows beneath the trees shifted, as if they wanted to come nearer.

Two people arrived carrying a large tasseled pillow on which sat something covered with a gauzy cloth. Jasper supposed it was the false crown, though it looked more like a cake.

Sibilla squirmed in her mother's arms, and Jasper took her.

From the manor house, trumpets sounded a fanfare. The bridegroom emerged.

They'd cleaned Trump up. Clean face, clean hands, clean jacket (blue velvet), clean trousers (they were ugly pantaloons), shiny shoes. But they couldn't do anything about his expression—shocked and horrified, as if he was living a nightmare in which he longed to run as fast as possible but his legs were glued. They'd taken off his handcuffs. But with one huge soldier on each side of him and three behind, there was only one direction Trump could go. Toward the altar where the wedding would take place.

Soldiers pushed Jasper and the others toward some chairs. The townsfolk stood, or sat on leftover chairs or cushions they'd taken from the carts. The pair with the fancy pillow and crown stood next to the altar, solemn and gloomy (though not nearly as gloomy as Trump).

"Oi," an officer called to Crispin Kent. "Get rid of that monkey!"

"I'd love to," Kent replied. "But she bites when she's upset. Vicious bites. Poison. Lose your arm. Or leg. You wouldn't want to have her bite your ear. You take her! I'd be grateful."

The officer backed off. Kent gave Beatrix a wink, and a glance at Jasper that said, We'll play it as it comes, okay?

What else could they do? Jasper shrugged. One thing he did notice—the townsfolk had seen the ghostly shadows in the trees. They didn't seem to know if they should run and greet the shadows or ignore them. Had Beatrix noticed? He didn't think so, and he wondered whether he ought to tell her.

But the trumpets blared again. The bride appeared.

~

All Jasper really noticed was the huge frill she wore that made her look like one of those lizards. She swayed and simpered toward the altar in a slinky white gown. She held a huge bouquet of pink and white roses in both hands, as if she'd use it to swipe anyone who dared stand in her way.

Instead of bridesmaids, on either side she had three black hounds with lacy ruffs around their necks.

ABSOLUTE LAST CHANCE

A tall man in a long green tunic stepped to the altar and unrolled a scroll. Jasper supposed he was the pastor who would perform the wedding ceremony. What he read out was awful lies:

Whereas on this day Lady Gall, Provisional Monarch of Fontania, and Lord Trump of the Northern Hills, have freely agreed to come together in royal wedlock ...

Trump closed his eyes and looked sick. Jasper wondered when he'd start yelling.

And whereas on this day, the people of the Eastern Isle do freely gather to celebrate the crowning of the Monarch ...

Several townsfolk shifted and groaned. Lady Gall stared coldly at them.

Therefore, the true wedding of Lady Gall and Lord Trump will now take place. Then the Monarch, wearing the New True Crown, will be anointed in the lake ...

Jasper looked at the wooden platform. Was Lady Gall meant to dive off it, or jump, or what? Before she had the crown, or after?

The minister asked in a loud but trembling voice,

Do you, Trump, of royal birth, take Lady Gall …

Trump took a deep breath and let out a shout. "I do not want … !"

An officer strode up and jammed a gag into his mouth.

Very pale, the minister asked a second time. Trump glared and shook his head. The officer unsheathed his sword, pointed to the wedding guests and drew a finger across his throat.

The bridegroom's shoulders slumped. He nodded.

Do you, Lady Gall Provisional Monarch and Provisional Commander-in-Chief of the Army and Navy, take Trump to be your royal husband?

She said she did, but Jasper could tell she didn't care a toss and wanted to hurry as fast as possible to the next bit.

The bride and groom had to put wedding rings on each other's fingers. Trump looked as if he was trying not to throw up behind the gag. Lady Gall wrenched his hand to keep it still while she shoved his ring on.

So that was over.

"Everyone stand!" bellowed an officer.

They did. Jasper held Sibilla.

The minister took a deep breath. "And now," he said. "The coronation."

The people carrying the fancy pillow approached the altar. The minister removed the cloth. There was a white crown with glittery pink stuff.

Sibilla whispered in Jasper's ear. "Hat."

"It looks like yucky cake," he whispered back.

"Hat," Sibilla said. She fiddled with his sleeve while the

minister lifted the sparkly crown.

Trump had turned so white that Jasper was afraid he'd faint. Lady Helen gasped and wavered. Dr. Ludlow put his arm around her. The minister turned to Lady Gall, held up the crown, and hesitated. It was obvious he really wanted to go home.

Lady Gall gave a tut of annoyance, stepped forward and took the crown herself. She turned to the audience, raised the crown, and lowered it on her own head. There was a smattering of applause. Lady Gall lifted her chin, and the clapping grew louder. It soon tailed off.

Sibilla wriggled out of Jasper's arms and dragged the wire puzzle from under his sleeve. The ground monkey screamed and dived at her. Kent scrambled for the monkey and stuffed it back down his jacket. The officer who had spoken to him earlier looked impressed. Sibilla settled against Jasper's legs and played with the puzzle.

The minister coughed and opened a second scroll. On his face was the sort of no-expression that said he was absolutely fed up to the back teeth.

Behold the monarch of Fontania ... blah blah ... the waters of the spring, symbol of truth, blah blah ...

He gabbled, as if he couldn't wait for the ceremony to be over. When he'd finished, Lady Gall gave a curtsey to the crowd, raised her arms to the side and turned to walk along the golden carpet toward the lake.

With a *whoop*, the monkey leaped out and tried a second time to snatch the wire circle from Sibilla's hands. Jasper jerked his sister aside, they fell against Beatrix and she yelled.

Lady Gall stopped halfway to the platform and gestured for soldiers to keep order. Kent caught the monkey, but it kept jabbering at Sibilla. Jasper picked her up again.

She scowled over at the monkey. "Hat!" she cried, and tugged the wire puzzle apart.

"Clever girl!" said Jasper.

She laughed and jammed one circle of the puzzle on her head. Then she pulled Jasper's hair. "Jasper hat!" He tried to stop her, but she jammed the other half on his head anyway. Then she turned in his arms and stretched upward. Clear as a silver bell she called out, "Please! Please! Please!"

There was a singing roar from the harbor, and the dragon-eagle from the *Traveling Restaurant* soared out of the anchor-well and spiraled up into the sky.

There was a louder singing roar, and the side of the *Excellent Hound* burst apart. The second dragon-eagle appeared, wings spread like huge silver-gold banners. Both dragon-eagles landed on the grass beside the lake.

Lady Gall's eyes shone with astonishment and utter glee. "The monarch will be anointed in the lake!" she cried. "In the presence of magic!"

The dragon-eagles bowed to the lake.

Jasper couldn't bear the look on his mother's face, nor on Trump's, nor on his father's, or on anyone's. They were all going to die. Everything had gone wrong. It was Sibilla who was the real monarch.

He stood and shouted. "Lady Gall caused the Great Accident! She blamed my father, and she blamed the children of the Eastern Isle. But she is to blame. I heard her speak about it to the dragon-eagle! Lady Gall's a liar! She's a cheat!"

In the silence, no bird sang. Lady Gall, her frightening face expressionless, pointed a sharp fingernail at Jasper. Soldiers unsheathed their swords. Other soldiers aimed their rifles.

Jasper was going to die. But he was determined to make his little sister Queen.

"Splash!" he said to her. "Come on!"

He held her hand, and they ran under the rose-covered archway, past the altar and along the golden carpet.

Lady Gall looked furious and waved her arms, but the soldiers didn't seem to know what to do. She hurried her walk toward the water.

Jasper and Sibilla reached the platform at the same moment as Lady Gall. Jasper shoved her hard, picked up his little sister and leaped into the lake.

They surfaced gasping and laughing.

In the air, spray hovered in a shimmering crown. It fell slowly, a glistening rain like watery fireworks, and Sibilla clapped her hands. With her in his arms, Jasper waded back to shore. He fully expected to be in trouble, but everyone— monkey, dragon-eagles, townspeople, soldiers and his family—stared past him at Lady Gall.

There she stood, knee-deep, soaking wet and beautiful. In her drenched robes and new crown, she looked truly regal. "I am Queen!" she cried. "Queen at last! Forever beautiful!"

Then the young dragon-eagle spoke in a great voice that was no voice.

~ But the Prince and Princess wear the crowns ~

An older, greater voice that was no voice said ~ And who holds the sign? ~

Jasper's hand went beneath his dripping jacket, and drew out the dagger. He raised it high (it was Sibilla's, they must know that) to show the dragon-eagles. They bowed their mighty silver-feathered heads to Jasper and Sibilla.

~ A King ~ the dragon-eagles said ~ and a Queen ~

"I am Queen!" insisted Lady Gall. "No more nonsense. Guards, do your work and take the brats away!"

She waded to shore. As she set her foot on land, a shiver went through her. The look of victory in her exquisite face increased. But then her outline shuddered. She raised her hands to her crown, and her fingernails went right through it as if it were pudding. The crown had started to dissolve. It trickled onto her hair. Her hair melted too, and then her face, her shoulders—dissolving, seeping—her arms, her clothes. Lady Gall was a melted pool upon the platform—steam sizzled from it.

She reared up again, and for a few seconds was the ugliest, most horrible creature anyone could imagine. Actually, it would be best not to imagine anything so horrible. But when she collapsed a second time she looked like a puddle of sour vegetable soup with chunks nobody could identify.

Then Lady Gall was gone. Utterly gone. Not even a last wisp of smoke or a nasty smell. For a long moment everyone was still.

Jasper clutched Sibilla. Would the dunking in the lake do

that awful thing to her? To him?

Sibilla laughed at him, and waved at the dragon-eagles. "Bird," she called. "Two bird!" Then she touched her crown. Because that circle of dull wire and red beads was the true crown. The wire was brighter than the brightest silver now, and the beads were stones that throbbed with crimson fire. And— this was not a good bit—Jasper was wearing the other half.

"Oh no," he whispered. "No."

~ It is no mistake ~ said the dragon-eagles in a soundless singing chorus. They put their silver metal-feathered crests together as if they were companions who had been forced to live apart for far too long.

~

AND SO ...

That was it, really. Sibilla butterflied her arms at their mother, and Lady Helen ran to hug them both. She said she was so happy that her heart broke all over again. Jasper understood, but he didn't want her to go on about it.

He hugged his father, his grandfather Dr. Rocket, and his Aunt Polly. He hugged Trump too. Trump had ripped his gag off, and was so faint with relief that his knees kept collapsing. Dr. Rocket said that Lady Gall had been so self-serving and mean-hearted that the water of the lake had revealed her as she truly was.

Jasper's hand flung at his own heart.

"You, however," said his father, "look exactly as you are inside."

The others smiled at him and nodded. Jasper gave a half-shrug. That meant he was an ordinary boy. He'd had some good and bad adventures, and now he really truly wanted a quiet life with his cart and a few ball games.

Beatrix had disappeared—no, she was stepping toward the trees with other people of the Eastern Isle. They seemed surrounded by the shadow figures who were greeting them, consoling them. He could tell it was a private moment of joy and sadness.

"Food," said Polly. "We're all starving. We need a feast, but I don't fancy any of Lady Gall's wedding breakfast. Does anyone else?"

"Feast?" asked an officer, which surprised them, because they'd forgotten about the soldiers. "She didn't order any feast. For her, yes, but not for us. We were going back to the barracks to have beans and cabbage." He pressed a hand low on his belly.

"What we could do," Jasper said, "is see what's in the *Traveling Restaurant*."

His father grinned. "That's my boy." He sounded genuinely proud.

"Did you know about the crown?" Jasper asked his mother.

"Emily and I thought the sewing box was the best place to hide it," she replied. "But nobody had ever known it came apart. My clever son."

It was "clever toddler," actually, and just that Sibilla had seen him wrestling with the puzzle. He ruffled his sister's hair, using that as an excuse to whisk off her crown as well as his own. The circles wouldn't fit together again, and he hid them back in his mother's bag. Then he yelled to Beatrix that they were organising lunch.

It turned out to be a barbecue on the shore. There wasn't room in or on the *Restaurant* for the officers and soldiers, the Admiral and sailors, all the ex-pirates (who were very relieved to be released from other parts of the manor-house dungeons), not to mention the dragon-eagles and townsfolk. Polly and Lady Helen rustled up salads. Dr. Rocket and Hannibal Ludlow did the potatoes, though Dr. Ludlow kept losing the peeler.

Trump tried to light the burners. The dragon-eagles lumbered up to help him out.

~ Steak ~ they said ~ a side of lamb. Sausages. Pure magic ~

Beatrix and her long-lost cousins did the trifle, carrot cake and apple pies. The ex-pirates fed pie crusts to the bridesmaid hounds, who wagged their tails.

The sun shone, just hot enough. The wind blew, the lightest of breezes. The waves of Old Ocean lapped the shore. Birds in the lake waded and waddled, quacked and sang. Sibilla patted Dr. Rocket's beard, and squeaked then ran about, someone always close behind to keep her safe (Lady Helen, Beatrix, Polly, Darkblood, Murgott, and Jasper).

Trump had a quiet word with Polly. Jasper figured there would be a wedding after all, before too long.

Crispin Kent, with a full plate for himself and the monkey, had a word with Trump as well. Jasper sidled up to overhear.

"You'll be wanting an official court reporter?" Kent asked.

Trump shrugged. "I'm just the monarchs' uncle. Better ask them." He grinned at Jasper.

Jasper frowned to show Trump he'd rather it wasn't talked about. "I think Mr. Kent should try writing stories," he said. "He's very good at making things up."

Kent looked a little ashamed, but his eyes still twinkled.

Jasper noticed Beatrix watching. "Did you hear what he said?" he asked her. "I'm still not sure if Mr. Kent is good or bad, but he is funny."

Beatrix's voice was huskier than ever. "Your mother was really nice to me. But you're too important now. I understand. Um … thanks. Very much. For bringing me home." She gave a small bow and walked away.

"No!" Jasper ran after her. "Honestly …" He checked that nobody could overhear. "I don't want to be King. I want them to forget it. It will be awful. Maybe Polly could adopt you."

Beatrix blinked at him, then burst into laughter. Lady Helen, smiling, had her eye on them.

Jasper smiled too, and went to see what was left for second helpings. Around him was birdsong, the sound of Beatrix's flute in a merry melody, sizzling from the barbecue, and little screams as the sausages burst their skins.

THE END

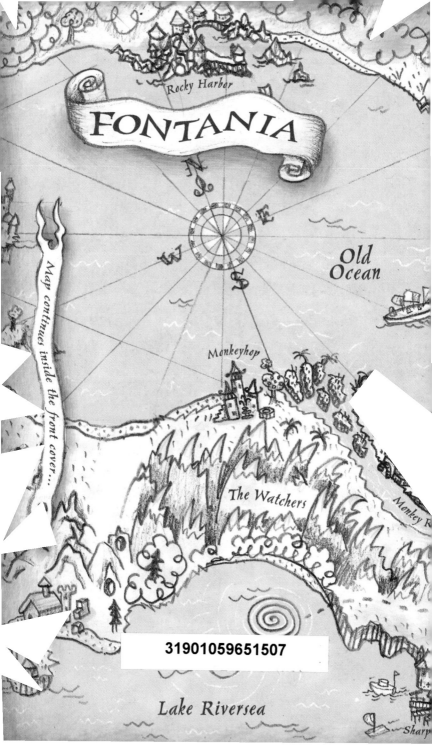

FONTANIA

Rocky Harbor

Old Ocean

Monkeyhop

The Watchers

Monkey R

Map continues inside the front cover...

Lake Riversea

Sharp